LEGACY OF LIES

A PSYCHIC COWBOYS WESTERN ROMANCE

COPPER RIVER COWBOYS
BOOK ONE

JILLIAN DAVID

Book and cover design by eBook Prep
www.ebookprep.com

March, 2019
ISBN: 978-1-64457-046-3

ePublishing Works!
644 Shrewsbury Commons Ave
Ste 249
Shrewsbury PA 17361
United States of America

www.epublishingworks.com
Phone: 866-846-5123

CHAPTER 1

*T*he *thunk* of cowboy boots increased in volume. Bad news heading down the hall.

Bad news but good memories. Holy moly.

Sara gripped the edge of the desk and pretended to pay attention to the parents sitting across from her. She managed to maintain eye contact, while inside, her heart rattled against her ribs.

Come on now. Stay focused.

She was a take-charge professional, able to handle any curveball thrown her way. The long day of parent-teacher conferences was almost over.

Thank God. She'd had about as much as any person could take of making polite chitchat, telling parents the good and the not-so-good things she observed in their children, and pretending not to notice the parents' silent accusations. Because how could someone like Sara Lopez sit there with a straight face and judge *their* kids? Maybe one day, her faulty parentage, stupid teenage acts, and relationship disasters wouldn't cling to her neck like cold, heavy chains.

Until then? Continue to smile until her face hurt. Pretend she didn't care that most folks in the tiny town of Copper River never left and never forgot anything. Bide her time until she could move on with her life.

One meeting to go, and it promised to be a doozy. That chill crawling up her spine had nothing to do with the Wyoming mountain weather. It was only early November. Going to be a long, frigid winter.

The stomp of leather on linoleum grew louder outside her door. The rhythm of the steps slowed. The sweat cooled on her forehead.

"Ms. Lopez?" Sitting across the desk, the vaguely familiar man in his late thirties shifted in his seat next to his wife and shot Sara a questioning stare behind his thick glasses. Sara knew most folks in town by sight at least.

They knew her by reputation.

"I'm sorry, what were you saying?" Heat flooded her neck and face. Damn her past, but as the new teacher in town, she needed to prove herself and handle the pressure. These parents in front of her deserved her attention.

In this small town, any misstep on Sara's part would travel through town and back before she got home tonight. Always did. Even though she'd grown up for the most part here, her family, or lack thereof, gave her permanent outsider status, and her adolescent hijinks provided the icing on the cake for most folks' poor opinion of her, despite the years that had passed.

Hope passed over the face of the father in front of her. "We were asking if Lucas is reading at his grade level. We worked with him over last summer." The man glanced at his tired wife. She was pregnant with their fourth—or was it fifth?—child.

Sara swallowed a lump in her throat and deliberately placed her hands on the desk, one on top of the other. Perfect. Now look at her. She was relaxed, focused, and most assuredly *not* distracted by what awaited her outside her classroom.

Resisting the urge to glance at the door, she responded, "Lucas is a pleasure to have in class. In comparing notes from Mrs. Johnston's assessment from last year, I see your son has advanced his reading skills to very close to second-grade level. He's confident enough to read out loud in class now. You're doing a great job, so keep up the nightly reading—it's helping."

Both parents smiled as their shoulders relaxed. At least these parents were involved. Caring.

"Our son talks about how much fun he has in school now. We're so happy. It's great to have new teachers in the community, even if you're—"

His wife jabbed him in the ribs.

And just like that, her past popped up and pulled an ugly face. With such a small town, even her absence while she attended college hadn't erased the citizens' collective memory.

Suppressing as sigh, she kept her facial expression neutral and gave the man time to recover from the slip.

He cleared his throat. "Thanks for believing that our son can improve."

"Of course. All kids have potential. It's our job to work together and find out how he can learn best."

The footsteps in the hallway stopped, and a scuff transmitted through the classroom door. Like the person walking had pivoted. A shadow flashed by the small window in the door.

Her voice came out too high-pitched. "Well, if you have any other concerns about Lucas, please let me know. We'll meet again in the springtime. But for right now, keep up the good work with the reading, especially over the holidays coming up."

The couple stood and shook her hand. As he exited the room, the man placed his hand on the small of his wife's back.

Something unpleasant, like emptiness mixed with jealousy, pinched in Sara's lower back. She tried to ignore the discomfort.

But she couldn't ignore the new hand that caught the door right before it closed. Big, square fingers with trimmed, work-roughened nails blanched as they gripped the metal. A flannel sleeve encased a thick wrist dusted with reddish hair. Sinews flexed as he pushed open the door.

Hail Mary…yum.

Sara blinked hard. *Stay professional.* She needed all her faculties with her today. She knew a little about Garrison Taggart's life since he graduated high school five years ahead of her: his wife, his son, the sudden breakup and divorce. Heck, she had appreciated that the people in town had someone else to talk about for a while there.

All day, she'd wondered how it would go, meeting her adolescent crush, all grown up. A rush of terrified giggles threatened to burst out of her lips.

Get a grip on yourself. He had no clue about her teenage infatuation, and he didn't deserve to walk into a parent-teacher meeting where the teacher was all aflutter. Besides, both of them were older, hopefully wiser, and world-wearier. She had that police record and a less-than-respectable family background. If the gossip could be believed, Garrison now had his own demons.

A colleague had warned her about Garrison Taggart's unwilling participation in parent-teacher conferences. He disliked meetings, he didn't have time for teachers, and he resented anything that took him away from his ranch. And God help anyone who said a critical word about his kid.

Odds were, he wouldn't like what Sara had to say.

The man filled the doorway, blocking the light behind him for a moment. As he entered the room, he removed his tan cowboy hat, and short, wavy hair the color of burnt sienna became visible. Beneath thick slashes of reddish-brown eyebrows, his amber-colored eyes took her breath away as he broke eye contact long enough to dip his head in a curt nod. He raised an eyebrow and waited.

Her dry tongue unstuck enough to form words. "Please come in, Mr. Taggart. You're right on time."

"Of course I am."

She flinched. The frigid tone rivaled the wind chill outside and made her glance at the clock on her wall: 4:22. She had run two minutes late for his time slot.

He crossed the worn linoleum floor in three strides, bringing with him scents of horses, hay, leather, and hardworking male. She inhaled, triggering fond memories of watching rodeo competitions which featured a certain steer roper.

4

Too bad her pleasant thoughts didn't jibe with the scowling man standing next to the chair.

Keep it professional. Stay cool. You can do this.

Sara wiped damp palms on her black slacks and stuck out her hand. "Mr. Taggart, I'm glad you were able to take time to meet about Zach."

His strong hand wrapped around hers.

Rough skin against soft. His ruddy, weathered skin against her light olive tone. Opposites all around, but damned if their hands didn't look perfect together.

Seriously? She slid her hand out of his grasp, trying hard to ignore the zing of excitement traveling up her arm.

"Garrison."

"Pardon?"

"Call me Garrison. When you say Mr. Taggart, I start looking around for my old man."

Garrison Taggart was anything but old. He must be, what, a few years past thirty now? Other than some weatherworn fine lines around his eyes, nothing else about his fit physique indicated he was anything but in the prime of his life.

When a twinkle lit the gold flecks in his eyes, her neck warmed up. It had been a bad idea to wear her thick hair down today, if the heat building up at the nape of her neck was any indication.

"All right, then. I'm Sara."

"Didn't you go to high school with my kid brother and sister?" His low voice flowed over her like wind blowing through pine trees, and she inhaled, despite herself.

"Kerr and Shelby? They were a year ahead of me."

"Thought so. Most everyone in town knows everyone else, one way or another. It's a small town." He pinned her with an uncomfortable stare.

"Sure is." If he didn't name her past missteps, no way would she serve up the bait. "Kerr and Shelby might not remember me. Um, I kept mostly to myself. But, yes, I was acquainted with them from school."

"You were acquainted with the Wonder Twins, you mean?" When he smiled, honest-to-God smiled, all of those harsh lines morphed into a handsome, wry expression that made her weak in the knees. Wow. For a moment, this grinning guy was the Garrison she had pined after in high school. Laughing, carefree, confident.

"Your siblings were nice. Other kids liked them."

He mumbled something and fell silent, staring at her. His brows drew together, and the light, smiling demeanor bled away. Just like that, the illusion of the high school Garrison dissolved, leaving a tired, bitter man.

The conversation dropped like a dead fish on the desk between them. Small talk, done. Message received.

Pulling a file from the stack, she opened the cover. "So, anyway. Um, let's get to work." Holy rosary, could she be any less smooth?

He relaxed into the seat across the desk from her. The chair next to him remained conspicuously empty. When he rested a dusty-booted ankle on his knee and balanced his Stetson on his solid thigh, she sighed and made a superhuman effort not to stare at the taut denim covering his...

Wow, she needed to stick with the parent-teacher routine and ignore how the guy made her ovaries tremble with excitement.

A stormy expression settled on his brow. "I agree. Is this going to take long? I have to get back to work."

Hard muscles tightened the fabric of his checkered work shirt and worn jeans. Every inch of him brimmed with rugged vitality and scents of the outdoors.

This man was the opposite of Sara. Although she had participated in the occasional teenage bonfire in the summer, no one could accuse her of being an adventurous sportswoman. Her idea of roughing it involved sleeping in her house with a window open.

With effort, she tore her gaze away from his gold-flecked eyes and said, "Uh, well. This time is yours to do with as you wish. But I'd like to discuss Zach."

"What about him?" That calm, low voice switched to knife-edge sharp in the space of a second. A warning.

She flipped through the papers, cursing under her breath as one page floated to the floor. With fumbling fingers, she retrieved the paper and pulled out her evaluation.

"So, Zach is a very bright young man. I'm sure you're proud of him."

A grunt. Possibly the Garrison equivalent of approval.

"He's above grade level in math and reading…"

A square finger flicked the worn leather hat brim.

"And, ah, he gets along with most of the kids."

"Most?" Garrison leaned forward and narrowed his gaze.

Stop it, she commanded her tapping foot. "Yes, he has some friends, and they get along well."

His glare hit the balance between cold assessment and irritation.

Sweat collected between her breasts, and she prayed the dampness wouldn't show through her pink button-down shirt. She tried not to pull a chicken-wing move, but paranoia and warmth were pretty good reasons for the deodorant to fail.

This man had her tied in more knots than a macramé hammock.

"But?" he said.

Damn her pounding heart, she hated confrontation more than anything—practically had a Ph.D. in avoiding it, for all the good that had done. Heck, she'd rather dust off her treadmill and jog a few miles than share unpopular information with this big, grumpy man.

"You and Zach live on the ranch."

"Yeah, so?" His response hit quick, like the lash of a whip.

She swallowed. "Are things, um, pretty okay at home?"

"Of course."

"Is his mother involved at all?"

"Number one, this is a small town, and unless you've been under a rock, you know damn well she left us last Christmas. Number two, my personal life is no one's business." He paused to take a breath. "Why? What are you getting at?"

She flinched. "Look, Garrison, I understand about your situation. It's just that some kids come from homes where the parents are separated—"

"What's that have to do with the price of cattle?" His jaw tightened as his mouth pressed into a hard slash. No more just handsome, now his face darkened like a thundercloud about to burst.

And Sara stood right in the path of the storm.

"No, what I mean is, sometimes children in families without a parent present have a hard time processing things emotionally. Sometimes those kids might act out. They don't know how else to express their feelings when they're upset."

"My son misbehaving?"

"More like he doesn't know how to handle certain situations. When stressed out, like if another child teases him, Zach overreacts."

"How?"

"Well, he yelled at one of his friends the other day and shoved another kid. And this isn't the first time he's lashed out at a classmate."

He snorted. "Must've had a good reason."

"Possibly. I do think there is some bullying that's part of the problem, but Zach's reaction is why I'm asking about his home life, so I can understand how best to help him. Sometimes things going on outside of school affect my students. Does he act out at home at all?"

"No. He knows the rules and follows them." A hard, blank expression descended upon his face. The emotional shutters were firmly closed.

She'd bet her left shoe that Garrison didn't tolerate anyone who didn't follow his rules.

Well, rough terrain ahead.

"So then, is his mother involved?"

Fwap, fwap. He flicked the edge of the hat brim. "You asked that already. It's not your business. But, no, she's gone for good. I thought people in town knew everything about everyone else's business."

She ignored the implied jab. The folks sure knew about her family and her mistakes. "How did he react when you and his mother split up?"

"What's it matter?"

That bead of sweat on her chest tormented her. "Because I think that's part of the problem."

"We split up almost a year ago."

If Garrison kept tapping on the hat, she'd have to reach over the desk and grab his hand. Everything about this man drove her to madness. Even worse, she swore he did the action just to be annoying. She rolled her hands into fists on her legs.

Keep going.

"Was it a rough separation?"

"Again, what does it matter? Ancient history. Everyone has a past they'd rather not remember. Wouldn't you agree?" His amber stare pinned her in place.

So, to answer her question, yes, he knew about her poor choices, probably every one of them. Copper River being a small town and all.

Fair enough. He had a right to be irritated when someone invaded his privacy. But he didn't get to shrug off his son, no matter how many buttons Garrison and Sara both ended up pushing.

She struggled to keep her comments to herself.

Trying a relaxation technique, she clenched and unclenched her hands in her lap. The technique failed.

Shifting to the edge of her seat, she stabbed the stack of papers with her index finger. "Don't you get it? This discussion matters because your son matters. If he needs help dealing with the fact that his mother is gone, and if that helps him continue being a good student and a good kid, then I want to get him that help."

"Fine. I'll take care of it." Blotches of red crept up his neck and face, and a muscle jumped in his neck. Good. Hopefully he felt as uncomfortable with this conversation as she did.

"I'm not telling you this information so that you'll simply 'handle it.' Zach's a good kid, but his behavior suggests there is something more going on inside of him that needs to be addressed. I recommend we get Zach in for regular sessions with the school counselor."

"Absolutely not," he gritted out from beneath a tight jaw. "My kid doesn't need a head shrink."

"Okay, welcome to the modern age. They're counselors, not head shrinks. And it might be nice to have someone for Zach to talk to outside the family."

"Son of a—Why would he need that?" He bit off the epithet like he was ripping through a piece of jerky. He froze, brows pulling together. "Is he behaving uh, weird or something?"

Her head came back. "No, not strangely. Look, Zach's acting out suggests that he might be internalizing the turmoil of his mother leaving. He may be feeling insecure. If we don't help him now, he could have problems down the road."

"Suggest? Could have? May be? Sounds real definite." Garrison snorted. "My family and I give him all the support he needs."

"Of course you all do. I just—"

"Is there anything else *important* that we need to discuss, Ms. Lopez?" The way he said her name…like it tasted foul.

Heat climbed her face. How the hell had she lost control of this meeting? No question, the train was well off the tracks. "No, but—"

The chair scraped backward as he stood, towering over her and the child-sized desks surrounding him. Stunned, she stood with him and circled around her desk.

"Thank you for your time." He shoved the hat back on and headed toward the exit as she followed. As he grasped the doorknob, he spun around, his thundercloud expression turning darker. "Say, don't you date Hank Brand?"

An imaginary fist tightened around her throat. Did they date? What a joke.

"I used to. What business—"

"What? You can pry into my past, but you don't like that dish served to you?"

"No, it's not—"

"Didn't you get your teaching job here a year or so ago?" His loud voice cut through the room, loud enough for other teachers or her principal down the hall to hear. She fought the urge to shush him.

"Yes. The beginning of last year." Before Hank dumped her.

"Isn't Hank's brother, Butch, the principal of this school?" Garrison pressed his mouth into a harsh line.

"No, that has nothing—" Blood drained to her feet until her head swam.

He strode back to her until he stood a foot away. "So. Let's see if I understand. You say my son's acting out and you think my kid needs professional help to fix him. There are bullies involved, and the principal hasn't stepped in to help. This same principal whose family doesn't like mine? That's pretty damn convenient. Hell, ol' principal Butch Brand probably wants my kid kicked out of school, out of spite. And this is the same Principal Brand whose brother you were dating? Who probably got you this job? Interesting."

Sure, she knew what it looked like. Didn't matter that her hiring had nothing to do with any family connections and everything to do with her obligation to repay her university loans to the school district. But at the end of the day, all that mattered were appearances, same as before. All her work, useless in the court of public opinion. If Garrison thought her job came from favoritism, other folks thought the same thing.

"Interesting? No," she whispered. "Listen, I care about your son. And for your information, I got here on my own merit and hard work, damn it."

No one, but no one, had worked harder to climb out of a past full of bad choices and zero family support to create a solid career than Sara. Now this rancher with his anger issues tried to negate her efforts and accuse her of benefiting from preferential treatment? Not happening.

As she opened her mouth to rebut him again, his intense golden stare slammed into her like an invisible wall, stopping her in her tracks. All of her muscles locked up. She felt sucked into a whirlpool but couldn't look away from the swirling gold flecks in his eyes. A roar, like rushing wind, engulfed her mind, and a stabbing pain made her blink back tears. Pressure built up beneath her skull, as if her brain swelled and ached.

What the heck? Maybe the stress of the day had given her a sudden migraine.

A brief spasm twisted Garrison's expression into something like sadness and resignation. Pain creased his brow, and then his features hardened into cold, impassive stone again.

The throbbing in her head eased by half, and her shoulders clenched, like she couldn't properly stand upright.

With the briefest motion, he nodded. "I know what you've said is true."

As if she would lie about his son? Or her job? What the hell had happened to this guy that he didn't even trust his kid's second-grade teacher?

"Of course it's true," she snapped. Pressing her fingertips to her temples, she willed the headache to go away.

"I'm sorry." He lifted his hand halfway to her, then dropped it back to his side.

Funny, it almost sounded like he apologized for her pain. She lifted her head and willed her shoulder and neck muscles to relax. Testing her legs, she made sure they worked before shifting her weight from one foot to another.

"*Mister* Taggart, my personal life has nothing to do with my professional life."

"You're right. Again, I apologize." He brushed his hand over his forehead, almost mimicking her movements. "Now you understand why I feel the same way about you prying into my family's business."

She flattened her palm on a nearby locker for support. "No. It's not the same. Just because I'm concerned about Zach and my recommendations are unpopular does not make the information less valid. His well-being has everything to do with his history. And my personal life has not a thing to do with any part of this discussion, thank you very much." Damn it, her voice had started to crack. Stupid nerves. She should have known better than to try to go toe to toe with this man.

His smile twisted into a cruel sneer. "Sure, your personal life has nothing to do with this discussion, Ms. Lopez. You keep right on thinking that. As for me, I'm going back home to my kid who, by the way, has nothing wrong with him, and I'm going to forget that this unpleasant meeting ever happened."

He spun on his boot heel, stomped to the door, and slammed it. As his footsteps faded away, she walked backward and bumped into the edge of her desk in an effort to reach her chair before her legs gave out on her. Slumping in her chair, she put her face into shaking hands. She pulled a tissue from the box on her desk and wiped her sweaty face. Tiny pieces of white tissue balled up and drifted onto her black pants.

After brushing the remnants of tissue onto the floor, Sara fished around in her purse for a compact. The high color in her cheeks reflected in the mirror had nothing to do with the morning's makeup application and everything to do with the furious woman staring back at her. The woman who now had bits of tissue on her forehead. She groaned and flicked the pieces away.

One day, she'd learn not to react when someone pushed her buttons. One day, but clearly not today.

Taking several deep breaths, she envisioned her stress levels dropping, but that didn't stop the tension pulling her nerves to their limits. With any luck, another teacher wouldn't drop in to investigate the shouting and door slamming.

She touched up her makeup and snapped the compact shut, tossing it back into her purse. What a day. God, only Monday.

Even better news: four more months until the next parent-teacher conference day.

CHAPTER 2

*G*arrison squeezed the handle of the open truck door like he clutched a roped steer. The familiar scents of the ranch welcomed him home. Dirt, hay, fresh air, and the sting of frigid air that heralded the cold front coming in tonight.

The Gros Ventre mountains with their snow-topped peaks reached up to the heavy, gray skies. Snow due tonight. Too early this year.

Shit. He had way too much to do before winter hit. The fresh air soured in his chest, and he let it out with an unhappy *whoosh*. Outside held cold and endless work. Inside the sprawling ranch house, with its large, handcrafted logs and glow of light, were more tasks he would rather avoid.

What the hell was he supposed to do about Zach? Was his son starting to manifest an ability like Garrison's? Damn it.

He lurched out of the truck and slammed the door, resting his fist on the icy metal.

Son of a bitch, he didn't have time for psychology mumbo jumbo. Any rational human could see that Zach was perfectly fine.

Anyone but his nosy teacher.

Worst of all, he'd bent his own rules today and used his ability to detect the truth back in that classroom—the same ability he should have fully used on his ex-wife last year. But who would have thought his wife would betray him?

The same guy who now thought his son's teacher would lie to him.

Hell, he didn't care how bad Sara's and his heads had ached afterward; he needed to know if she was telling the truth about Zach and about her relationship with the Brands.

Damn it all if her aura didn't glow a bright, confident pink. Not lying. Utterly sincere.

Sara Lopez. From the hint of a mischievous dimple in one cheek down to her ample curves, she personified everything Garrison wasn't.

He had no rounded edges. No gentle approach. No soft touch.

And he'd hurt someone who didn't deserve it.

Wretched power. Good only for invasion of privacy and continuous paranoia. Great.

So Sara was completely correct: What she did in her spare time was none of his goddamned business.

Even if he found himself a little curious about her personal life.

But not jealous.

He pressed his fist harder against the icy metal of the truck.

Bottom line: he had doubted someone. Again.

Sparing a brief glance at the cloud-covered mountains to the north and west, he pushed off the truck. On his way up the steps to the porch, he paused.

Instead of enjoying the clean mountain air and the lowing of distant cattle, instead of appreciating the handcrafted knotty wood beams and soaring roofline, all he saw was the looming to-do list from hell. And problems. Craploads of problems.

Stomping up the front porch steps, he pushed open the heavy wood door.

"Dad!" Zach slid on socked feet as he tried to stop near the front door but missed and bumped into the opposite wall. Seemingly unaffected, he bounced back in front of Garrison and grinned.

How had he not noticed that his son's curly, red hair had grown into an unruly mop? Time for a haircut.

Add another item to the to-do list.

An invisible vice clamped onto his heart and squeezed. His son wasn't something to check off a list.

Zach chattered away as he held on to the living room doorjamb and ran in place on the smooth floor. "Did you meet Ms. Lopez? Isn't she nice? Did she tell you I got two stars on my art project? Did she?"

Garrison eased the door closed, placed his hat on the hook, and took a deep breath. An eight-year-old with unlimited energy was a force to be reckoned with. What he'd give to harness that exuberance.

He rubbed his neck. "Yes, son. She is a very nice lady. Smart, too."

"Does she like me?"

In spite himself, he smiled. "Of course she likes you." He crossed his arms. "But she also talked about your behavior."

Zach's open, grinning face crumpled.

"What behavior?" Zach said. "I listen. I have good marks for staying in my seat. Um, and I only get marked down for talking *sometimes.*"

Shit, he sucked at this parenting thing. "Uh, did she ever say anything about you acting up with the other kids?"

Zach stared at the floor. "No."

"Want to try that answer again?" He would *not* use his ability to find the truth on his own child. Thankfully, he could read his open-book son without the help of any extra powers.

"Maybe." Zach slid his socked toe in an arc on the floor. "Some kids aren't that nice."

"Are they picking on you?"

"Naw." The corners of his mouth drawing down canceled out the attempt at a light tone. Bony arms peeked out from the sleeves of the shirt Shelby had bought Zach at the beginning of the school year.

"Really?" Garrison asked.

"Well, a couple of kids were kind of mean."

"How?"

"Nothing." He stared at the floor, puffed out his cheeks, and blew out the air. "They said stuff about how I don't have a mom."

When Zach raised his head, the depth of sadness in his light brown eyes nailed Garrison like a sucker punch to the jaw. How much had his kid been hiding? How much had he dealt with on his own? What kind of father didn't see how much Tiffani's leaving had hurt Zach?

His son toed the base of the wall. "And about not having a mom? That's crap."

Garrison snapped. "Who taught you to swear like that?"

His son's head whipped around, and he flushed red. "No one," he mumbled.

"Zach..."

"Well, Kerr was saying 'crap' a bunch when he and Eric were breaking that new horse." He dropped into a whisper and darted a glance behind him. "They said badder words, too."

Damn it, Garrison would have to talk with his younger brother, Kerr, about his language in front of Zach. Again. Garrison should talk with Kerr's business partner and honorary Taggart member, Eric, too. Add that item to the growing to-do list.

"So don't use that word. Just because other people say bad words doesn't make it right, okay?"

Zach's pale brow furrowed. "Okay."

"So. What about these kids in school? What happened, and what did you say back?"

"I said they were dumb, and..."

"And what?"

"And I maybe sort of pushed one of them."

"Sort of?"

"Really did," he whispered. Even his ears turned red.

"Remember what we talked about, duck and water?"

"Yeah, their words are water and I'm a duck, and those words just slide right off me and go into the pond."

"So can you work on that more?"

"Yeah."

Even though Zach had agreed with him, why did he feel like his son was still going to slug the next bastard who mocked him? Garrison's college major was business, not child psychology, damn it.

Silence stretched between them. Zach licked his lips. "So, um, want dinner?" Good grief, now his son had to throw him a bone. Garrison wouldn't win parent of the year any time soon.

CHAPTER 3

*T*hey followed their noses through the silent dining room into the bright, cheery kitchen. The moment he set foot on the shiny red-and-white tiles, his spirits lifted. Memories of past meals, crowded around the kitchen table, chattering and laughing, anchored him to this room. Better times, back then.

"Hi boys!" Garrison's sister, Shelby, blew an orange curl off her forehead and waved the hand that didn't hold a spatula. She flipped burgers in a skillet and stirred a steaming pot. The sizzling pops and scents of hot, fresh food tantalized his ears and filled his nostrils as his belly growled loudly.

"No calls? You're on dinner duty tonight?" he asked. "Thanks."

With a grin, she answered, "Yup, stupid hiker season ended a month ago, and the snows haven't started yet. So search and rescue gets a break before stupid skier season starts. I'm technically on call, but it's unlikely I'll be needed for another few weeks."

Garrison crossed his arms. "No one's happy you're still going into the Tetons, especially with the increased earthquake activity."

She shrugged. "Even more reason to get in there and help folks. Look, just because some mountain on the West Coast exploded is no reason to assume the Tetons are going anywhere."

"The Tetons don't worry me. It's the earthquakes kicked off from that caldera of lava next door that sits on a fault line: Yellowstone."

When she glared at him and flicked her gaze at Zach, Garrison clamped his mouth shut against any more misgivings. Didn't matter if she was a grown woman, Shelby was still his baby sister.

Straightening, she said, "And about dinner? You're welcome. If I don't cook once in a while, you all would never get anything green to eat, ever."

"Yuck, green stuff." Zach pulled a face.

Shelby crossed her eyes, looking even funnier with the wild curls that had escaped her ponytail and framed her face. A fake tuxedo apron engulfed her tall, slim frame.

"Broccoli." She raised the spoon in a mock menace at Zach between stirs.

"Oh, no!" Zach said in a high-pitched voice as he pretended to cower.

"But with ooey-gooey awesome cheese all over it!"

His son licked his lips again. Hook, line, and sinker. Shel was pure manipulation when it came to Zach, and Garrison loved her for it. She'd filled in as best she could over the past year after Tiffani left.

"Cheese! That sounds great, Auntie Shelby."

She pressed the ground meat patties with a spatula. "How about you quit your drooling, little man, and set the table?"

"Okay!" He ran around the kitchen like a dervish, slamming drawers and clanking plates so hard that Garrison cringed.

Damn, if only he could get that sort of enthusiasm out of Zach. How great would it be if things were easier between them? They would have good, solid father-son talks while riding horses or eating dinner. But good parenting took time and practice.

Time. Something else he lacked.

While Zach scampered around the table, Shelby pinned Garrison with a gold-flecked brown gaze beneath an arched eyebrow.

"So, how was the meeting today?" she asked.

Garrison gave her a curt shake of his head and eased into a spindled wood chair at one end of the table. She pressed her lips together with a wary expression and turned back to the food on the stove.

With a frown of concentration, Zach filled four glasses with milk and set one next to each plate. No spills. A wistful swell grew in Garrison's chest. His son was growing up too fast.

"Hey, Zach Attack, go get Grandpa," Shelby called over her shoulder.

He took off at full tilt, careening around the doorway and disappearing into the depths of the big ranch house. Garrison winced at the bangs and slams that drifted back to the kitchen.

"So?" She turned away from the stovetop and crossed her arms. If not for the serious frown, he would've laughed out loud at the tall version of Little Orphan Annie glaring at him.

"Teacher says he's acting out some."

"How come?"

"Who knows? Kids picking on him because of his mom."

"What a bunch of little pukes."

He loved her fierce mama-bear streak when it came to Zach. While it didn't take the place of their mom, gone these last five years, or his ex-wife Tiffani, Shelby's supportive presence had steadied his son.

"Just kids being stupid."

"You sure it's not anything else?"

He scrubbed his face. "Like Zach developing an ability?"

"Yeah."

"Hope not. You notice anything?"

"No. And you'd think I would get a sense if something was going on with him." She tapped her head.

A breath whooshed out. "I know. And the teacher didn't mention anything...suspicious...about his behavior." Maybe he could figure out a way to get Ms. Lopez to observe his son's behavior a little more closely. Eye in the sky, so to speak, in case the Taggart gift was starting up in his son.

"Well, that's good. So what did the teacher recommend?" She wiped her forehead with the back of her hand.

"Nothing helpful. Something about counseling and stuff. Dumb."

She faced him squarely. "Dumb? You think Zach talking with a counselor is dumb? Might help him. Tiffani only left a year ago. He still remembers."

"I know. Tiffani hasn't contacted us since she left, and I haven't been able to track her down." Truthfully, he hadn't given the task a ton of effort. She had what she wanted, and what she wanted didn't involve Zach or him.

"And you don't think his mom being gone bothers him?"

"Sure, but we're his family. We look after him."

"You're an idiot." Shelby blew another curl off her forehead with a scowl. "As good as the Taggart clan is, being here for each other, Zach may need more…professional help than we can give him. That's all I'm saying." She squinted at him. "You *were* nice to that teacher, right? Didn't go all grumpy, I-can-do-this-myself caveman on her, did you?"

Guilt socked him like a one-two punch to the midsection. "Uh, no."

"Uh, yes, you mean. That poor lady. How bad was it?"

He stared at the red-and-white-tile floor. "Not my most commendable moment."

"You should apologize."

"She's probably used to it."

"Used to getting abuse from parents? Have I mentioned lately that you're an idiot? No one deserves for people to be mean to them."

She studied him for another long moment, her eyes unfocusing in that eerie way of hers when she accessed the part of her unique ability that allowed her to read emotions. After a brief wince and a few blinks later, she smiled.

"What in the world?" She laughed. "You like the teacher!"

"Show off. Quit rooting around in my head just because you can." He leaned back in the chair. "Besides, you're wrong. Projecting. Wishful thinking."

"Ouch. Bitter, much?"

"No. Just saying you've missed the mark on this one. If you can't read me, maybe you can't read Zach, either." Satisfaction smeared a grin on his face. Take that.

Pain creased her brow. Then a dangerous scowl appeared. "All right, Zoltar, all knowing. You think you got me pegged and I'm making up what my power tells me? Then why don't you use that truth-or-lie ability on me and find out for sure?"

Well. Shit.

"What? No answer?" She lifted her hand. "Actually, why don't you use that lie-detector power on yourself? Because with each denial, your nose is growing, Pinocchio."

"Shel—"

"Can it. You know when you've been beat." Good point. After turning off the burners, Shelby pointed a wooden spoon at him. "So? Going to ask her out? Sara Lopez seemed like a nice kid in high school, minus some brushes with the law. But who doesn't have some kind of past, right?"

"No, I'm not asking anyone out. And what the hell is that supposed to mean?"

"One bad decision does not a character make. Wouldn't you agree?"

When she gave him that stare, broken up by some winces, it unnerved him, mostly because he could tell she was filtering his emotions the whole time. Anytime the Taggart siblings used their powers, it hurt, and Shelby was no exception.

"So?"

"So what?" he spat.

"Are you going to ask her out or what?"

"No. I have things to do here. And with Zach, there's no time...I'm still waiting to see if he's going to develop an ability."

"I don't think so. We all had ours by his age."

"Good. No kid can function normally with our family's weird powers."

"Uh, I manage fine." Shelby wrinkled her nose.

"You think avoiding close relationships is *fine?*"

She didn't meet his eyes but raised her hand when he opened his mouth. "Shut it, big brother, or I'll spill to everyone else about you and teacher."

"Doesn't matter, Shel. I'm never going to do anything about any feelings I might or might not have. Besides, there's too much work to be done here."

"You're kidding, right?" Lifting her hand, palm in, she presented three raised fingers. She lowered one finger at a time. "First, you have help: us. Second, you need to get out there. Date. Go, be a regular guy. Enjoy." Only her middle finger remained extended. "Third, you've been a zombie since Tiffani left. Even before then."

Well played, little sis.

He bit off a curse. "I wouldn't say 'zombie,' Shel."

"Get back in the game. Take a chance. Ask pretty teacher out. You might enjoy it."

"You're one to talk, avoiding—"

She hissed and pressed her lips together as Zach strolled into the kitchen, tugging Austin Taggart behind him.

With a groan, their father eased himself into the chair at the head of the table. He patted his belly; it was still only a small paunch. "Smells great, Shelby." The ranch work kept him fit, though he had slowed down considerably after Mom died.

She grinned and laid her apron on the counter. "It'll taste great, too. Zach, come get this plate."

They set the food out on the table, and for a minute, the only sound was the clank of serving spoons on bowls and the scrape of forks on plates.

After a few bites, Garrison looked up. "Did you get the back forty fence repaired, Dad?"

His dad ruffled Zach's hair. "Sure did. Your boy was a big help today, too."

Zach's beaming smile had orange cheese smeared all over it. Garrison fought the urge to wipe his son's face.

At his father's quick frown, Garrison tensed. "Did you find the lost cattle?"

He flicked a glance at Zach, who was busy creating orange tracks with his fork.

Lines, deeper than Garrison had seen before, creased the skin around his dad's watery blue eyes, suddenly aging him. "No, but the fence break was pretty extensive. Looked intentional."

Shelby stared at him.

Garrison put down his knife. "What do you mean?"

"A big section of fence had clean cuts in the wires, enough to let an ATV or someone on a horse to pass through. And there were some tracks in the open section."

"Exactly which section were you working on?" Garrison's hand curled into a fist.

"Top of the property, north section, where the mountains start."

"Near the national forest? Abutting the Brand property?"

"Yep." His dad raised a bushy eyebrow and passed a weathered hand over his face. "Something's going on over there."

"Like what?"

"Don't know. The Brands never liked us, ever since I moved here in the seventies and outbid them for this property. But they've been acting more squirrely than usual over the past year, especially after we turned them down on their offer for our ranch." He swiped at the circles under his eyes. "Now? Big equipment moving in and out of their property, but no one in town knows anything. Ol' Wyatt who runs the supply store was acting weird when I came in to buy feed the other day."

Shelby sat up straight and leaned forward. "Acting weird, how?"

"Cagey. Won't make eye contact. Snippy. Won't extend us credit anymore. He says no more local discounts, but it seemed personal. I don't know. Maybe I'm getting old and paranoid."

"What's 'paranoid'?" Zach piped up.

"Paranoid is what you're going to be if you don't finish your homework," Garrison said.

"Can I be excused?" Zach lifted his plate. "Look, Auntie Shelby, ate all my greens. They're all goooone."

"Good job!" Shelby's tight smile didn't reach her eyes.

"Wash up first," Garrison said.

Zach jumped out of the chair and was halfway to the kitchen doorway.

"Dishes!" Garrison called out.

Zach spun around on his socked feet, grabbed the plate, dumped it into the sink with a clatter, and dashed out of the kitchen. The thud of his feet on the stairs stopped, and the water ran in the bathroom upstairs. Full blast or nothing. That kid didn't have a second gear. If only Garrison had that much energy, he'd make a dent in the endless list of things to do.

"Dad, I don't like you taking Zach out there if the Brands are acting weird."

"Agreed. Didn't think fixing my own fences was dangerous until I saw the ATV tracks coming through the opening in my fence. And cattle tracks."

"You sure it was the Brands?" Shelby pulled on the end of an orange curl. "And what about any other ranches? Would they take the cattle?"

Their father rubbed the loose skin on his jaw. "Haven't heard of anyone else, and it makes sense. Given the area of fence cut, if someone else wanted to take our cattle, they'd have to cut through the Brand fencing, break through our fencing, take the cattle out, and run them through rough terrain in the mountains before getting back to flatland. That's if no one saw them. So, it's damned unlikely to be anyone else."

Garrison took a bite and swallowed. "To hell with them. We have enough to do without needing to deal with those losers. What's going on over there? Why can't they just leave us alone?"

His dad shook his head. "No idea, but Hank Brand called again today, asking if we'd sell our ranch to them. Again."

Shelby's head whipped up to stare at their father.

Garrison's vision blurred. Damn it, they'd already told that man no. "He did what?"

"Said he reckoned we might be losing money, and they could help us make up the losses if we sold."

Cheeks blazing red, Shelby leaned forward. "It's odd how much he knows about our financial situation. It's none of their business. I hope you told him to go shove it."

"Not in so many words." The lines next to his eyes deepened. "But yes, 'not interested' was the general message."

Garrison set down his fork and knife on the empty plate. "They have a good-sized spread. Why does he need ours, too?"

"Don't know," his dad said. "Might have to do with whatever project is going on over there. We need to keep our eyes and ears open."

"Damn it," Garrison cursed. "We can't do anything about his little project. But what about the cattle? Can we go looking for our ear markings and tags?"

"We'd be trespassing."

Garrison snorted.

"I believe they trespassed, too, son, since that livestock is gone. Any smart cattle thief wouldn't hesitate to tear the ears, remove the tags, or slaughter the cattle by now. We'll never get proof. All we can do now is prevent them from stealing more."

"Son of a bitch. That means we'll have to move our herd down sooner this year. This week. Soon."

"Yep."

"So we're going to need more hay, earlier than usual?"

His dad nodded.

"Going to cost more money." Garrison scrubbed at his face. So much shit piling up. He turned to Shelby. "What's your availability this week?"

Maybe he could convince her to help. God knew, there was enough work to go around. She liked to bury herself in volunteer duties on the area's search-and-rescue team. Due to her extra ability, she never came back from a mission empty handed. Of course, none of her teammates knew about her gift; they simply thought she was incredibly lucky.

She had the strongest abilities of all the Taggart kids, no question. Even if she hated the part of her gift where she could read others' emotions, her second ability to find anyone more than made up for it.

If only she didn't drive herself to near collapse trying to find each victim.

He sure as hell didn't want her back up in the Tetons with the increased seismic activity in the region. If tourists were dumb enough to go off-trail despite the heightened danger, then they could damn well rescue themselves and not make his sister put her life on the line for them.

However, making Shelby do anything fit on the scale of impossible things right between finding Bigfoot and discovering Atlantis.

She raised her hands. "It's unlikely I'll get called out on a rescue. Don't worry, I'll give you a hand moving the herd down."

"I'd appreciate the help." Garrison drained his glass. "Speaking of help, when's Kerr coming back?"

She rolled her eyes. "He's on an elk hunt with a group of guys from Texas. Fancy gear. Big mouths. He'll be back in a few days."

Their dad smiled. "Don't laugh, Shelby. Those flatlanders might get off the plane with the sales tags still on their brand spanking new Cabela's gear, but they bring in a lot of money."

"Is Eric guiding with Kerr?" Garrison asked.

"Think so. Those guys are two peas in a pod." She smiled. "I told Eric the other day he was our brother from another mother."

"Pretty accurate."

She pressed her hands to the table. "So, when do you want the cattle moved?"

"All right, then." He wiped his mouth and crumpled the napkin on the plate. "We'll wait until Kerr and Eric are back, then move the herd. Hopefully Eric will help, if he also doesn't have to work search and rescue this week."

"I don't know his schedule." Her answer was too abrupt.

With a weary set to his shoulders, Dad pushed back from the table. "Thank you for dinner, honey. It was delicious." He dropped his dishes into the sink and trudged out of the kitchen.

Shelby frowned. "He's still not the same after Mom died."

"He's slowing down. It's been five years. But it takes time. One day he'll move on."

"Like you and Tiffani? Yeah, I agree. Time to move on."

Time. Hell, he'd barely had time to process the whole exploding mess that was the end of his marriage. Maybe when he dug out from under the work here, he could sit on the beach, sip margaritas, and mull over his stupidity.

"It's nothing like my situation. And moving on is easier said than done. Discussion over."

"What about the ranch issues, Vaughn leaving, and Kerr being back home but not totally okay? All of it's wearing on Dad. I'm worried about him."

"Son of a bitch, Shel, I can't fix everything."

After a pause, she tapped her chin. "What about the dreams? You still having those?"

Garrison wanted to deny it but couldn't. "Yeah. Erupting volcano. Dark cave. Red eyes. Lava. And a woman's hand stretched out to me."

Shelby pinched the bridge of her nose. "Me too. I can't see her face. It's like she wants to help me. But then there's blackness that swallows her up."

"And pain?"

"And pain." She swallowed. "Kerr's having similar dreams, too. No idea what they mean. What do you think?"

"How the hell should I know?" he snapped, a red film covering his vision. "I'm up to my eyeballs in bullshit. Why don't you work on figuring out the dreams?"

If only he weren't so worn out, he'd try to take the pain away from her expression.

"So, poor ol' you, then? You've got some nerve," she spat. "Like you have a corner on worry and stress."

Nasty silence crackled between them until she put a hand to her forehead, no doubt trying to deflect his steaming anger. Too bad for her, he couldn't tamp down his feelings. Too worn out. He was so tired, his eyeballs ached.

So she absorbed the full force of his emotions, with only her innate filters damping the onslaught.

When he opened his mouth to apologize, she scooted back and raised her hand. "Let me know when you want to move the herd."

A pile of manure stunk less than he did right about now.

"Look, I'm—"

"Shut up, Garrison. I know you're stressed and worried about Zach and the ranch. I get it. Go to your happy place or think about cute teacher, but don't take your crap out on me, okay? I can only filter so much raw emotion. Once I get tired, I end up absorbing all of the feelings people throw off—you got it?"

"Yes." He couldn't meet her eyes but took a breath to say more.

"Damn you. Stop talking. Please." As she rubbed her temples, her wild hair stood up in crazy curls. "I'll be ready to help tomorrow, but right now, I need to sit by myself and air out my brain."

"Understood. And I'm sorry." He massaged the back of his neck. "Do whatever you have to so you'll be ready. I'll need you to find every last one of our remaining cattle. We can't afford to leave any behind. Our margins are beyond tight."

Her mouth turned down briefly. "Got it. Radar's ready." She tapped her head. Too brightly, she said, "All systems will be 'go' for the roundup."

He didn't fault her for nearly running out of the kitchen. No one wanted to be around his black thoughts, least of all his sister. He rubbed his own temple in empathy. At what point would she tell him off for his request to exploit her bloodhound skills? At least she had a useful power. All he got out of his lie-detector ability was a headache, self-loathing, and zero trust in other humans. No climbing mountains, no lives saved. Just supernatural levels of cynicism.

As much as he hated to put Shelby through more pain by asking her to use her power, he needed to get those cattle if the ranch was going to stay above water this year. So, greater good, lesser evil.

Damn it, he didn't want to think about the ranch anymore this evening.

Not an option. He pushed to his feet and headed out to do the never-ending chores.

CHAPTER 4

"*I*zzy, I'm telling you, that entire meeting was weird." Sara inhaled the minty essence of her mojito before sipping. The evenings after parent-teacher meetings always deserved a stiff drink or three.

"Garrison was probably having a bad day." Isabelle Brand pushed her long, golden hair back over a shoulder. She appeared oblivious to the glances from several men in the bar.

Some women had all the luck. If Izzy weren't the nicest person in the world and Sara's best friend, it would be much easier to hate her. Sara blew out a breath full of frustration. Her friend would have handled Garrison Taggart better than Sara had.

Okay, seriously? Quit the pity party already.

"So what else about the meeting?" Izzy asked.

"Garrison brought up how I had dated Hank."

"Yikes. In a parent-teacher conference? Can you say, 'inappropriate'? Besides, you and Hank broke up a year ago."

"Yeah, what a mess." She glanced over her shoulder as invisible cold fingers walked up her neck. "Sorry. I know Hank's your brother and all."

"You can't offend me. Besides, he's a moron for leaving you."

Sara dabbed at the condensation on her glass until the bead of water ran down onto the bar. "Thanks."

Izzy drained her beer before propping her chin on her fist. "Ever wish you and Hank could get back together?" The sincerity in her sky-blue eyes took away the question's sting.

"No, we're done. That fact was made crystal clear. To be fair, we didn't have a future, especially after he started acting strangely." She used the straw to bury the slice of lime beneath the ice in the glass. "I mean it. Breaking up was for the best. It was just frustrating to have my past raked over the coals by Garrison."

"I bet." She pushed her empty bottle away and lifted her chin at the bartender for another beer. "Man, I know he's my brother and all, but I still can't get over the fact that Hank was a jerk to you. He's gone kind of nuts over the past year."

"How?"

"You know how a few weeks ago, I said he was cooking up some get-rich scheme? Well, he's got two of my brothers totally wrapped up in the idea, and they've become all secretive. Somehow it involves the Taggart's ranch. But the guys don't say much around me, even when I ask."

"Really? That's weird."

"Yup, I end up stuck at home doing all the housework and dealing with Mom and her health issues. They're not helping with Mom anymore, which kind of sucks. Now, they're out in the hills, dreaming up God-knows-what harebraned plan. And they won't tell me anything." Izzy scraped her long hair off her face. The corners of her mouth dropped.

"That stinks."

"At least I still have you to talk with."

Sara covered her friend's hand with hers. Anything to erase the sad downturn to Izzy's mouth. Ever since Sara showed up in first grade wearing mismatched thrift shop leftovers, with no parents to drop her off, Izzy had been right there. *Like peanut butter and jelly,* they used to giggle to each other.

Even after Sara's stupid shoplifting phase as a teenager, Izzy had stood up for her—unlike most folks around here who still ruminated over the new teacher's checkered past.

"Of course. I'm always here to talk," Sara said.

The new beer arrived, and Izzy wrapped her long fingers around the frosty bottle. "Thanks." She blinked and her expression went from unhappy to mischievous. "Speaking of topics that are interesting, I haven't seen Garrison in a long time. He mostly stays at the ranch, and I haven't had as many shifts at the hardware store lately. Is he still hot and available?"

At Izzy's eyebrow waggle, Sara laughed despite herself. "Ha. If you mean is he a stubborn and surly cowboy, then the answer is yes. We didn't get to spend much time discussing the particulars of his relationship status."

"You know his wife left him last year."

"Yes. It's not a secret. But no one seems to know why."

Izzy sipped her beer. "True. Most folks figure she ran off with someone. But who'd want to leave such a fine hunk of man as Garrison? Rough break."

"I don't know. Takes two to tango, as they say. A woman would have to be pretty unhappy to leave her husband and child."

"Maybe."

Sara crossed her arms. "What if he brought a lot of the problems down on his own shoulders?"

"What? Just by being...the way he is?" Izzy shrugged. "Could be. But really, we don't know the whole story about everything that happened and why she left." Damn her friend's accepting attitude.

Just like the people in town didn't know all of Sara's story, yet judged her. Suddenly, the drink soured against the shame coating her tongue. She had judged him without trial. Hypocritical much?

She swallowed. "Right about now, I'm mostly worried about Zach." Weak recovery.

"Maybe there will be a chance to meet again and help his son out?"

"Hopefully not until next spring. I can't take another parent-teacher conference like that one."

Izzy paused, then her blue eyes shone. "Hey, remember when we were in high school and we went to the rodeo finals to watch him? Man, I'd love for a cowboy like that to rope me any day. He could keep me tied up for more than the mandatory five seconds!"

Sara snorted, the drink burning her nostrils.

The effervescent sound of Izzy's laugh drew even more male attention. Cowboy hats rotated in her direction.

Of course the men would want to look at Izzy. Not Izzy's fault, either.

"Five seconds. That's hilarious." Sara laughed.

She whispered, "Wonder if all that pounding in the saddle messes up, you know, a guy's other parts?"

Sara nearly spit out her drink and had to cough to clear her throat. "You're impossible."

"And that's why you love me!" They leaned their heads together until Izzy's face relaxed. "Did Garrison mention how his brother was doing?"

"Kerr?"

Izzy's cheeks turned red. Ten dollars said the blush had nothing to do with the alcohol. "You know, after the military and injury and all, how he's getting along."

"If I didn't know better—"

"You don't know better. Just curious to see if he's doing okay after he got hurt, that's all." She took another swig. The laughter in her voice flattened into something like resignation. "Never mind."

"Izzy—"

Pressing her perfect, pink lips together, she gripped the neck of the bottle, her knuckles turning white. Izzy stared at the brown glass. "Man, I don't want to go back home tonight."

"So move out. You can stay with me or get a rental in town."

She blew out a deep breath. "Can't right now. They're all guilt-tripping me. Mom, my brothers. They say I can't leave now; Mom needs me there. What with the drilling—"

"What drilling?"

"Part of that stupid plan I mentioned. Idiot brothers. Got a wild hair that there's riches in them thar hills."

"Just like that?"

"I don't know, exactly, but Hank's got them all fixated on finding something. Invested all their savings to put in some equipment near the foot of the mountains."

"Why?"

"Why do men do anything? Probably because it's there and they've dreamed up a plan. God only knows." She waved her hand. "Enough about my stupid family. Let's talk more about your rodeo boy."

"Izzy, he's a parent of one of my students. I was having a professional conference with him."

"Throw me a bone here. Make something up. I need to live vicariously."

"Since when? You can have the pick of the litter any day." Sara gave a small gesture to the sets of eyes that followed Izzy's every move.

She shrugged and shook her head. "So were his jeans tight?"

Sara dropped her voice and put her hand to her mouth. "Are you serious?"

"As a heart attack. I need details." She sipped on her beer. "Come on, spill."

And now Sara's heart went pitter-patter. Great. "Um, well, maybe a little tight. I mean, I wasn't really looking…"

Izzy grinned. "Your denial is hilarious. Garrison's hot. Don't you think so?"

Sara spun on the stool to face her friend. "Holy mother of God, of course he's hot. But I'm not interested in anyone right now."

"I thought you weren't Catholic anymore."

"I'm recovering. It's still a crutch for cursing."

"Got it. So, not interested in anyone because of Hank?"

Sara said nothing as a blob of unhappiness spread out from her chest until her whole body ached. It wasn't only because of Hank, but that epic fail hadn't helped. She had to choose: successful career, loan repayment, and her professional future versus dating in this small town. She'd already wasted years before going to college; well, she'd been kind of a directionless bum for a while, heaven help her patient and kind aunt and uncle, and God rest their souls. She'd had no direction, no plans, but at least she'd kept out of more legal trouble for those lost years.

With college behind her, she wanted to get on with creating a normal life. As eagerly as her biological clock encouraged her to find a good man and settle down, reality dictated that she avoid making any more missteps with her reputation. Which meant extreme caution with any relationship.

Besides, she had a plan for her future. And that plan did not involve Copper River. A plan that would take her far away from this place and to teach in an upscale suburb of Atlanta with a friend from college. She just needed to finish her obligations to Copper River, and then Sara could follow the path she'd mapped for herself. Any entanglements here would only derail her goals.

Izzy squeezed her hand. "My brother's such a dope."

"You've already mentioned that."

"It bears repeating." She removed her hand and tapped her chin. "Fine. Let's say you weren't gun-shy from Hank. Would you date Garrison Taggart?"

"Shush! People will hear you." Sara absently touched her lips, then shoved her hand in her lap. "Maybe. But he's not interested in me, and besides, I don't want to date anyone right now."

"How could he not be interested in you? You're super cute."

At least her friend was supportive. Sara played with the coaster edge. Enough. No thinking about activities with a certain rancher that would never happen.

Besides, if a rugged rancher wanted a partner, he didn't need to look further than Izzy. Even now, all of the male attention in the establishment focused on those unfairly long legs, glossy blonde hair, and other assorted assets.

Sara waved her hand. "Doesn't matter. He's pissed off at me from the unpleasant parent-teacher conference."

"Why?"

"Can't share that info. It's protected. Let's just say he stormed out of the meeting."

"Ouch. Maybe the next meeting will be better."

"Couldn't be worse."

"True." She spun her stool away from the bar. "Want to dance? Those guys are getting frisky." Izzy tossed her blonde hair over a shoulder and smiled. One of the men tipped his hat and pushed away from a booth, his dark eyes locked on her.

"You go right ahead. Looks like you're about to have some options for your evening. I'm headed home. Work tomorrow."

"You know what? You're right. And I should get home, too. I'll walk out with you." She pulled out her phone and typed.

"Sure you should drive?"

"No way. I texted Wyatt, and he'll be by in a little while after he closes the hardware store."

Another Brand brother Sara didn't want to interact with. Her stomach clenched. What a mess. It would be centuries before she dated again, at least in Copper River.

The problem wasn't that she had loved Hank. He was someone to date while she spent the required four years in Copper River, fulfilling her obligation so she could pay off her loans. If she was truthful with herself, she had never imagined meeting him at the end of a church aisle with her in a white dress. Hell, she had never gotten butterflies over their next date.

It wasn't even that he'd become erratic and downright mean, which led to her breakup with him.

What hurt was how he had responded and why.

For such an initially pleasant guy, Hank Brand had been cruel and detailed in his retaliation, shredding her reputation and ego like a sharp cheese grater. It was like he'd been taken over by another person altogether.

You're a piece of bastard trash, he had said. *You came from trash, and that's what you'll always be.*

In this day and age, that kind of thinking should have gone the way of the horse and buggy, but apparently not in Copper River, Wyoming. At least not for Hank Brand.

According to him, she possessed no value as a person or as a lover, and he'd only dated her for something to do. Someone to do. A cure for his boredom. In fact, if he could be believed, then he already had someone else waiting in the wings.

God, how he'd smashed the emotional supports she had finally built one piece at a time over the years.

All that hard work to try to prove herself: going to college, earning her degree, and creating a respectable career and life. All done to negate her upbringing and her adolescent mistakes.

Still not good enough.

She hugged Izzy good night before a Brand brother could show up and make a bad day even worse. Tucking her arms around herself in the chilly air, Sara trudged the few blocks to the rental house one street over from Main.

The silence in the home didn't welcome her this time.

CHAPTER 5

The next afternoon, for the second day in a row, dread clenched at the center of Sara's chest.

She squeezed the arms on her office chair as she stared at her classroom, which had stood empty for an hour. Since the students left, she had pretended to work but accomplished nothing.

Suddenly, her knit top and cardigan became too warm.

How was she going to tell Garrison?

What he'd alluded to at yesterday's conference, some kind of bad blood between the Taggarts and Brands, appeared to be true.

The two Brand kids had once again bullied Zach at recess, and she had gone to Butch Brand, the principal and the boys' uncle. She expected Butch to maintain objectivity. She thought he would see the problem and offer a solution.

Nothing. He gave her nothing but platitudes. No disciplinary intervention. No support for her concerns.

With a flippant "boys will be boys," he'd brushed her off and consigned Zach to continued torment. And Butch's thinly veiled ultimatum to "mind her own business" had made it clear: If she valued her job, she shouldn't intervene.

Good Lord, of course she wanted to keep her job—had to, if she wanted her school loans forgiven. Besides, no way would she fail at her first job. But as a newly minted teacher, she had no leg to stand on. She couldn't fight the administration.

Yet she'd be damned if a kid would get bullied on her watch.

Sara knew how it felt, knew how being a victim of bullying would affect Zach later in life. She'd been the only Latino kid in school in Copper River. Double whammy for her, and extra ammo for the kids in school. You'd think times had changed, what with bullying aware-ness and all, but Zach's situation took her back. She was the kid, standing on the edge of the playground, hoping to be noticed, but not by the mean kids.

Still, she could only imagine what that kid endured. Teachers saw only a fraction of the actual bullying.

So. Decision time. Stick her neck out for the kid, or keep quiet and preserve her career?

Taking a deep breath, Sara dialed the number on file.

"Hello?" Garrison's rumbling voice came through the earpiece, sliding shivers up her spine.

"Yes, uh, this is Sara Lopez, Zach's teacher."

"Is he in trouble again?"

She pulled the phone away at his barked response. "No. And he wasn't in trouble when we talked yesterday, either."

"Is he acting weird?"

"No. Not at all. Why would you think that?" Seriously, talking with this man was like facing a rapid-fire interrogation.

"Doesn't matter. Never mind."

"Okay…"

"So then what's the problem?"

She flinched at the curt tone.

Her tongue turned to sand. "Um—"

He interrupted. "You know what? Forget this phone call. You and I need to talk about some things. Are you at school?"

"Yes, but—"

"I'll be over there in a half hour."

"No, you don't—"

"Stay put."

The line went dead. Her heart rapped a staccato beat on her ribs. Good Lord, he sounded pissed.

Forty minutes later, Sara gave up on waiting and headed to her car. The parking lot was empty as frigid twilight turned the school grounds gray. Garrison Taggart probably had a million things more important to do. Zipping her winter coat closed, she bent into the biting wind. The heavy clouds threatened snow.

A rumbling dually sped onto the asphalt. The truck had barely stopped when Garrett burst out of the vehicle. The parking lot light cast shadows beneath the brim of his hat and enhanced his dark glower as he stomped over to her. Sara shuffled backward until she bumped into her sedan.

"Why are you leaving?" he said, not bothering to button his sheepskin and leather jacket. His narrowed gaze raked over her, like she'd been indicted and found guilty before the trial.

She gulped. "You said thirty minutes. I thought you'd changed your mind or were detained."

"I'm here now, aren't I?"

The aggressive stance made her shy away, but it was at odds with how his low voice wrapped around her like a toasty wool blanket. Come to think of it, no blanket ever made her pelvis tighten.

"Well, yes." The cold air crawled under her coat.

He ground his booted toe into the pavement and shoved his hands in his jacket pockets. "Um, I need to apologize."

"What?" He'd gone from mad to contrite in a millisecond. Her neck hurt from the emotional whiplash. Was he playing some game with her? She stepped forward to better study his face.

"Apologize. Say I'm sorry. That kind of junk." He grimaced and shifted from foot to foot. At least his discomfort rivaled hers.

"Junk, huh?"

"Um. Son of a bitch. Not quite the right word."

Hugging her arms to her chest, she tried not to quake as the icy air worked its way through her cotton slacks. "Okay, I'll bite. Why do you need to apologize, Mr. Taggart?"

He stared at the ground. His tense jaw relaxed, and his mouth turned downward. A softer, younger Garrison emerged from that rigid, angry facade.

"I was, uh, a little short with you yesterday."

And you call today's attitude warm and fuzzy?

"If you say so."

"Look, Zach means the world to me, and I get mad if things aren't going great for him. That's all."

"He's a good kid. And I expect some parents might get upset in the conferences if what I tell them isn't 100 percent positive. But in the end, it's all for the benefit of my students."

"I get it. So—" He held his work-roughened hands out, palms up. "Look, I'm sorry."

"All right, fair enough. Apology accepted. So about—"

"So can I take you out to dinner?"

With a step back, she bumped into her car door. "Come again?"

"Out? To dinner. Together."

How in the name of God had this man switched gears so quickly from a grumpy, half-assed apology to propositioning her for a date? Keeping up with Garrison's moods was like watching a human tennis match.

"No, that's not why I...Look, I called you because I wanted to discuss Zach."

"I understand that." He squinted up at the darkening sky. "It's too cold to have this conversation outside. Your workday is over. I'm hungry. You might be hungry, too. Let's talk about this over dinner."

"I'm not sure that's a good idea."

"Why not? It would give us time to chat about Zach."

Since when did Garrison Taggart *chat?* "I don't know..."

"It'll give me a way to make up for being a jerk."

"Well, you have a point there."

At his lopsided smile, her heart flipped in her chest. *It's not a date, damn it.* They were only going to discuss his son. So why, then, did she have trouble catching her breath? Had to be the cold air.

"So?"

When he stared at her like that, all focused and with a determined lift of his chin, he made her hungry, and not for dinner.

She hit the button on her car fob, unlocking the door. "Fine. I'll meet you at the Hungry Moose."

A shadow of a smile bent the slash of his mouth upward.

CHAPTER 6

A few minutes later, Sara slid into the vinyl booth seat at Copper River's local diner. Garrison sat across from her. What in the world was she doing? Nothing like giving folks in town something else to talk about. Damn it, coming here was a stupid move. Even now, Sara felt the eyes of other diners on her, making connections.

New teacher? Check.

Shoplifting past? Check.

Questionable parentage? Check.

And, oh look, now she's out with Garrison Taggart, whose wife recently left him. Isn't that interesting?

Fabulous. It didn't matter that this was work related; it only mattered what people saw.

Ducking her head, she studied the menu instead of the man sitting a few feet away. Even after she ordered and no longer had a menu to hide behind, she couldn't figure out where to rest her hands and eventually chose to stuff them between her slacks and the worn vinyl cushion.

Garrison stared at her with those amber-colored eyes dotted with gold flecks, a frown forming between his brows. What the hell was he staring at? She smoothed her cardigan and pushed her hair back over her shoulders.

With his hat off, his hair glinted like banked embers. Curling back off his forehead, his hair remained wild despite his brushing a hand to smooth it. His thick fingers wrapped around a glass of water, and she fixated on the dark red hair on his wrists, peeking from under the edge of his thick flannel shirt. What would his skin look like under that sleeve? Would his arms have ropes of hard muscle, brushed with ruddy hair? Would his biceps tighten under her touch?

He raised the auburn slash of his thick brows; her breath caught. "So?" he asked, startling her out of her unprofessional thoughts.

They were having a work-related dinner, that's all. She cleared her throat. "You recall my concerns about Zach and the other kids?"

"Clearly."

No one could accuse Garrison of being verbose. Her face warmed. "He got bullied again today."

"Explain."

"After it happened, I took my concerns to the principal, but he blew it off."

"Butch Brand?" He bit out the name. Hopefully, no one in earshot heard.

Whispering, she continued, "Yes. And, um, the kids picking on Zach were the Brand twins."

"Tommy Brand's kids? Butch's nephews? What did those hoodlums say?"

It looked like the glass would break, so hard did he grip it.

She needed to be careful.

"They said stuff about Zach not having a mother around."

He cursed under his breath. "Those kids were out of line, but damn their parents. That's who influenced them." He shoved his hand through his hair, giving it a wilder, even more untamed look.

"I'm so sorry. I broke the kids up, but it was clear that what they said bothered Zach."

"The Brands have it in for our family. No idea why."

"Seems odd, since I had those two kids in class last year and they seemed like good boys."

"Something changed in the past year."

"With the kids?"

"With all of that family." He took a swig of water and set the glass down with a clunk. "The kids might be fine, but their parents are not. That whole family. They're not nice people."

"I don't know all of them. I'm good friends with Izzy Brand, and she's nothing like her brothers."

"Sooner or later, she'll join her family in hating us."

"That can't be true, Garrison."

"Just you wait." He dropped his hand on the table hard enough for her to jump.

The food came—thank goodness she could focus on taking a few bites instead of trying to deflect Garrison's anger.

When his Adam's apple bobbed with a bite, a quiver worked its way through her belly. Dragging her eyes from his corded neck, her gaze passed his stubbled chin and rested on his firm lips. Which moved as he talked.

Pay attention.

"...why are you sticking up for my kid? I mean, since you have ties to the Brand family—"

"I have no connection to them," she snapped. A patron at a nearby table glanced over. She took a steadying breath. "Trust me. I don't want anything to do with Hank, and the feeling is most definitely mutual."

"Why?" Garrison held up his hand. "I'm sorry. Forget it. It's not my business."

"No, that's okay. I'll answer your first question. I'm sticking up for Zach because I understand why he got bullied." She folded the napkin in half and half again, so neatly. "I grew up without a mother or a father." The napkin morphed into a crumpled ball in her fist. "I spent my childhood being told I wasn't good enough because of living with my aunt and uncle. You'd think nowadays, kids wouldn't get picked on for having single parents or absent parents. But yes, when I saw Zach being bullied, I couldn't stand by and do nothing."

Silence stretched as he studied her face. A muscle ticked in his jaw. The intense focus…no. She wouldn't squirm beneath the weight of his stare.

She shifted in her seat. Damn it.

"Thank you for watching out for my boy." His voice, like coarse gravel, scraped over her raw nerves, and she shivered.

"Of course," she mumbled, concentrating on the drop of water scudding down the outside of her glass. Anything to avoid meeting those mesmerizing eyes.

He shifted in the seat, drawing her attention. The harsh set to his mouth compressed into a grim line. "So, what happened when you talked with the principal?"

"Simplest explanation? He blew me off."

"How do you mean?"

"When I tried a second time to explain my concerns about Zach, Butch insinuated that my job was at risk if I intervened. And that was the end of the conversation." Something about Garrison made her want to open up, just a tiny bit. "I feel like I failed Zach."

When Garrison grazed her wrist with his work-roughened fingertips, she jumped.

"Hey. Are you okay?" he asked in a low voice.

"I care about my students." Damn it if her eyelids didn't burn. What was it about this man? Maybe she was more upset about the very real possibility that her job was at risk.

The corners of his mouth bent downward as he rubbed the back of her hand, sparking sensations up her arm that also fell into the "unprofessional" category. His touch had the added bonus of triggering a sudden urge to cry. For her own sanity, she needed some space. When she withdrew her hand, the absence of his warmth created a strange emptiness inside of her.

"Let's change the subject, okay?" he said.

The tightness lodged in her throat released. "Sounds good to me."

"You grew up here, right?"

The one subject she didn't want to discuss and he had to pick it? "Um, yes."

"Where did you move from?"

"Texas."

He closed one eye and squinted. "But you lived with your aunt and uncle."

And now the urge to squirm started up again. "Yes. They've both passed away."

"That's right. That was after high school, right?"

What the heck, Mr. Twenty Questions?

"But you came back after college? Even with the trouble you'd had earlier…" When his voice trailed off, two patches of red tinted his hard cheekbones. "Son of a bitch, I stuck my foot in, didn't I? Look, never mind. Forget I asked anything. Damn it, here I get all mad at you for prying and look who's the Nosy Nellie now?" The repentant half-smiling guy across from her made her heart flop over.

Sara ducked her head and put her hand to her temple, blocking her words from prying ears. "It was hard enough growing up here where everyone knew my family's dirty laundry and my mistakes. When I came back, it was important to project a solid, respectable life." She snorted a tiny laugh. "Little good that did, with the whole Hank thing."

Garrison frowned. "I've been out of the loop, obviously. I knew your aunt and uncle raised you, and so what? But what kind of trouble did you get into?"

"You were wrapped up in rodeo and off at college then. Shelby and Kerr were a grade ahead of me and probably know a lot more." She systematically shredded the napkin on the table. "I never had a father, and my mother left me here when I was around Zach's age, when we moved here. Or rather, she dropped me off here. I never saw her again, but I kept hoping she'd come back and get me. Years later, when I found out about her death, I gave up and kind of rebelled."

"How?"

Was that…sincerity in his eyes? Like he truly cared about what she had to say. Like he wasn't judging her. Long may Garrison's acceptance last. She resisted the urge to cross herself.

"Um, I shoplifted a few times in high school. Stupid stuff."

"Why?"

She sniffed. "The *head shrinks* said I was acting out because of abandonment issues. But what do they know, right?" She continued to deconstruct the napkin into tiny pieces.

"Yeah, about what I said yesterday about the counselor. That was stupid and—"

Holding her hand up, she said, "It's okay." When he opened his mouth, she added, "Please. Let it go."

After mock wiping his brow, his expression softened. "So I'm having dinner with a hardened criminal?"

"One petty theft away from wearing an orange jumpsuit. Or so I've been told."

He nodded and folded his hands on the table. "What about your family here?"

The neat pile of paper continued to grow. "Staying with my aunt and uncle was safer than living hand to mouth and dealing with the never-ending line of Mom's mean boyfriends. Problem was, most everyone in town here knew how messed up Mom was."

"Why did you return to Copper River later on, if you wanted a fresh start?"

"No choice, unless I want to be in debt for the rest of my natural life. I'm working here through a program with the county department of education. To combat a shortage of teachers, they paid up front for my college. In return, I owe them four years of teaching, and then I'm footloose and fancy-free. That is, if I can keep my job. God, if I lose this teaching job, I'm on the hook for the full four years of college. Immediately."

He tapped her arm, startling her into halting her shredding activity. His crooked smile turned her to boneless goo. "Hey. It'll be fine."

She folded her hands in front of the paper pile. "Sure."

"So how was it, coming back to Copper River?"

"While I was in college, my aunt and uncle died in a car accident.

So returning here wasn't the homecoming I'd hoped for. But I have some friends in town, and dating Hank was nice for a while."

"Really?" The gold in his eyes turned to crystals of yellow ice.

"Yes, seriously. Believe it or not, he started out as a fairly decent guy. Last year, around this time, something changed. Like a switch flipped."

"Did he hurt you?" White lines formed at the corners of his mouth.

When was the last time a man truly cared about her well-being? Damn it if her ovaries didn't do a tiny tap dance in response to his protective tone.

"No, nothing physical. I initiated the breakup, but he got pretty mean." Although she aimed for a casual, couldn't-care-less tone, her voice broke. "He said I came from nothing, I'd amount to nothing, and I am worth nothing. End of story."

Garrison grasped both of her hands in his strong, steady grip and squeezed. Warmth and unexpected pleasure flowed up her arms.

"Look at me," he commanded, and she complied. "Hank's wrong. You and I both know it."

"Of course." With reluctance, she pulled her hands out of his. "Look, can we talk about something else? This conversation has veered way off course. We're not here for a pity party, and that's not what you signed up for."

"Okay, but I'm, uh, glad you shared that stuff with me." He looked about as comfortable with her sharing as a balloon in a room full of porcupines.

"Sure you are." She tamped down the sarcasm. He didn't deserve it. "But we *are* here to help Zach."

Leaning back on the seat, he rubbed his jaw. "I agree, but how?"

Ignoring how his big shoulders flexed under the shirt fabric, she pressed ahead. "Not sure what's best that doesn't somehow draw unwanted attention to Zach."

"Or you."

She swallowed. He wasn't wrong. If she didn't tread carefully, her job and possibly her entire career could be at risk. "For now, I'll keep an eye on him and try to make sure he's around good kids."

"Unfortunately, that doesn't stop those Brand kids from talking." He crossed his arms, and his brows drew together. A wave of anger seemed to radiate off him as his expression darkened. A muscle in his jaw jumped.

Garrison pissed off. Not something Sara wanted to experience again any time soon.

"No, but there's not much I can do about what kids say." She took a sip of water. "So I understand the whole situation, does Zach have any contact with his mother at all? Does she call or write?"

"No. She left just under a year ago, before Christmas." His casual shrug contradicted the drawn expression. "Sent me divorce papers and a letter that said she was gone for good. That was it. I haven't heard from her since."

"Nothing? Just like that?"

"Said in the letter that she didn't want anything to do with Zach or me. Asked that I sign the papers and 'leave her alone' or she'd get custody of Zach and take him away."

"Wow."

"And right after I signed the documents, she drained our accounts. Almost like she knew when I mailed the papers."

"Did you get your money back?"

"No. All calls went to a lawyer in Salt Lake City. That assho—sorry, jerk, wouldn't tell me anything else, citing client confidentiality."

"I've never heard of anything like that happening."

"Me neither. But frankly, I was so scared to lose Zach, I just gave up."

"Really? Because you don't seem like the giving up type," she blurted.

"What's that supposed to mean?"

Heat flooded her neck and face. "Nothing. It's not my place to say anything."

He stared at the condiment holder for a long, uncomfortable minute. Almost like he wanted to set it on fire with his mind. Right as she was about to apologize, Garrison swung his head back and locked his eyes onto hers.

"Anyway. So that's the basic story." Flat tone. No emotion.

"Sounds strange to me."

His glinting gaze narrowed. "Did your Mom call or write after she dropped you off?" he snapped.

"Well, no…"

"Then Zach's mother leaving isn't strange at all, is it?"

Boom. Boom. She could almost see the walls coming down around him. Tough and strong and defensive. She'd pushed too much.

Message received.

After a few awkward restarts, she finally steered the conversation toward benign topics like weather and ranching, but the tension remained.

After he set his empty glass down, he threw a few bills onto the table. "This was nice."

"Well, mostly."

He tapped the table. "Hey, we all have our pasts. No worries about anything that was said, okay?"

"Sure."

"And yes, it was a nice evening. Two adults having a dinner together."

"Like normal people?"

"Normal. Exactly." He scooted out of the booth and turned his palm up. "Ready to go?" Was that a double entendre? His dark gaze danced as he studied her.

Her heart thudded as she eyed the tall rancher. *You have no idea.* Putting her hand in his, she let him help her out of the booth and into her coat.

Despite herself, she smiled. Then froze.

"What?" He turned around.

"Sara?" From the front of the restaurant, a man ambled toward them, with that wide, confident stance.

Hank. She would know that sneer anywhere, and she knew better than to trust the smile. His behavior could turn on a dime. The meal burned in her stomach; she would pay good money to be anywhere but here right about now.

"I don't want to talk with him," she muttered.

Garrison gave a sharp nod. "Done. With pleasure."

Hank hadn't changed much. Same beard, same unkempt brown hair, same attitude, like a man who wanted to pick a fight with everyone. Handsome to look at but ugly when he opened his mouth. Even now, he planted his feet and crossed his arms over his broad chest.

But then he smiled, all charm. Classic Hank. "Hi, Sarita."

She didn't use that name, and he knew it.

He sniffed. "You're looking lovely as usual this evening."

"Thank you, Hank. This isn't the best time to chat, so you have a good day."

"How have you been?" He grinned.

"We're just leaving." Garrison tugged her toward the door.

"Good luck, Taggart." The sneer slid from under his curled lip.

He whipped around. "What?"

Crap.

"You know she's a loser, right?" At least Hank had the courtesy to keep his voice down. Judging by the darting glances and whispers, way too many patrons found the meeting far too interesting for her comfort.

A muscle popped in Garrison's jaw. Holy mother of God.

"Hey, now, that's uncalled for, Brand. Come on, Sara, let's go."

She pasted on the blandest smile she could muster. "Hank, so nice to see you. Please give my best to your family. You have a good night now."

His eyes bulged, and the pleasant facade melted into true, red rage. "Your best isn't good enough for my family, or anyone."

"Hank, that's enough," Garrison said, voice low and controlled. Too controlled.

They were so not doing this...drama in a public place. She forced the words out around her tight throat. "All righty, then. Well, you take care now."

Garrison turned his back on a leering Hank and held open the door for her. Despite her coat, she wanted to cover herself up even more.

As he walked at her side across the parking lot, she welcomed his solid presence even in the safe community of Copper River. Tiny flakes of snow fell in the early evening. Besides the few cars moving down Main Street, no one else was outside. The chilly air remained still around them.

Pausing at her car door, he said, "Pardon my French, but Hank's a massive asshole."

"So says Mr. Obvious." Despite herself, she giggled. The genuine smile felt good but didn't erase the hurt deep down. "Life is better without him anywhere in the general vicinity."

"Agreed." Garrison rubbed his neck. "For you and for me."

"So, thanks for helping me deal with…"

"No problem." He flicked his hand like the memory of a certain jerk could be tossed away.

If only it were so easy.

He cleared his throat. "Well, uh, thank you for trying to help my boy."

"Of course. I'll keep trying to figure out a solution for him."

"Whatever you decide, don't put your job in jeopardy. Please."

"I'll be careful. And I'm sorry for the comment about your divorce."

"It's long forgotten, along with the ex-wife. You're fine. Believe me."

"Oh." She looked around for something useful to say. Nothing came to mind.

He toyed with the edge of his jacket. "So, Sara…?" The smooth rumble of his voice set her insides quivering.

The top half of his face hid in shadow beneath the hat. She could barely see his eyes but felt them boring into her face.

"This evening was nice," he said. "Besides the Hank stupidity."

"I agree. God, he's a jerk."

One boot toed the gravel. "You think we could try another dinner together sometime? Minus the dumbass?"

Her heart stumbled two beats. "Like a date?" she blurted. "Even after what Hank—"

"Anything that man says, I tend to think the exact opposite. He's not worth the oxygen wasted to speak his name."

"True."

Puffs of vapor drifted up between them as they breathed. "So, then," he said. "Dinner later? A...date?"

"Uh, sure. Yes." Typing his number as he recited it, she texted him her info. Her stuttering heart continued to trip along.

There wasn't much to do, but she didn't want to leave. Not yet. The silence stretched for too long.

He tilted his hat up an inch with his thumb. "I'd like to give you a kiss good night, if you'd oblige."

"What?" Back on its feet, her heart now scampered in place. "Okay," she whispered.

He moved forward until his body heat reached her exposed face and neck. The scent of good food, leather, and hardworking man blended in a heady mixture.

"It's been a while, so I may be rusty." His low voice sent jolts of anticipation down her spine.

Her lips waited, just a few cruel inches away from his mouth...was this some kind of evil torture? Would she have to wait, a millimeter from heaven, while she froze to death?

No thank you.

Never let it be said that Sara couldn't take charge of an iffy situation when the chips were down.

Or help knock some rust off a fellow.

She grabbed his sheepskin and leather jacket lapels, yanking him toward her as she stood on tiptoes.

When their lips met, a zap of *holy wow* shot clear to her feet, then returned to settle in her pelvis, swirling in the most delightful way. The heat from his mouth flowed like warm liqueur through her body. After a moment, her calves protested the height difference, and she staggered back a step. Her hands remained clamped onto his jacket.

She licked her lips, her taste buds instantly craving more of his spicy male essence. A comparison between the taste of his lips and the rest of his body would be fine, too. "Yes, well. So there you go, no more rust. Like riding a bike," she babbled.

With difficulty, she unclenched her hands from the crushed jacket lapels, then smoothed the worn leather, like it was a suit coat. A flash of desire hit her. Oh, baby Jesus, what would this man look like in a suit? With *those* shoulders?

When he leaned down, his stubble brushed her cheek, sending ticklish, delicious sparks skimming over her skin. "I might need more practice." His breath slid up her jaw and drifted over her ear.

He wrapped his leather-clad arms around her upper back and waist and pulled her close again, this time dictating the timing and pressure of the kiss. Had she thought his mouth hard and cruel before? Because right now, his strong and soft lips sent flickers of excitement right into her own mouth.

When he tugged her flush against him, even through their coats, she sensed the iron muscles of his torso, flexing as he adjusted his stance. She melted against him. Despite their differences in height, they fit perfectly.

Moving his mouth into a fabulous new angle, he stroked with his tongue until her lips tingled.

In the name of the Holy Spirit, amen. This guy kissed like a pro, his kisses a perfect mixture of gentle and possessive.

Rusty? Out of practice? She'd love to bear witness to his expertise when he regained proficiency. Kisses any better than these could kill a woman. Dead.

She floated for what seemed like hours, cocooned in his steady arms, and savored the sensations that arose beneath his ever-changing lips. Just when she got used to one angle, he shifted and nudged her mouth open for more. The confident strokes of his tongue and nips of his teeth made her toes tingle.

When one of his hands snaked up into her hair and massaged her scalp, every muscle in her body short-circuited. For the first time in her life, her knees nearly gave out on her. Amazing.

After minutes—hours? days?—he pulled back. "Wow," he said. Vapor from his breaths created puffs in the winter air.

Was he breathing as quickly as she was?

"Well. This has to be the best parent-teacher meeting, ever," she said.

The vibration of his answering chuckle rolled through her ribcage, making her breasts perk up and take notice.

"I believe this is the part where I tell you I'll call you?"

Dazed, she managed to respond, "Only if you mean it." Crap. Dumb answer.

Even dumber? The part where she wanted to hang out with him more. Stupid idea, if she wanted to protect her job and her loan payment, given that her boss's family hated Garrison's. Hey, it was just his phone number. No requirement to answer. That's what caller ID was for.

He whipped his hand around to the back of her neck and planted one more toe-tingling kiss, followed by a playful nip that removed any question of his intention to call.

Okay, maybe she would consider one more date. Then she would stop. Because work. Life plans. Things that didn't involve a sexy rancher.

With a sheepish grin, he opened her car door and stood there while she turned the ignition. Once she'd closed the door and put on her seat belt, he stepped back.

It took every ounce of willpower not to touch her lips until she had pulled onto Main Street. Or circle back and beg him for more yummy kisses.

Once home, she kicked off her shoes, set down her bag, and tried not to swoon like a cartoon princess. But what an unexpected end to her evening.

How long could she block reality from stomping on her happiness?

She spun back as the doorbell rang.

Garrison? Here? Her heart fluttered.

She flung open the door.

A seething Hank greeted her.

CHAPTER 7

Son of a bitch, he actually manned up and kissed a woman. Not just any woman. Zach's cute teacher. Okay, mild conflict of interest, but when presented with such a lush set of lips like that, what kind of man could resist?

Garrison hesitated before opening his front door. Responsibility, stress, and more problems awaited him inside the house. If he could only stay outside, he'd get to revel in the evening.

After spending time with Ms. Lopez, he felt like a man who had been walking through the desert and had finally found water. Delicious, fresh water. Water to drink, to roll in, to swim laps.

As he brushed his jacket, a faint scent of flowers made him want to wrap his arms around that body all over again. He hadn't been able to properly explore all the ways she fit against him, due to the coats they wore. But he had tasted paradise.

Now he wanted seconds.

Funny, he'd always gone for the petite, blonde, sexpot types back in the day. A lot of good that had done him. This real woman with real curves and really hot kisses revised his selection criteria in a millisecond.

Maybe it was time for him to make new, better decisions.

He entered the kitchen to find Shelby and his dad sitting at the table, plates half empty. As one, they looked up at him with twin expressions: tight and haggard.

"Want leftovers?" she asked, already pushing her chair back.

Garrison raised his hand. "No, already ate. Don't let me interrupt your dinner."

She tilted her head and raised her nose, as if sniffing the air. When she pinned him with an inscrutable expression right before her eyes unfocused, he couldn't maintain eye contact.

She winced, blinked, and then grinned like a Cheshire cat.

Busted.

Thank goodness his father was generally immune to the psychic activity swirling around him. Although he knew about Garrison's and his siblings' abilities, Dad mostly ignored that there was anything strange about his children. As long as they didn't flaunt their abilities, Garrison and his siblings pretty much did whatever they wanted with their gifts. No rules.

Good. Because no rule would stop him from threatening to dump horse hockey on his sister when she read his emotions like a billboard on the highway. Once again, she flashed that cheeky expression, devoid of repentance.

Refusing to meet Shelby's knowing gaze, Garrison cleared his throat and pulled a chair out to sit at the table. "You two talking about anything interesting?"

His sister's and father's faces fell. Garrison leaned forward, elbows propped on the edge of the table. The sinking feeling in his gut had nothing to do with any psychic ability and all to do with Murphy's Law.

"Got another call a few hours ago from our 'neighbor' asking if we'd sell the property." Even Shelby's finger quotes were sarcastic.

"Again? What the hell? You just told them no." Garrison's hand itched to pick up the phone and give Hank Brand a piece of his mind.

Their father's lips curled up, but the lines of strain on his face told a different tale. "I'm getting a little weary of the pressure to sell. So, I took Shelby's advice. In the most polite language, I told him to go screw himself."

"Polite?" Garrison asked.

Shelby grinned.

"Maybe less polite this time…and more descriptive."

"Must've been a short conversation." Garrison smiled.

"Yessir, pretty much ended our chat. That guy couldn't take a hint if it ran him over on the road."

Austin Taggart wasn't a young man. He'd married and had kids later in life than most men. But even being in his late sixties, his father's arms still had muscle from years of ranching. His hair had gone from dark brown to white only in the past few years, what with Mom unexpectedly dying, Garrison's older brother Vaughn flying the coop, Tiffani's departure, Kerr's military injuries, and now all the problems with the ranch. How much could one man take?

Garrison ran a hand through his hair. "True. What else?"

When his father remained silent, Shelby finally piped up. "More cattle loss."

His father sagged in the chair. "I was checking the fence again this afternoon."

"With someone?" Garrison asked.

"No, on my own. I can still ride." The older Taggart drained his glass.

"Where's Kerr?"

Shelby's head came up sharply and flicked a glance around the kitchen. She and Kerr had an odd connection. Whenever they were separated, they both got on edge until they could reestablish that connection again. Must be a twin thing. All Garrison knew was that the time Kerr served in the military had been hell for Shelby.

"He's not back yet," she said, rubbing the back of her neck.

"He's late. Supposed to be helping here on the ranch." Garrison gritted his teeth.

With a shrug, she said, "Hey, the clients were determined to get elk, so the guys stayed out another day. It's good pay. Besides, we need any extra money we can get."

He flinched. *Because my ex-wife sucked the accounts dry.*

His father's eyes narrowed. "Why the hell can't I ride my own property, son?"

"It's not specific to you, Dad. I don't want anyone going out alone. Those Brand folks are getting weird. Unpredictable. Hank came up to me at the Hungry Moose this evening, half-cocked. Of all the stupid things."

"Why? You barely know Hank," she said. "And what were you doing at the diner?"

He wasn't about to spill about his evening with cute teacher. Shelby would needle him forever. "Why does Hank do anything? To be an asshole. But we've got to be careful. Until further notice, only go out with another person. And carry a firearm."

"You're kidding? Here, on our own property?" Shelby asked.

"I'm dead serious," Garrison said. "Anyway, Kerr should be back tomorrow, and he can help."

Shelby murmured, "Man, I wish Vaughn were here."

Son of a bitch. She'd come out and said it. If their oldest brother, Vaughn, were here, they wouldn't be in this mess. That's what she meant. Shelby wasn't incorrect, which made the statement hurt even more.

The hackles on Garrison's neck rose, and he squeezed his jaw closed to try to control the frustration. Even though Garrison had taken over responsibility for running the ranch, the specter of his older brother always remained. Never mind that Vaughn had split for New York City over a year ago and never called home. When the going got tough, everyone still wanted to call Vaughn.

Garrison had always come in second place.

His father pushed away from the table and stood up. "Maybe he'll return home soon."

And maybe pigs will fly.

"Yep." Garrison bit his tongue.

No use arguing with his dad. It wasn't his father's fault that Vaughn left, their neighbors had lost their minds, and the ranch was going down the shitter. He curled his hands into fists, watching his father leave the room. For a guy who claimed to be fine riding the property, his old man shuffled like...an old man. Was he becoming unsteady on his feet? Damn it.

Shelby pinched the bridge of her nose, then shot Garrison a nasty look before storming out of the kitchen. Absorbing all of his foul emotions probably made Shelby's brain feel like it was getting sandblasted with glass shards. At least Garrison's power worked like an on-and-off switch. Poor Shelby couldn't pick which emotions bombarded her. When she was tired or stressed, she picked up all of the feelings around her.

He wanted to go after her and apologize, but he stayed put.

Garrison had no time to add her to his to-do list.

Sara's insides shook like Jell-O as she clutched the front door handle, but she tried to remain polite. No way was she going to give Hank the satisfaction of seeing her intimidated.

"What are you doing here, Hank? I believe our conversation from this evening already ended."

"That's the best welcome you can give your former ball and chain?" His calm demeanor clashed with the uncontrollable snicker that erupted from his mouth. "Ball and chain, get it?"

"No, I don't. And we were only dating, Hank. What do you want?"

Serious now, his cold stare raked up and down her body. "You're looking...healthy as usual."

It would be so much easier if he didn't hide behind this polite veneer, despite the fact his voice was like sandpaper across an open wound. Even when they'd been dating, he always made backhanded compliments about her weight. Some things didn't change. But she couldn't very well slap a guy making seemingly pleasant conversation, could she?

And no, she would not tug at her clothing. Instead, she jammed her foot under the inner edge of the door, preventing it from opening any farther.

"Did you come here to insult me, Hank, or do you have some purpose to this visit?"

"Insult you? Why would I do that, Sarita? You're such a special woman."

Steam must be coming out of her ears by now. Her full name always slithered out of his mouth. He'd never said her given name in a positive way, ever.

As for "special"? The only way she'd be special was if she grew a third eyeball.

"Cut it out, Hank."

"Anyone tell you how defensive you are?" His attempt at a handsome, innocent expression never reached his eyes. Those brown eyes remained cold and dull, like mud.

Damn his emotionless face. Damn his platitudes. "Good night, Hank."

When he stopped the door with his hand on the casing, her heart pattered against her ribcage, but she stood her ground.

"I'm not done." He flexed his grip on the wood, shoving the door back open. All with a blank smile on his face. If anyone were out on the street, they would hear nothing more than polite chitchat on his part.

While she came across rude and angry.

Was he drunk? She inhaled. He didn't smell like booze. Hank was 100 percent stone cold sober. He stared like he could slice her in half with his gaze.

And he was calm. Too calm.

Holy Christ.

"Friendly warning, Ms. Lopez."

Every inch of her skin turned to ice.

"You *will* stay away from Garrison Taggart and his family." His voice crawled over her like a lovers endearment gone all wrong.

"What's Garrison to you?" It took all of her courage to resist taking a step back.

"Shut up and listen." He rapped his knuckles on the door casing, and she jumped. "Pay attention!"

The air caught in her throat as she focused on the man in front of her. Hank scooted his foot into the foyer.

The hammering in her chest reverberated in her ears.

"You like your job?" He smiled.

"What?"

Stars crowded the corners of her vision. Her job, the students she loved, her loan repayment. Forget the money. Could her career recover if she got fired only a year out of school? Probably not.

"What?" she whispered.

He grinned and shifted a hip into the house, leaning on the door-frame. "My brother's your boss. He'll do what I tell him. And I hate the Taggarts. You hear me?"

"Yes."

"So, if you get involved with anything to do with the Taggart family, including that giant dickhead Garrison, you can kiss your career good-bye. I will personally see to it."

"Why are you doing this? You never mentioned issues with the Taggarts before."

Hank curled a hand into a fist and propped it on the door handle. An eerie flash of uncontrolled rage twisted his features. "It's none of your business. I have a score to settle with Garrison Taggart. He ruined something of mine. So I'll ruin something else of his."

"Huh?"

"I've been called to destroy them all, you know."

"What in the world are you talking about?"

"In the world? It's what's *not* in the world that's important. Get it?" He shook his shaggy head. "You wouldn't understand. No one does. But the Great One knows." After a big breath, his energy dropped from crazy back to surly. "But you? You're nothing to me. Nothing to this town. No family, no respect. Your reputation as a thief still hangs on here. All you have is your job. Barely. So you'd better do as I say or that'll be gone. Hell, I could accuse you of stealing my Kershaw knife collection. Bet the charge would stick, what with your history."

"But I didn't—"

"Guaranteed that law enforcement would find the collection here." His ugly grin held the warmth of a jail cell.

She whispered, "I hear you."

"Good. Now give me a kiss for old time's sake."

Rearing back, she tried to close the door. He shouldered into the entryway, grabbed her neck and jaw in a vice grip, and squeezed hard. Then he put his cold, damp lips on her forehead.

All while remaining calm. Damn him.

Then with a nasty smirk and a shove, he was gone.

She worked her jaw, sore where he'd clamped his fingers.

The threat was clear. She had a choice to make regarding Zach and also now about Garrison.

Keep her head down, pay off her loans, and get out of town.

Or take a stand and risk everything.

CHAPTER 8

"Yep, looks like more damage." Kerr's light tone belied the seriousness of the situation. He shifted on the horse like he was born to ride. Nowadays, Garrison's younger brother moved more naturally on the horse than on solid ground. That damned IED in Afghanistan had taken his brother's right leg, but it hadn't taken his tracking skills.

Or his sharpshooting abilities.

Kerr pushed up the brim of his hat so a bit of curly orange hair, the same color as Shelby's, appeared. Then he adjusted the scope on his rifle. "I see some people over in that next valley. And cattle."

"Our cattle?"

"Whoa there, trigger. I'm good, but I'm not magic," he said, while continuing to look through the scope. His slow, shallow breaths sent streams of vapor into the cold air. At least it had stopped snowing this morning, leaving only a few inches of light snow on the ground to contend with today.

Not that Garrison ever worried about getting lost with Kerr around. His brother's GPS power was an odd gift that served him well on missions in the Middle East. And that ability sure came in handy when he guided clients into the mountains for days or weeks at a time. Always exited the forest right where the trucks and horse trailers were parked. Uncanny.

He could also disappear. Well, not exactly disappear, but fade away to where no one noticed him. Kerr rarely used that ability. Too painful, he said.

"You're not magic? That's not what I've heard from the ladies," Garrison needled his brother.

Relaxing away from the gun for a moment, Kerr flashed a rakish grin. "I bet you have heard, Mr. Polygraph. And of all the people on this earth, only you know for sure it's God's honest truth."

Good to see Kerr finally back to his old randy self. The last two years had been pure hell on him and rough on the whole family. Kerr's warped sense of humor had been a big factor in his successful recovery.

Garrison snorted. "Humility is one of your greatest qualities."

Puffing out his chest, Kerr swept invisible dust from his shoulder. "I resemble that remark." He winced as he kneed his horse over. He blew out a lungful of air and squinted again into the scope. Brow furrowing, he muttered, "I can't see the tags or ear cuts on the cattle from here."

"Can't you dial up more magnification or something?"

"I know they say there are no dumb questions, but man." He pulled a face and said in a voice that was almost too manly to be believed. "Yeah, you've caught me. I've been holding out on you. Let me pop my bionic lens into the scope."

Garrison growled.

Kerr scrubbed the orange stubble on his chin and spoke in his normal tone. "Dude. I'm exhausted. After spending ten days up in the high country wiping the hineys of those city slickers from Texas, I'm beat. I can only kiss ass for so long before my lips start to stink. And you know I'm still having those stupid dreams we're all experiencing. Consider yourself blessed that I was willing to track with you today." He glared at him.

"You think I'm lucky, having you here? You smell like armpit and rotten horse." At the offended gasp from Kerr, Garrison shrugged. "But in all seriousness, thanks for helping out."

Yeah, Kerr didn't have to turn right around and come with him to the back of the property. But damn it, Garrison was running out of options for help.

Dad had wanted to rest at home. Very unusual behavior for an active guy like his father who rarely missed out on any action on the ranch.

Dad had refused to see a doctor, which was typical. But Garrison had caught him shuffling aimlessly and staring into space a few times. Damn it. He needed to get checked out by a professional.

More items on the to-do list.

"Not a problem. Happy to help." Kerr popped his hand onto a hip. "Speaking of body odor, smelled yourself lately?"

"Fresh as a daisy."

"I did notice the thick musk of bad cologne there. So. Who's the lucky lady?"

Warmth, like thick, delicious molasses, spread out from his chest. "Uh. There's no lady."

Garrison avoided making eye contact. Kerr couldn't read emotions, but hiding anything in this family was nearly impossible.

"That's not what Shel says."

"Come on. When did you two get a chance to talk?"

Kerr tapped his forehead beneath his tan cowboy hat. "Don't need to."

He turned his upper body square to his brother. "What? Your power changed? You two can communicate mentally now?"

"Naw, I'm just screwing with you. Shel told me how you're hot for teacher right before we rode out today."

"That traitor."

"So, tell me the story, because you smell like a high school dance. All teenage flop sweat and bad cologne." He sniffed and pretend sneezed. "Holy Axe overload there, Batman."

Garrison stopped trying to check his scent when his brother laughed out loud.

"Whatever, Kerr. Look, there's nothing to say. There's no 'us.' In fact, I tried calling her last night after I got home from our dinner together. Then I called a few times today, but she didn't answer her phone or return my calls."

"Maybe milady is busy?"

Damn it, when Kerr started to poke at someone, he never let up.

That pleasant, molasses sensation in Garrisons gut congealed into cold, unhappy concrete. "Where else would she be? I left two messages this morning and again at noon. It's a cell phone. It's with her all the time. And it didn't go straight to voice mail, so it's not like she didn't know there was an incoming call."

"Or twenty calls?" Poke, poke.

"I'm not that bad. Look, it's fine. I can take a hint."

"Methinks he dost protest too much."

Novelty of having his brother back? Gone.

Thankfully, Kerr must have read the scowl because he backed off. "Okay. Let me get real with you, dude. First, she probably thinks you're a stalker, calling her right after your non-date and again while she's at work. So, strong work with the self-restraint to wait the standard forty-eight hours to call her. Second, which really bothers you more: the fact that she didn't *answer* you or the fact that she didn't answer *you*?"

"Fuck you."

"Stand in line and wait your turn like everyone else." Always a thorn in the side, Kerr. At least he retained his sense of humor and swagger. Garrison couldn't have stayed positive after losing a leg and almost dying.

Garrison nodded toward the specks in the distance, trying to get his brother to focus on anything else but his own nonexistent skills in the woman department. "So what do you recommend?"

"I recommend that you go to this lady's house and beg her forgiveness for whatever you did to piss her off. Don't even worry about being specific, just keep saying 'I'm sorry' and hope to hell she buys it. If you are exceedingly lucky, she might lay a wet, sloppy one on you. Maybe even on your lips, if you play your cards right."

And just like that, with a tip of his hat and an impish grin, Kerr pushed Garrisons last button. The horse shied under Garrison, and he had to force his hands to relax on the reins. If he didn't need so much help with the ranch, he would throttle his younger brother.

He took a deep breath and blew it out. Nope. Didn't calm him down. "No, Kerr. What do you recommend? With the cattle." He slapped his leg, making his horse jump. "And no, I didn't piss her off."

"Doesn't sound that way to me." Kerr put a hand on his chest. "And trust me, I know women. It's best if you start every conversation you ever have with 'I'm sorry'. Really sets the groundwork for the makeup sex later."

Garrison's jaw hurt from clamping down on it. "Enough with the advice on women. The herd, man. What should we do about the missing cattle issue?"

"Well, why didn't you say so?" He winked. "Let's fix the fence first and then disappear." He flipped down the lens cap and carefully stowed his rifle on the saddle.

"Disappear? Like what you do?"

"No." He winced. "Disappear. Like, you know, make a show of working, pretend to leave, and then pop up over there." Kerr inclined his head toward a high point a mile away just inside their property line, near the national forest. "And see if we can't get a better look-see."

"Sounds good." Garrison patted the Ruger in his waist holster.

After an hour of patching the fence for the second time in less than a week, they backtracked toward the ranch house for half a mile and then turned sharply to the north. They rode up a hill that gave a better vantage point over the neighboring valley and property.

As the horses topped the hill, Kerr raised the rifle and peered through the scope once more. Then he swung it toward the foothills bordering the national forest to their right.

"What's that equipment off in the woods down there?"

Garrison rolled his eyes. "You've got the scope. I see nothing but little shapes."

"Hmm." He clicked his tongue. "Looks like a big truck, a metal frame with a conveyor belt, and…"

"What?"

"Holy industrial machinery, Batman. That looks like an excavator. Everything's been painted dark gray and brown to blend into the hills. But I can see some patches of yellow they missed. Wow."

"Okay, that's interesting. But what about the herd?"

"The herd. Always the herd. Fine. Cows. So, I could swear that's our cattle, but without checking tags, there's no way to be sure."

"Do we need to know for certain?" Garrison asked.

"Probably." Kerr scanned the valley. "We've got a few more hours of light left. Maybe we can work around a bit farther to get a better view."

They traveled to the part of their ranch that bordered national forest land and then passed through a section of barbed wire fence into open mountain country beyond. Years ago, Garrison's father considered going all free range grazing like most folks in other parts of Wyoming, but issues like this bullshit with the Brands made Garrison happy for the decision to fence their large tract of land, despite the maintenance headache.

Patches of snow from last night's squall stippled the ground. More snow was forecast. At least their tracks wouldn't be as obvious with bare ground today, but that advantage would soon change.

They paralleled the Brand fence line for another fifteen minutes, the creak of leather and clank of bits punctuating the cold silence.

"What the hell are you doing?" A voice shot out of the forest.

Spikes of ice speared Garrison's neck as he focused on the sound of a gun safety clicking off.

He stared down the barrel of a rifle and then to the man who held it.

Hank Brand.

Glancing behind him, Garrison spied Kerr carefully laying the reins on the pommel and lifting his hands up as another man trained a weapon on him.

Wyatt Brand. One of Hank's equally nasty brothers.

Son of a bitch. Worst-case scenario.

CHAPTER 9

"How's it going, Hank?" Garrison aimed for a tone somewhere between neighborly happenstance and mild irritation.

"I'm asking the questions, Taggart. Why are you out here?" His wild eyes darted away, toward the open fields, and then back to Garrison.

"Us? We're just taking a nice ride before the snows come."

"Yeah, right. You're on our property."

"Actually, Hank, I believe that we're on national forest property, same as you. Over there"—Garrison pointed to the fence—"is your property."

Hank leveled the gun at him.

Sometimes it was smarter to be quiet rather than correct.

"I don't like you snooping around this close to our spread," Hank growled.

"There's no law against us being here, my friend."

"I'm not your friend, asshole. Not you or any of your pissant family."

Garrison locked his mouth shut against a rebuttal. A loaded

weapon trumped logic. Besides, even if he could get to his pistol fast enough, Kerr would get shot.

Damn that family. The only thing that would make this better was for their older brother, Tommy Brand, to join the fun. But he was too busy telling his kids to torment Zach.

Son of a bitch, he'd love to beat the hell out of these men. Hank had been nothing but a burr under Garrison's saddle for the past year. Wyatt had stopped extending credit to the Taggarts at the hardware store. Nothing would relieve stress like a good brawl.

But Kerr couldn't maneuver well off his horse. Fists and threats wouldn't get them out of this mess. Not today, at least.

"Seems like this is a big misunderstanding, guys," Garrison said.

"Only thing you misunderstand is basic information," Hank sneered. "Stay away from our property—we won't give you a friendly warning next time."

Friendly, his ass. But wasn't about to split hairs while sitting in the crosshairs.

Hank hawked and spat. "And while I'm thinking about it, stay away from that slut teacher you're mooning over. She's off limits."

It took a lot to get Garrison so mad he couldn't function. Calling a good person a bad name was one of those methods. His blood pounded in his brain. His ears buzzed. "Ms. Lopez is. Not. A. Slut," he gritted out. "Don't you ever talk about her like that again."

"I'll call her whatever I like. Just leave her alone." Hank shifted from foot to foot, still glancing toward his property. Odd.

"You don't date her anymore. Why should you care?"

"We're getting back together, ass clown. So that means you're out."

"News to me. You must have started dating since I saw you yesterday."

Stupid to even continue this discussion, given the weapon pointed at his chest, but damn it, Hank's macho shit crossed a red line three miles ago. His hand twitched with the instinct to break Hank's jaw into tiny pieces.

No way she could be dating him. Right?

This wasn't the time to consider Sara's relationship status.

Garrison would rather beat the hell out of the asshole in front of him instead.

When Garrison glanced back at Kerr, his brother shook his head, only a tiny gesture. If they tried anything stupid, one or both of them would get hurt. Like in the song, Garrison knew when to fold 'em.

Hank's mouth twisted into what generously could be called a smile, and he reset his aim. "See, Taggart, your family took something that was my family's. And you took something that was mine. So I took it back. But just wait until you see what I've been called to do. Now I'm going to—"

"So, Hank, how's Izzy?" Kerr piped up.

Damn his brother. They should have kept Hank going with his crazy talk. It might have given them clues as to why those guys wanted the Taggart ranch and the reason for the equipment on the Brand property.

"How do you know our sister?" Hank shouted.

Kerr raised his hands up farther. "Hey, simmer down. We went to high school together. She was a nice girl."

"You're not running around to see our 'nice girl' sister, or we'll kick your ass," Hank spat.

Garrison's internal alarm system shot to red alert. His brother was goading the guy. Or trying to distract him. Why?

His heart slammed against his ribs.

Kerr shrugged and brushed his knuckles over his jeans-clad leg. "Kick my ass? Who are you kidding? Obviously, you were unconscious for the past two years and never listened to town rumors. Else you'd know that I couldn't run around for any reason. Now can I, Wyatt?"

Wyatt's eyes cut away from Kerr's prosthetic leg locked into the stirrup.

"Hell, boys, I can't even kick my own ass." When he smiled, there was pain behind the jokes.

Wyatt swallowed and dropped the tip of his rifle. "Hank, come on, man, let's go home. You made your point."

Hank stared at Garrison down the barrel of his gun for a full minute before taking a step back and dropping the tip of the weapon. "Fine. Just stay away from our property." He glared at Kerr. "Keep your hands off our sister." With another hawk and spit, he pointed his chin at Garrison. "And stay away from that teacher. Got it?"

Far be it from Garrison to argue with a loaded gun, but it took an inhuman amount of self-restraint to keep his mouth shut in the face of such an asshole.

Garrison and Kerr turned the horses around and slowly rode away. His skin crawled. At any minute, he expected to hear the crack of a rifle and feel the pain of a bullet tearing through his back. Wouldn't put it past that bastard.

Hank was cagey. Out of proportion with reality. Paranoid.

Those guys had to be hiding something.

Why did Hank hate the Taggart family so much?

The family quarrel, Garrison could understand. Dad had purchased the ranch back in the day, fair and square, and later found out the Brands had wanted it but couldn't afford it.

But what else had Hank been about to say? Garrison had taken something of Hank's, and now the guy wanted to take it back? What the hell was he talking about? Damn it. Nothing came to mind.

Even stranger, he wanted Garrison to have zero contact with Sara Lopez.

What lengths would Hank go to, to make sure his orders were followed? How much danger were Sara and the Taggarts in right now?

What was the connection?

Sara shut the front door after Izzy left her house. They'd eaten pizza while Sara enjoyed a therapeutic vent session. Okay. Vent session minus a description of the steamy kiss. She wanted to keep that detail as her own little secret, at least for now. Also, her friend was still Hank's sister, even if their friendship placed Izzy firmly on Sara's side.

Blowing out a long, slow breath, she dragged herself back to the kitchen to clean up the dishes and pizza box. Once she put everything away, Sara collapsed on the couch, rolling the tension from her neck and shoulders. Even nice company, simple carbs, and oozy cheese couldn't completely relax her.

God, today couldn't end soon enough. Last night's roller coaster hadn't ended with Hank leaving. Between the hours spent staring at her bedroom ceiling, she managed to sleep a little bit, but her dreams oscillated between hot rancher and creepy ex-boyfriend. Safety and fear. Confidence and humiliation. Desire and repulsion.

Her whole world kept tilting from side to side.

When the two men had finally morphed into one, she had given up and gotten out of bed.

If she had more days like today, her poor performance would attract undue attention. Not only did she nod off during class, but it took more energy to maintain vigilance for Zach's safety.

With every knock on her classroom door, every flicker of movement behind the school windows when she monitored the kids at recess, she teetered on edge. When would the principal take action and relieve her of her job?

To make matters worse, she wanted to see Garrison again, but not if doing so put him or any of his family in danger. Not if she'd get fired in the process.

Maybe she could go to the police?

What would she say? Her ex-boyfriend came by her house, remained calm, and said some mean things. Impolite behavior, sure, but not illegal. Besides, Tommy Brand, the bully kids' father? He was the sheriff. Convenient. With the close-knit law enforcement in this area, she wasn't likely to get a sympathetic ear.

Drawing attention to herself was not an option. Would it be too much to ask to keep a low profile and hush the town rumor mill? Didn't matter what she wanted. Hank would paint this picture in a way that made him look like a saint.

Would it be too much to complete her contract, move away from this place, and move on with her plans for a teaching career that had nothing to do with Copper River?

Damn. She rubbed her jaw and flinched. The spot where Hank's thumb had pressed into her face last night still ached. Makeup had covered the bruise, but his mark went much deeper than the color. Hurt on a deeper level.

Silence wrapped around her as surely as Hank's cruel grip.

The still, dark living room brought no peace tonight.

A buzz sounded on the end table behind her, too loud in the quiet house, making her heart *rat-a-tat* like a snare drum.

The phone glowed. Another voice mail from Garrison popped up on the screen.

Every inch of her body yearned to connect with him again, relax in the strength of his arms encircling her, and taste his heated lips.

What would be the harm?

Ice cold fingers of fear dug into her neck.

Hank.

Her career. Her carefully planned future.

Zach.

Forgive me. I can't.

She turned off the phone and threw it on the couch.

Even after taking a long, hot shower and changing into sweats and a t-shirt, her eyes still burned. But she couldn't go to bed and face another night of disturbing dreams. Not now.

Barefoot, she wandered through the living room and flipped on a lamp. She rearranged the few knickknacks on her bookshelf. She didn't want to watch TV, didn't want to curl up on the couch to read. In no mood for cleaning, instead she floated past a faded picture on the kitchen wall. And stopped cold.

Her own smiling seven-year-old face, full of hope and joy, pressed next to her mother's face. Only her mom's eyes didn't sparkle with happiness; they stared, glassy and fearful, into the camera. Her mother's smile came across as more of a frozen grimace.

The rest of the image wasn't visible in the picture, but Sara remembered this moment. Christmas. No decorations, no presents. But there was a new boyfriend to hurt her mother.

And a one-way trip to Copper River for Sara to stay with her aunt and uncle waited on the horizon, only she hadn't known it then.

The last day she saw or heard from her mother.

Merry freakin' Christmas, Sara.

When she blinked, the sting under her eyelids didn't go away.

Tears now, after all these years?

Garrisons gold-flecked gaze overwhelmed her mind's eye.

She touched her lips.

Her jaw throbbed where Hank had grabbed her.

Hot, wet tears gathered, floodwaters behind a dam wall seconds before it burst.

Absolutely not. She would not cry.

After putting the picture back on the counter, she sank to the kitchen floor and sat cross-legged, her forehead in her hands, breaths coming harsh and rapid in the quiet house. The hard refrigerator surface provided her unyielding support.

With an ear-splitting crash, glass exploded from the window.

CHAPTER 10

*S*tupid move, coming here.

Gravel popped under the tires as Garrison parked his truck a hundred feet up the street from Sara's small, one-story bungalow. One advantage to living in a place like Copper River? Easy to find out where people lived. Tonight's data on Sara's house location came courtesy of Shelby and her excellent memory for town gossip.

Disadvantage? Everyone would know about this visit before he got back home.

He threw his hat on the front seat and pushed the truck door closed. Hesitating next to the vehicle, he peered a few houses down to Sara's home. Stars twinkled in the cloudless sky. Maybe 8:00 p.m. had been too late to come calling.

A yellow glow from Sara's living room window spilled out into the cold, clear night air, like a beacon drawing him to a sanctuary.

When he took a few steps closer, he stopped in his tracks. He shouldn't be here. His mouthy brother had been right: Garrison *had* turned into a stalker.

But, son of a bitch, he wanted to make sure he hadn't upset Sara. Had he moved too quickly when he kissed her last night? Or had he become so starved for female attention that the first polite and eligible woman he met had him instantly whipped? Same leash, different master. What a joke.

What about the idea that she could keep an eye on Zach? Not to protect his son from bullies, but to be on alert for any emerging powers. If Garrison could get close to Sara, she could provide the objective assessment needed.

So, what, now he was a stalker who wanted to use her for his personal gain?

Pretty much.

An ethical man would turn around and leave. A smart man wouldn't have come here in the first place.

Didn't matter. Even if he was relationship challenged, after the bizarre conversation with twitchy Hank Brand today, Garrison had to make sure Sara was okay. Once he completed that task, if she didn't want to see him again, he'd respect her wishes and leave her alone.

A high, tinkling crash stopped him in his tracks. Glass? The cold, clear air made it easy to get a direction.

Sara's house.

As he rounded the mailbox in a dead run to the porch, a deep engine rumble emanated from the alley behind her house, followed by a clatter of what sounded like gravel beneath spinning tires. The sound of a vehicle faded into the night.

Then silence.

Sara.

The blood froze in his veins.

He reached her front door in two steps and pounded on the door.

"Sara? It's Garrison. Are you in there? Are you all right?"

A small yelp was followed by a thud.

He rattled the door handle. Locked. Shit.

Air caught in his chest as he strained to listen.

"Sara," he called again.

A distant voice came through the door. "Just a minute."

What the hell?

"Who is it?" came her muffled voice, louder now.

Her voice. Thank God. He sagged into the doorframe, but he jumped back when the porch light came on.

The door opened a few inches, revealing her bloodless face and wide eyes. "What are you doing here?"

"Are you all right? I heard a sound."

"How did...What are you doing here?" she repeated. Her voice wavered, too breathy, as she darted glances past him, toward the street. "You shouldn't be here."

"What's going on in there, Sara?"

He wanted to move heaven and earth to erase that frown.

"Nothing."

"I heard a sound. Are you hurt?"

That dazed expression on her face? Not good.

"Glass. From a window. The window. You know, the window in the kitchen." Her hand shook as she rubbed the front of her neck. The door opened a few more inches. "And the picture is broken. All broken."

The lost look on her face, her dilated pupils. Was she in shock?

"What happened? Sara?"

"I don't know." She swallowed convulsively. A strand of damp hair clung to her neck.

Gooseflesh prickled along his spine, and he whispered, "Is someone in there?"

Licking her lips, she pinned him with a haunted look. "I don't know."

When he glanced around her into the house, dark shiny smears dotted the hardwood floor. "Shit, are you bleeding?"

When she lifted her foot, blood dripped from the sole. She opened her mouth, but no sound emerged. Her dry lips went pale, and her eyes rolled back in the sockets.

He shouldered his way into the house and grabbed her before she hit the floor. Kicking the door closed with one booted foot, he half carried, half dragged her limp frame to the nearby couch and eased her head onto a cushion.

Propping her feet up on a pillow on the arm of the couch, he examined the cut sole. A piece of glass protruded from a two-inch gash that oozed blood. He'd take care of it as soon as he made sure she was otherwise okay. At least when he placed a hand on her sternum, her breathing was even and her heartbeat a little fast but steady. Maybe she had passed out from the sight of blood or pain?

What about the fear etched on her face? Embedded glass didn't cause fear, did it?

Not wanting to leave for long, he hurried to follow the blood track to the kitchen, searching for supplies for her foot. Frigid air drifted into the house, thanks to a shattered window over the sink. A faded photo of a woman resembling Sara and a young girl lay on the floor within a broken picture frame.

More glass crunched under his boots as he grabbed a cup of water and a towel.

As he turned, his foot bumped an object on the floor. He used one of the cloths to pick it up. A melon-sized rounded stone, like from a river, with a dull metal chain lashed around it. What the hell?

At a soft groan from the living room, he dropped the rock on the table, rushed back to Sara, and knelt next to the couch.

The wings of her dark eyelashes swept shadows over her tan cheeks, tempting him to rest his lips on the flawless skin. Other areas of his anatomy decided to use this inappropriate opportunity to take notice of her lush curves as well. Damn his starved libido; this was not the time.

Her head lolled toward him, her eyes fluttered open and widened, and she gave out a strangled cry.

"Sara, shh. It's Garrison." He patted her shoulder closest to him.

"What?" When she tried to sit up, her foot hit the pillow. "Ow! Crap."

He tucked a dishtowel under her foot. "Yeah, looks like you got some glass in there, honey." He sat up straight, ready for her gratitude. Maybe she'd give him a kiss for his gallantry.

"You have to leave."

What?

His puffed up chest deflated. Just like that, he went from hero to stooge. Not the reception he'd expected.

"What?"

"It's not okay for you to be here. My—" She pressed her trembling lips together.

Like a man slowly drowning, reality dawned on him.

Of course. How stupid could he be?

In his companionship-starved brain, Garrison had built up their dinner and sexy kiss into something it wasn't: a date. He'd never thought to ask about Sara's relationship status; he had assumed she was single.

She had a boyfriend.

He gritted his teeth and studied the green-and-brown cloth pattern on the couch.

Second best. Again. Son of a bitch.

Story of his entire life.

He should leave. Now.

His gaze locked onto Sara's shimmering eyes. She was in pain. He might be the perennial runner-up, but Garrison wouldn't leave her injured. Wait. No. If she had a boyfriend here, why hadn't he come running to help her? The situation made no sense. Shoving his pride to the side, he kept his hands to himself and stared at her, not certain what to do.

"I can help you."

"No, please. You can't be here." Her head whipped back and forth; no doubt she searched for something—or someone.

"Can I call anyone for you, then?" he asked.

"No, there's no one to call." One tear slipped from a corner of a soulful brown eye.

Damn it, what was he supposed to do?

"A boyfriend?"

Her rattling laugh twisted something inside of his chest.

He shrugged. "I assumed."

"No. There's no one."

The bitterness in her voice raked across his nerves and lifted his spirits at the same time. Which was worse? He wanted to use his ability to get the answers so badly. He'd even sell his own sister's powers to the highest bidder at this moment if it meant avoiding ethics in this damned situation. Which made him a complete bastard all over again.

"Um, okay." Pat, pat on her shoulder. Like that was the only part of her body he could safely touch without being too tempted. Shelby was correct. He *was* an idiot.

How about seeing to her well-being and security, asshole? Why don't we try being unselfish?

Now Garrison was talking to himself. He took in a shaky breath and exhaled a steadier one.

"Sara, let me get this glass out of your foot and help you clean up the kitchen."

"The kitchen." Tears flowed. "Oh, no. The picture…"

A woman crying. His kryptonite. "It'll be fine. Just needs another frame."

"No, you don't understand. It's broken."

Even, white teeth chewed on her full lip, which riveted his attention. Not good.

"Never mind." She didn't meet his eyes but took a deep breath.

Unfortunately, the action pushed her breasts up against the thin t-shirt fabric. It was clear she didn't have a bra on, as the night air chilled her skin. Obviously. Good grief, he needed to help this woman, not ogle her enticing assets.

You could do both, his libido prompted him.

He kept his voice calm, despite the effect her sweet-scented, braless proximity had on him.

"Okay. I'm going to get this glass out. Let's start there." He laid his coat on an armchair and knelt at the end of the couch.

Resisting the need to trace the delicate arches of her feet, he gently grasped her toes, grimacing when she yelped. After repositioning the towel over the pillow, he held her foot still as he flushed the area with water. There, a piece of glass protruded from the wound.

Without saying a word, he pinched the glass and snagged it out of her foot.

"Yowch! Hey, some warning!" She jumped back, but by then, he had the shard.

Holding up the blood-coated shard, he grinned. "Done." He wrapped the towel around the ball of her foot. "Do you have some peroxide or alcohol?"

"Mother of Christ, no way you're putting alcohol in there!" At least she had firm control of her faculties now, as the stubborn lift to her chin attested. She rubbed her cheeks, then pointed. "Bathroom around the corner, first aid stuff under the sink."

He took the opportunity to check the rest of the house for anything else out of place. A quick glance in her lace-trimmed bedroom and her closet reassured him that no one else hid in the house. The bedroom smelled like flowers, and he inhaled.

Which is to say, he'd lost his mind.

Returning with supplies, he washed out the wound once more and dressed it with gauze and an elastic bandage.

"You might need stitches."

"It's fine." Swinging her legs off the couch and onto the floor, she winced. Her expression, clear but guarded, held him in place. "Thank you. But—"

Buts always nailed him like a kick to the groin.

"Yeah, I know, you need me to leave. Got it. I'm sorry to have bothered you." He ignored her raised hand. "Can I at least help you clean up the floors and the kitchen?"

She hobbled to the kitchen. At her sharp intake of air, he grabbed her upper arm, worried that she would faint again.

Beneath the harsh fluorescent lights, glass sparkled all over the floor. She trembled beneath his hand.

"You okay?"

"It's just...a mess. And the window." Even though her lower lip quivered, her eyes narrowed and she straightened her shoulders. Trying to be strong.

All of a sudden, he needed something to occupy his hands. "Broom?"

After retrieving it from the closet she indicated, he had the floor cleared in no time. Taking care to remove the pieces of glass, he wiped down the counter, table, and chairs.

"What's this?" she asked. The rock he'd found swung from the chain.

"Not sure. You have any idea who might have done this?"

She set the stone down on the kitchen table and made a show of straightening up the counter items. "No. Maybe."

"Sara." He grasped her arm, and she flinched. "Has someone hurt you?"

"No, not—"

Son of a bitch, she was lying, wasn't she? It took everything in him not to dig into her mind and get to the truth. But no. Fucking ethics and all, even when he knew where that had gotten him so far in life.

The problem with his power? He had to intentionally activate it. He had to make the effort to invade someone's mind. Tonight, that wasn't happening. Not with Sara.

The blood drained into his feet. "Yet?"

"Yeah. Maybe. Yet."

"We should go to the police."

"No!" When she looked up and away from him, her hair fell back to reveal a quarter-size bruise on her jaw. The way she'd lain on the couch earlier had hidden the purple oval on her skin.

"Shit. What's that?"

Careful to move slowly, he brushed her hair back farther. Turning her face the other way, he found smaller bruises speckling her opposite jaw. The fingers of a big hand would line up perfectly with those bruise marks.

She stared somewhere off into space, face blank. Who would do this to her? He might be a temperamental boor, but he sure as hell never laid a cruel hand on a woman.

He could only stand there, frozen in place.

Neither his need to rip the hands off whoever had touched Sara nor his desire to yank her into his arms would solve any problem tonight, but those were the only emotions he had to work with right this minute.

What kind of asshole would do such a thing?

Asshole. Yep. Bet he knew who.

No way was she in any state to discuss certain dickhead ex-boyfriends.

Then she blinked and turned to face him, her head barely reaching his chin, and the crystalline moment of his fury and her fear met. And cracked.

He shoved his hands into the pockets of his jeans.

She stepped back. "You can't be here. Please leave." Her breathy voice riled his nerves like a breeze skimming his skin.

"But, I still have to fix the window—"

"I need you to leave."

"Uh, can I take you home with me instead?"

Her head shot up, mouth dropping open. Stumbling back a few feet, she wrapped her arms over her chest.

Crap. Wrong impression.

Clearing his throat, he started digging. "No, not like…Um, we can use a guest room. Not for 'we.' Only for you. Or other people if they stay. But you can stay there. Alone. For safety. I mean, I'll be in the house but not in the room. Because it's not safe here."

And *boom* went the dynamite. What a colossal babbling idiot.

The best thing to happen to this conversation would be for him to shut the hell up.

"I'll be fine here, thank you." Just like that, she stepped around him and limped to the door.

And just like that, he followed her swaying hips across the living room, snagging his coat on the way out.

"Sara, I don't like this situation." He motioned with his palm up. "You sure I can't call the sheriff?"

Her eyes downcast, she shook her head. "That would be the worst idea ever."

"Please reconsider my offer to come to the ranch."

"Thank you. No."

"You have my phone number, right?" From the ten times he'd called, yeah, she could probably figure out which number was his. "Call if you need anything, anytime. Please."

"Fine."

Like a drowning man, he flailed for a life buoy. "Can I check on you tomorrow?"

She raked her fingers through her dark hair. "I don't know. Maybe. Look, you shouldn't come back here."

That answer would have to count as a "yes." Before he could try again to convince her to come with him, she closed the door in his face, leaving him to study the weathered wood. Then the porch light turned off, leaving him alone in the dark night.

CHAPTER 11

*A*fter a cold and cramped night in his truck watching Sara's house, Garrison's mood sucked. Even if she didn't want to go with him, he couldn't leave her by herself. So he'd stayed and watched her house.

He'd arrived back home in the morning to see Zach off to school and then buried himself in hours of the never-ending ranch work.

Didn't matter if he brought the herd down, put out the hay, or repaired the barn. His mood stayed black, and nothing distracted him from thoughts of Sara.

Maybe he didn't have the gift of reading emotions like Shelby, but he sure as hell could tell when a situation felt wrong. And he didn't need a psychic ability to figure out that something was off with Sara. Whatever happened last night had resulted in her getting hurt, damn it. He wasn't Superman, but if he had to spend more chilly nights in his truck to keep her safe, he'd do it.

She intrigued him. He craved more of...everything about Sara. Which was probably the exact opposite of what that woman needed right now, and the exact opposite of what he needed in his complicated life these days.

Like a human punching bag, he would go back over there again, where she would probably reject him again. But he had to ensure her safety, especially if Hank's retaliation against her had anything to do with Garrison. He still wanted to see if she had noticed anything different about Zach as well. She'd become his spy in the classroom, because Garrison and his siblings couldn't objectively assess his son. Great.

He cleaned up and, right as the sun set, pulled up in front of Sara's house.

On this quiet street, one block off Main, all the houses appeared similar. Small single-story structures and a few wood and brick two-story homes. Stepping onto her wood porch, he rang the doorbell.

A light step preceded the porch light turning on. His heart jumped when she opened the door.

Although she'd piled her hair on top of her head, some escaped tendrils framed her frowning face. Jeans clung to her curves, and a sweatshirt couldn't hide the swell of her full breasts. The entire adorable, sexy package made him hungry, and not for food.

But when she glanced down the street with a frown on her face, suddenly dropping in didn't seem like such a good idea, like a bad rerun of last night. Maybe she had plans. Who was the pushy guy now?

He stuffed his hands in his pockets. "Um, hi."

Great opening line there, Romeo.

"Hi. What are you doing here, Garrison?" She bit her lip; ah, how his tongue would glide over that light indentation, tracing the curve.

"After last night, I was worried about you." So not smooth. "How's your foot?"

"Well, my foot's fine, and I'm fine…" The pulse jumped at the base of her throat, and a flush climbed her smooth, honey-colored skin. Her socked toes curled on the hardwood floor.

Shit. He didn't need to use his ability. He knew.

She was lying.

A woman lied to him again. His gut clenched. At what point would he learn his lesson?

He stumbled back a step. "Look, this was a bad idea, my coming over here. I'm clearly intruding, and I should go."

Reaching an arm toward him, then dropping it, she blurted out, "No, it's not you."

"It's not you, it's me? Is that the line?" He shoved his hand through his hair.

Her dark brows shot up.

Yeah, he'd dumped all of his resentment right at her feet. He didn't give a shit if that wasn't fair. "Fine. I'm sorry I enjoyed our kiss the other day. I thought we had something good starting there, but I must have imagined it. And I thought you could use help last night since someone threatened you. Wrong again. So, dumbass me, I'm here because I wanted to make sure you were all right after last night."

Tears sparkled in her deep brown eyes. Damn it, if her chin didn't quiver. He had no defense against womanly emotional stuff.

"No, I can't...because of my...it's not your fault. Seriously. You have no idea." Her knuckles whitened on the edge of the door.

"Then what?" he gritted out.

With another jerk of her head to look up and down the street, she stepped into the house and held the door open. Her shoulders sagged. "I give up. Come in."

"Don't act so happy about asking me in." He ignored her flinch. Instead, it was the fear etched on her face in the living room light that drove a spike into his chest. No more of this guessing game. "Are you talking about what happened last night? Something's wrong here, Sara."

"I, um...oh hell." She wrapped her hands over her upper arms and burst into tears.

Son. Of. A. Bitch.

What the hell was he supposed to do? Was Sara manipulating him, like Tiffani had?

And how screwed up did a guy have to be to doubt the sweet woman in front of him?

In daily ranch life, he strode through knee-deep horse hockey and made decisions without doubt or hesitation.

Now? What should he do with this woman going to pieces in front of him?

No idea. Drew a blank. Shit.

He paused. Tears rolled down her face, reappearing even as she wiped them away. Shit.

Fuck it all. He hadn't comforted her last night, which was the wrong decision. Time to try the opposite approach. He yanked her into his chest and wound his arms around her back and neck, absorbing her sobs with his body. Sliding his fingers into her hair, he eased her head to rest on his chest.

When a truck roared down the street, she startled and clung tighter to him.

What the hell?

Muttering to herself, Sara pulled out of his arms and ran to the kitchen and living room windows, pulling all of the blinds. He followed her, noting the cardboard duct-taped over the broken window, which of course didn't provide any security against anyone who wanted to enter the house. Sara, unsafe in her own house. Unacceptable.

When she stood back in front of him, her hands shook, and she didn't meet his eyes.

He rubbed the back of his neck. "All right. I know you don't want me here—"

"No, it's not—"

Damn him if he didn't want to wipe her soft cheeks until they were dry again. "I got it. Not me. Not sure I believe you. But something isn't right here. What sort of trouble are you in?"

She brushed a tendril of hair back behind an ear. "Can I get you something to drink? Want to sit down?"

"No, I'll stand, thanks." He planted his feet.

Her complexion paled as her eyes widened. "Okay. Mother of God, where to start? So you know about Hank?"

"Uh, yeah. We've all met. Remember?"

"Yeah. Sorry." The tip of one manicured thumb tapped her lower lip. His mouth went dry.

"What about him?" Damn it, his tone made her flinch again. "Last night, was that him?"

"Maybe."

Before he could stop himself, he touched her shoulder. Thank God she didn't skitter away. He rested his hand there until she began talking again.

"The night after you and I had dinner...he came here and threatened me. He said there'd be trouble if I saw you again. He told me I'd lose my job." Her voice cracked. "Because Butch is his brother and all. I don't know what to do." She held up a hand. "And I'm *not* leaving my students, and especially not Zach."

The set of her jaw and tough stance made him want to cheer and then protect her, surrounding her with his body so nothing and no one could hurt her. Her fist on her jeans-clad hip made his hands itch to ride over those curves.

"So that's why I didn't return your calls, why I kicked you out last night. I took the coward's way out, and I'm sorry."

"No one would blame you for staying away from me," he said.

"It's not right. And you know what? I'm sick of the hiding and the fear. And no one is going to tell me who I can and cannot associate with."

A flicker of optimism popped up in his chest. "All right."

"I'm tired of being scared and intimidated. I'm tired of being told I'm not good enough." She punctuated each statement with angry slashes of her hands.

What the hell? Of course she was good enough. Too good for a guy with rough edges and baggage like him. And way too good for a bastard like Hank Brand. But good enough for a nice, normal man who could give her the time and attention she deserved.

Something shifted inside of him, like a car revved up and ready to speed off down the road. Hope. "So then, you don't want me to leave?"

"Not at all, I—" At a loud knock at the door, she yelped. "Open up, Sara." Hank's harsh voice drilled through the door. Her mouth opened and eyes widened as her hand fluttered to the bruise on her jaw.

Garrison hoped like hell there wouldn't be a crime committed here tonight, but he had no guarantees.

Her stomach dropped to the floor.

Hank. Here. And Garrison here.

Flashes of her job disappearing in a wisp of smoke, Garrison's kisses, Hank's wild-eyed visit last night, and the broken picture frame all hit her at once like punches to her sternum. She couldn't get enough air in her lungs. If ever she wanted to quit her life and go hide in a hole somewhere, it was now. No nice guy needed to get involved in her mess.

"Please, don't let him see you," she whispered as she motioned for Garrison to step away.

God, she was such a coward.

His burnished eyebrows rose as he moved next to the door. He crossed his arms, hands gripping his biceps as his mouth compressed into a thin, angry line.

Hail Mary, full of grace. Sara was screwed no matter what she did.

Panic created sweaty pinpricks on her skin. Her back twitched like a knife was about to be thrust between her shoulder blades.

Hank pounded on the door again until the windows rattled in the casings.

She took a deep breath, flicked a glance at the unhappy man standing next to her, and opened the door a few inches, keeping Garrison hidden behind it. Even then, she could still feel his disapproving stare.

"Hank?"

"Why didn't you listen to me?" he growled.

His voice remained so calm. Too calm.

"What?"

"I'm very disappointed, Sarita." The man fairly vibrated, so well did he hold his emotions in check.

But his darting eyes and vein pulsing on his forehead told a different story. He was about to blow.

And behind the door, Garrison was probably fuming.

Goose bumps rose on her arms.

Now everyone disapproved of her. She couldn't catch a break.

Maybe she could bluff her way out of this mess. "Seriously, what are you talking about?"

"Can I come in?" His voice was too sweet, too quiet. Not good.

"No."

His smile twisted within his bearded face. "Where's rancher boy?"

"Who?"

"That Taggart asshole. I saw his truck parked nearby. He's got to be in here."

"Please leave, Hank. It's late. You've said your piece."

"But you didn't obey me." Sick logic, but he clearly believed it. "I am to be obeyed."

She resisted the urge to wipe her sweaty palms on her shirt. "You're not my boss."

"Yeah, but my brother is. You don't do what I say, you'll be out of a job, maybe forever."

Nausea threatened to drive her to her knees, but she maintained a calm demeanor. No need to give him any advantage.

"My life is none of your business."

His eyes bulged as he looked into the house. Then he leaned back and sighed. Flickers of the old, genial Hank interspersed with this new, strange Hank.

"Taggart *is* my business, sweets."

The old endearment sounded like poison coming from him today. "Why?"

"I've been called to destroy them."

"Seriously, what in the world are you talking about?"

"In the world? It's what's *not* in the world that's important. Get it?" He shook his shaggy head. "You wouldn't understand. No one does. But the Great One knows."

"Who?"

He clapped a hand over his mouth, then whispered. "Can't say."

Was Hank experiencing some kind of mental breakdown? Maybe he needed professional help.

He stepped forward again. "Let me look around."

Breakdown or not, she'd had enough of his behavior. "No. This isn't your house, and you're not welcome here." She hung on to the door with one hand and put her other hand on the doorjamb, barring his entry.

He stared at her.

Sara froze.

The crack as he slapped her arm away vibrated up to her shoulder, bringing tears to her eyes.

Garrison flew around her in a split second and went nose to nose with Hank.

Standing behind Garrison, she had a front-row seat when the back of his neck turned an ungodly shade of red, contradicting his own much-too-calm tone of voice. "Don't touch her. Ever. Again," he growled. Only, unlike Hank, Garrison didn't sound nuts. He sounded dangerous.

Hank rocked back on his heels, as he stood a few inches shorter than Garrison's six-foot-plus frame. Fury and heat radiated off Garrison. One hand clutched the door while his other hand extended back to keep Sara behind him.

"Back off, Taggart." Hank sneered. "This conversation is between Sara and me."

"The conversation is over. You will leave the lady alone."

"She's no lady." Hank's face contorted.

Hard to tell which hurt more, her throbbing arm or the character assassination. Goddamn it, she couldn't control who her parents were, and she'd done her best to rectify her petty crimes. She'd made something of herself and built a respectable life and career. Any meddling was for the sole purpose of helping her students.

Holy mother of God, give a woman some credit.

Garrison had the posture of a man whose fuse burned half an inch from the stick of dynamite. "One more time, Hank. Get out, or I will remove you from this property. And I guarantee who will win this round." He invaded Hank's personal space. "Leave Sara alone." The cold control in his voice nearly shattered her own ability to hold her shit together.

Her heart pounded double time.

"Whatever. Neither of you losers is worth my time." Hank turned his head and spat on the porch. "Sarita, you'd better watch your back. And polish up your résumé." He tipped an imaginary hat. "Taggart, you and your family are all marked."

He stormed off the porch, slammed the door of his truck, and sped off in a pissed-sounding *vroom* that surely drew the neighbors' attention. How was she going to wave at her neighbor tomorrow morning and act like she didn't notice his stare, that "so, you can't get along with men, huh?" assessment? Her cheeks already felt hot.

Until Garrison spun on his heel, kicked the door closed, and stared her down.

CHAPTER 12

*S*he couldn't breathe.

Garrison's powerful hands clenched and stretched, over and over. A muscle popped in his hard jaw, in time with his hand movements. When he stepped toward her, she flinched away.

"Son of a bitch, I'm not going to hurt you. Let me see your arm."

"It's fine. Let's just…God, I don't know."

He gripped her elbow and hand, and she gasped. Strong but gentle, he eased the sweatshirt fabric up her arm. She couldn't move, but he wasn't hurting her. His thumb brushed over the tender, red skin, and like an idiot, she felt a surge of desire settle deep in her belly. Totally inappropriate response to the entire situation.

"You have ice?"

"I don't need anything." She extricated her arm. "Let's just forget this whole unpleasant incident." Damn it, he stood way too close for comfort. Besides, she had a life to plan that didn't involve sticking around Copper River. That life didn't include anything more than a passing interest in Garrison. The sooner he left, the sooner she could move that plan forward.

No chance of entanglement. Maximize the chance of her plan succeeding.

"What?" He rocked back on his heels.

"Which painful part would you like me to repeat?" The chill in her tone was the only way she could keep from breaking down in front of this man.

He shook his head like a man waking up from a trance. "What the...You actually believe you don't need any help?"

Sadness needled between her ribs like an icepick. She couldn't take a deep breath without it hurting. "Doesn't matter. Please go home to your family, Garrison."

"I want to be here." He lifted his hand as if to touch her again, checked himself, and ran his hand through his short hair. "And you shouldn't be alone with a guy like that coming by."

"I've managed so far."

"Obviously." The sarcasm dripped like acid from his tongue. "Look, let's at least get some ice on this arm."

He ignored her protest as he stalked into the kitchen. The sounds of the freezer door and cabinets opening drifted back to her as she stood, stunned, in the living room.

When he returned with a Ziploc bag full of ice, he grasped her hand and led her to sit on the couch. With infinite tenderness that belied the red color of his face and tension in his frame, he draped the ice over her purpling arm. She gasped at the cold.

"Sorry." One side of his mouth quirked upward. "It's cool."

She couldn't help but smile in return, damn it. "Supposed to be. It's ice."

Uneasy quiet stretched out around them, broken only by the clunk of ice shifting in the bag. Her heart rate had finally returned to normal, though little flutters of excitement skittered through her as she sat hip to hip on the couch with him. He still had her arm resting on his hard thigh, her hand much too close to a certain bulge.

Adjusting the ice to keep the bruised area covered, his businesslike demeanor gave no indication he knew or even cared about her proximity to any part of his anatomy.

"Why did you come here tonight, Garrison? Really?" Her voice sounded hollow in the stillness of the room.

"Because you didn't return my calls. And when I stopped by yesterday, you kicked me out." His self-deprecating smile lifted her spirits a bit. "So, basically, showing persistence in the face of certain defeat." He shrugged. "Guess I'm no better than Hank, huh?"

"You're a much better man than he is. There's no comparison."

He shifted a quarter turn to face her.

She tried to ignore the heat from their thighs pressed together.

His gold-glinting gaze held her in place. "I'm really here because I wanted to check on you. That's it. Honest. And I'm glad I came back." Pressing his mouth into a line, he added, "We also didn't get a chance to regroup on how Zach is doing."

"You're here for another teacher conference?" That certainly slapped a girl out of her mooning.

"No. Not really."

"But you said—"

"It's not...I only want for you to tell me if Zach starts acting strangely. Or something."

Never heard that request from a parent. "All right. Well, so far so good. Normal kid behavior."

"Good." He nodded. "Good."

"Is that mainly why you came here, then?"

"No."

She was unable to take her eyes off the unforgiving features of his face that had somehow softened. The flannel shirt strained as he brought an arm up to rest on the back of the couch, not quite touching her, but so close she could sense his fingers right behind her.

His low voice came out like a caress. "Maybe I'm also here... because I only got a taste."

"Pardon?"

"I can't stay away from you, Sara."

Had he lost his mind?

Hell, had she? This was so not part of her plan, damn it.

"What about the stuff Hank said? He told me the 'Great One' called him to destroy you. I have no idea what all that was about."

"Frankly, Hank can go screw himself for all I care."

She giggled. "He's not that flexible."

When he laughed, his entire face reflected a whole different Garrison. Still strong, but gentler, with more layers than the tough rancher most folks probably saw. "I came close to making him that flexible tonight."

"Thanks for helping out, by the way."

"I'm only sorry that it needed to be done and that I didn't step in until after he hurt you." The slow movement of his thumb over her fingertips as they rested on his leg created swirls of pleasure, waking up parts of her body that had slept for far too long.

"Well. Okay, then. No one's ever stood up for me like that."

He locked eyes with her. "You know what I care about? Who you are as a person. I couldn't give a shit about anything else. We all have our ancient history. I care about the sexy woman in front of me who believes in my son."

"Oh."

"Yeah, oh." He stared over her shoulder. "Besides, um, I have a sense for when people are lying."

"Really?"

He didn't meet her eyes. "Kind of have an instinct for it. Hank's not going to ruin your job. He's spineless."

"How can you know for sure?"

His warm breath fanned her face. "Like I said, I'm pretty good at telling when people are lying."

Squinting at him, she said, "Now you're teasing."

"Nope."

"Hmm, what if I tell you my favorite color is yellow?"

He squinted at her. "Lie. Try again."

A stab of pain, like a pinprick on her skin over the temple, came and went. How odd.

"I love my job."

"Truth. I don't have to try on that one."

"And if every day came with chocolate icing, I'd be in heaven."

"Oh, that's true. I don't even need to use my...instinct. All your feelings show on your face. You'd make a horrible poker player."

"Too bad."

"Why too bad?"

"I could pay off my student loans with the winnings."

"Care to share leftover funds?" At his wry smile, her heart skipped a beat. "Okay. Let's do an experiment."

"That doesn't sound good."

"You've got another few minutes to ice your arm. We need to kill some time. Close your eyes." He raised his auburn eyebrows. "Unless you're chicken?"

Her insides melted right along with the ice in the Ziploc bag. "No way." She shut her eyes. "What's the experiment?"

"This."

He rested his fingers on her shoulder and trailed them over her neck.

When he buried his hand in her hair, she sighed and leaned into the warm palm. Sparks of happiness centered on the back of her head, spread down her neck and chest, and settled in the space between her legs.

He brought his other hand up and massaged her neck and scalp. Slow sweeps released her hair from the clip that he set on the end table.

The man had a point. They'd only had a taste of each other. The kiss in the parking lot hadn't been nearly enough. She had wanted so much more. Maybe he'd consider more. After he finished rubbing her neck and scalp, of course.

"Sara, look at me." His voice flowed over her like warm caramel.

When she opened her eyes, his irises glinted with gold flecks. How long had he been staring at her? How had he come so close to her, with his mouth only inches away?

"Your face gives it away every time."

"Gives what away?"

"The truth."

He tugged her head closer and slid one hand under her chin, and she shuddered, not from fear but longing. The only sound was that of her breathing, much too rapid for calm, polite company.

"God, you're beautiful."

He stilled her protest with his heated mouth, his lips demanding her consideration.

He had her undivided attention.

The contact took her from toasty to sizzling in the space of a breath. His kiss, insistent and hard, stole her breath. He'd bypassed tender hesitation and gone straight to devouring her whole.

And she was A-okay with Garrison's devour mode.

She gasped, trying to keep up with his shifting, searching, tasting mouth. When her lips parted, he slid his tongue inside, swooping into her mouth and opening her to him.

The bag of ice dropped to the floor, and she grabbed the front of his shirt, pulling him closer to her.

His groan echoed her own as he stroked her neck and slid down to the sweatshirt. His rough fingertips left a trail of heaven as one hand drifted to her breast, warming her skin through the fabric. When he cupped her and rubbed a thumb over her covered nipple, she threw her head back.

"See what I mean? Open. Book."

He pinched the hard tip of her nipple again, and she squealed as her toes curled.

"You're too far away from me." He growled as he pulled her onto his lap, facing him.

The spread of her legs over his hot denim thighs felt naughty and perfect. And left a space that begged to be filled. By him.

When he snaked his arms under her shirt, she leaned in and kissed him with every ounce of appreciation for his caresses on her back.

He lifted the hem of her shirt and tugged off the garment.

In the past, this would be the point where she'd cover herself or turn off the light. Even her curves had curves, and for a hard body like Garrison, she might not be to his taste.

As he licked his lips and groaned, he palmed her full breasts. "So beautiful," he breathed.

Okay, maybe her body *was* to this rancher's liking. His hot palm seared the skin of her back until a fingertip reached her bra. He popped the clasp, and he drew the fabric down and away. He licked his lips again like a starving man eyeing a buffet.

She ran her hands up his arms to his muscled neck and gently raked her nails over the nape. He shuddered.

Instead of keeping her arms around his neck, he gently positioned her hands behind her, on his knees. With her back arched and breasts pushed forward, she straddled him. Excitement zinged through every inch of her body.

Without preamble, he raised her breast to his mouth and sucked the nipple in, hard, holding it in place with his teeth and flicking his tongue over the tight nub.

She gasped as a pulse deep in her pelvis throbbed in time with his tongue's motion.

Colors and light began to smear as he shifted to the other breast. He squeezed the soft flesh and rolled the nipples between his thumb and finger, drawing her closer to him. Harsh breaths filled the room.

Turned out, the rough panting was actually her own. Thrusting her chest toward him, she was greedy for him to taste even more, for his hands to roam over her skin. She thanked the Holy Ghost when Garrison obliged with his hot mouth and rough tongue on her breast once again. Who said seconds weren't healthy? She groaned as he switched his attention back to her other breast.

"God, I want you, Sara." His lips returned to her mouth, and he kissed her hard and deep as he continued to torment her breasts with ever-faster movements.

Too much sensation, everywhere. Her body threatened to burst into flame.

"Me too," she breathed. "Oh God, I so want you."

When she angled away from him, he unbuckled his belt, the clink of metal setting her nerves on edge. His amber eyes hadn't left her face for a moment.

A ringtone broke the silence.

"Shit." He fished in his back pocket, jostling her on his lap. Cramming the phone to his ear, he barked, "What?"

A woman's high-pitched voice followed. He threw the phone to the side and jumped up, pitching her off his lap onto the couch.

"The ranch is on fire."

CHAPTER 13

*F*orget a bucket of cold water.

Garrison righted Sara from where he'd dumped her on the couch. Between fear for Zach, who was at the ranch, and the abrupt interruption of sexy times with a hard, hot rancher, she teetered on the edge of sanity. She looked down. Right, and she was half-naked, too. Fabulous. She clutched her sweatshirt to her chest.

When she glanced up, Garrison stood halfway, his gaze riveted to her breasts.

Her mouth went dry.

His voice cracked. "Shit. I need to go. Now."

Somehow, she managed to string coherent words together. "I'm going with you."

"Like hell."

"You could use an extra set of hands."

"Might not be safe."

"Am I safe here? With Hank running around?"

"Damn it. You're right."

"Give me a second. Um." When he continued to stare at her, she twirled her finger. "If you wouldn't mind."

As he spun around, she whipped the bra back on and shoved her sweatshirt back over her rumpled hair. Hopping on one foot and then the other, she pulled on tennis shoes and snagged her hair clip and a coat on the way out of the house.

The ranch burning. How bad was it?

She slammed the front door closed and raced to the passenger side of the truck. Before she could buckle up, Garrison pushed the truck to maximum allowable speed as the vehicle roared down the side street and onto the state highway.

Shadows from the yellow dashboard lights gave him a haunted, corpselike expression. The hard line of his jaw in profile cut the moonlight coming through the driver's side window. Leather creaked as he gripped the steering wheel.

Too long. They wouldn't get there in time. *Faster, faster. But safely.*

He tried making a call en route, but it must have gone unanswered, since he flung the phone on the floorboard. A heavy web of dread settled on her shoulders until she wanted to rip the uncertainty off. What was burning? Was anyone hurt?

She rubbed her sweaty palms on her jeans and returned one hand to the door handle.

Sniffing, she caught a faint scent of smoke, getting stronger.

As they passed under the Taggart Ranch sign, a glow appeared over a low hill.

Garrison's intake of breath matched her own.

Holy mother of God.

"Goddamnittohell."

The phrase no sooner made it past his lips when the truck's speed jumped another notch. As they fishtailed on the gravel, she bit her lip while the moonlit world flew by. Tears welled in her eyes at the smell of smoke, much more acrid now.

As the truck crested a hill, Sara stifled a scream. Hungry flames leapt from what looked like a fully engulfed structure, possibly a barn, throwing cruel reflections on the ranch house windows nearby. The truck screeched to a skidding stop in front of the massive ranch house, about fifty yards from the inferno. A wave of heat blew Sara back when she jumped out of the truck.

Far back on the ranch road, flashing lights piercing the smoke heralded fire trucks' arrival, the red-and-white strobes bouncing off the clouds of dust as they approached.

"Oh my God." Sara coughed as she stopped near the front porch of the ranch house.

A figure dashed from the smoke and flames rolling out of the barn, her face smudged and orange hair flying in a wild nimbus.

"Shelby!" Garrison screamed and ran toward her. "Where's Zach?"

"In the house." She grabbed a hose next to the house and soaked a blanket before throwing it over her head.

Garrison's fingers dug into Sara's bruised upper arm, hard, and he spun her around. She tried to ignore the painful throbbing created by his grip. "Get in the house. Please. Make sure Zach is safe."

As she dashed in the house, Sara paused at the door in time to see Shelby sprint past three other men and back into the blaze via the far side of the barn.

Garrison screamed, "Shel, no!" He ran after her and directly toward the inferno.

In the yellow haze, Garrison blinked to clear his blurry vision as he stumbled toward the barn, searching for Shelby. Heat buffeted him in harsh waves. A horse whinnied from within the burning structure, and cows mooed in distress in the nearby small pasture behind the house. Bringing all the herd down out of the back forty now seemed like a bad idea, given the unhappy lowing going on in the field. Stressed cattle equaled more problems for the ranch. Son of a bitch, he had a bigger crisis right now.

Three figures dashed toward the blazing barn, throwing water and yelling to each other.

Garrison chanced a glance over his shoulder. The firefighters poured out of their vehicles and disengaged hoses and equipment at lightning speed.

It wouldn't be fast enough.

If only they could keep other buildings from burning. He eyed the large timber-constructed ranch house. Zach and Sara were in there. At least the light breeze carried sparks away from the structure for now. Garrison had to keep them safe.

Kerr limped over, leading two wild-eyed horses by the bridles. The rearing horses tried to pull him off the ground, but he persisted until he swatted them into the field with the cattle.

Garrison's father, bent over and coughing, doggedly kept filling water and hauling it over to the barn for Eric to throw. After a few more rounds, the men's shoulders slumped. The buckets dropped, useless, at their feet.

"Where'd Shelby go?" Garrison shouted as he reached the men.

"I thought she was getting more water." Kerr hurried back, limping more than normal. Like a magnet needle, he rotated right to the barn, using his connection with Shelby to find her. "Shit. There."

Cold terror warred with the waves of heat hitting Garrison.

"Damn her." Eric took determined steps closer to the scorching heat until Kerr clamped down on the man's arm.

An ominous creak of beams screamed into the night, popping over the roar of the inferno.

"Son of a bitch," Garrison whispered. He whipped around. His father swayed on his feet, gasping for air. "Kerr, get Dad in the house!"

"What about Shelby?"

"Damn it, Kerr, take care of him!"

Visibly torn, Kerr finally hobbled over and guided their dad through the doors of the house. Garrison's last image was of his brother's sooty face with the hard line of his mouth, tight like an over-tuned instrument. Garrison turned back toward the fire.

The train-engine howl of the conflagration rang in his ears. Firefighters approached the heat.

Eric stumbled forward. "I'm going in after her," he yelled.

Garrison hung on to Eric's arm. "You can't go in there. Let's—"

A large section of the roof collapsed in a howling whirlwind of sparks and heat.

God. Shelby.

With a gut-wrenching burst of disintegrating wood, one wall fell inward.

A horse and bareback rider burst out of the inferno as the remainder of the structure imploded. The horse's eyes rolled back in his sockets, and he reared on back legs. The rider lay on the horse's back and clung to the mane, cleared the fire and most of the heat, and then slid off to one side.

"Geezus." Eric got to his feet and skidded to a stop, grabbing Shelby before she could hit the ground.

She wheezed and hacked until tears ran down her soot-dusted face.

"Get her out of here," Garrison ordered Eric. "I'll put the damned horse in the corral."

"I'm on it," Eric muttred.

When she waved off a firefighter's offer of medical assistance, Eric cursed as he slung her over his shoulder and hurried her into the house. An EMT followed with his medical bag.

The firefighters began to spray the fully engulfed barn as clouds of steam and smoke thickened the air.

"Whoa, boy, I know you hate the fire," Garrison crooned to the panicking horse over the roar of water, flames, and sirens. "Let's get you to a safe place." He petted the skittish horse's head. A few sear marks on the animal's flanks would need to get treated with liniment this evening. After getting a better grip on the bridle, he redirected the horse to the corral on the far side of the main compound.

Kerr walked up to him and shut the gate after the horse. "Holy backdraft, Batman. What the fuck?"

Another large fire engine screamed to a stop, lights flashing. In rapid coordination, more firefighters dashed out, pulled a hose, and drained the tank in a matter of minutes.

The thick smell of water, mud, and burnt wood seared Garrison's nostrils. He turned to Kerr.

"Son of a bitch. What happened?"

Kerr scrubbed at his sooty face. "No clue. One minute we were sitting in the house having dinner; next minute, the damn barn was up in flames."

Garrison asked, "Where's Dad?"

"Inside. With Shelby, our boneheaded sister. Who nearly died. And since she's more stubborn than even you, she won't let anyone check her out." Behind his mad words, Kerr's wary expression told another tale. He was scared. No doubt, the inferno had triggered some of Kerr's carefully hidden PTSD.

"We'll try again to get someone to evaluate her. I'm sure she'll be okay." The confidence in his words? All for Kerr's benefit. Truth be told, Garrison was crapping himself.

Garrison blew out a breath, and then started coughing until his eyes ran. "You get all of the animals out of the barn?"

"With that last horse of Shel's, yes, it's clear."

Another whoosh of fire and sparks heralded the beginning of the end. Wood beams straggled upward, like charred fingers reaching into the cold night sky. Despite the firefighter's efforts, all that remained was a flaming, smoking, twisted hell of wood and metal roofing material.

The barn. Gone. And the supplies with it.

A weird sensation on the back of Garrison's neck made him turn around to peer into the dark fields and hills. He could have sworn he heard a deep chuckle in the distance near a far hill, but how could he have heard anything over all the yelling and roar of the fire?

He stared at the moonlit mountains, indistinct behind the clouds of smoke.

Could this fire have been set deliberately?

The engines departed after the flaming rubble had been reduced to smoldering ashes. Kerr and Garrison completed statements for the police arson investigation, and that was that. Silence punctuated by the occasional hiss of a hot spot in the rubble.

They checked once more on the horses and cattle, and, satisfied that the animals would be safe until morning, trudged back to the house.

The front door felt like it weighed a thousand pounds to push open. Tonight, they could have used Vaughn's power to anticipate danger. Would've come in handy. Damn his brother, running off. Dumping all the responsibility on Garrison's shoulders.

The last million wishes hadn't brought Vaughn back home; no chance today's would, either.

Tomorrow, Garrison would have to look into constructing a barn, and fast, with winter coming.

Great. More shit to shovel.

CHAPTER 14

*H*is father sagged in a recliner, skin ashen in the areas not covered in soot. Rode hard and put up wet didn't even begin to describe the level of exhaustion etched on the man's face. He kept shaking his arm and hand. Maybe he'd injured himself hauling buckets.

Although he stood, Kerr leaned on the back of the recliner with his bad leg lifted off the floor, as if he couldn't manage more pressure on the prosthetic. His eyes had gone blank, and sweat beaded his soot-smeared forehead. Shit. If Kerr had a flashback tonight, Garrison would have to talk his brother down again instead of monitoring the ranch. Too much to do.

From his position next to the mantel, Eric's scowl reflected exactly how Garrison felt.

Shelby leaned forward from her seat on the end of the couch, her head in her hands. The longer parts of her hair had been burnt off, and the remaining seared ends stuck straight out from her now mostly shoulder-length hair. Her harsh wheezes and wet coughs filled the room as she struggled to catch her breath.

On the opposite corner of the couch sat Sara, her dark eyebrows raised, hair piled back up in an adorable mess on top of her head. The fear in her eyes when her gaze locked onto his rocked him to his boots. When he opened his mouth, she shook her head and darted a glance downward.

Zach had fallen asleep, his burnished head pillowed on her lap, a small hand resting on her leg. With his son curled on his side, Sara rubbed his back. Her sweet smile twisted something inside of Garrison's chest. And just knowing Sara and Zach were safe in his house? The tightness over his neck and shoulders unclamped by a few degrees.

Then the sensation changed into a different kind of tension: desire and unfinished business.

What would it feel like to relax with her fingers running through his hair, his own head resting on Sara's soft thighs?

Preferably, she would be naked.

He took a sharp breath and choked; the stinging scent of smoke drilled him back to harsh reality. Someone could have been hurt or died. Thank God everyone was okay.

Zach was safe. In the peace of sleep, his son appeared younger, like he looked years ago.

No. One year ago. Before Tiffani left.

Son of a bitch.

Kerr repositioned his stance with a *thunk* and leaned over, shaking their dad awake.

"You need to get to bed, Pop."

Dad groaned as he leaned forward, forearms propped on the sides of the recliner. "Christ almighty, what happened th-there?"

"A large chunk of our property went up in flames. No idea why. But you look like hell. Sure I can't take you to get checked out at the hospital?" Kerr asked.

"What use have...for a hospital?" He pushed up from the chair and trudged out of the living room, listing to one side. Kerr trailed behind him, hands up as if to catch him if he stumbled.

Dad asked, "Can you take care of everything, son?" He braced a hand against the log wall and peered at Garrison.

Out of the corner of his eye, Kerr flinched, dropped his hands, and returned to the living room.

Get used to it, little brother. I know how it feels to be inadequate. Only reason he's talking to me is because Vaughn's not here.

"Sure, Dad. Get some rest," Garrison said. "If anything comes up, we'll let you know."

His dad shuffled with an unsteady gait down the long hall. It was unusual for him to agree so easily to go to bed.

A prickly sensation crawled over Garrisons neck until he firmly stuffed it in his mental "deal with it later" box.

He had enough bad shit going on right now.

"So?" Garrison said as he walked between the chairs and the fireplace. "What really happened? Anyone know?"

Shelby's head came up. When she opened her mouth, another coughing fit stopped her cold.

Eric took a breath, opened his own mouth as if to make a comment, froze, and then melted back into the wall.

Breathing finally calm, she spoke, her voice hoarse. "Someone was out there."

"Be more specific," Garrison said.

"I got kind of a feeling"—she peeked at Sara from under her singed eyelashes—"so I went out to check on the horses. I heard footsteps in the barn. Before I could find out who it was, the back corner of the barn exploded in fire."

"Shit, Shelby. We don't know who was out there. One, take someone out with you when you get one of your feelings." Garrison raised his hand as she opened her mouth. "Two, what the hell kind of stupidity possessed you to go back into a burning wood structure?"

"What?" Shelby gaped. "I'm not a kid, and I'm not a delicate flower, so drop the caveman crap. Why wouldn't it be perfectly safe to walk around on our own property?" Her orange, ash-dusted hair glinted dully in the living room light. "Second, those horses are part of our family and part of our livelihood, you moron. Someone had to save them."

He glanced toward the couch but couldn't meet Sara's eyes. She shouldn't have to hear all of the Taggart family dirty laundry. Or the family secrets.

But any rebuttal was lost in Shelby's paroxysm of coughing. One hand gripped the arm of the couch while another pressed against her chest. Finally, she stood up and stared him down, still gasping for breath.

"At least I was here to help, unlike some folks," she said in a whisper. "So you're welcome, you big jerk."

No one moved as she left.

After long minutes of hearing nothing but Shelby's footsteps receding up the stairs and then the shower running, Kerr broke the silence. "What's the plan, then?"

"Get the assholes who did this, man." Eric's gaze darted toward Sara and a still-sleeping Zach. "Sorry. I know, I know. Language."

Kerr rolled his eyes and snorted.

"We have to consider all possibilities. It could've been a freak accident," Garrison began.

Kerr dropped into his father's vacated recliner with a groan and straightened both legs in front of him. "Unlikely."

"Garrison?" Sara's soft voice cut through the room like molten silk, riveting all three men's attention on her. "What if the fire had something to do with what happened earlier today?"

Eric frowned. "What?"

"Explain. Now," Kerr said.

She swallowed, and her hand drifted over her neck. "Hank Brand threatened me earlier this week and then again at my home today."

Kerr rubbed his hair. "Why?"

"For hanging out with Garrison. For standing up for Zach against Hank's older brother and his kids. For the fact that, um...Hank and I used to date."

The glistening in her eyes begged Garrison to take her in his arms, but somehow he managed to stay put.

Kerr raised an eyebrow as his head swiveled from Sara to Garrison. "Well, that's interesting information. Because we had that episode with Hank and Wyatt two days ago while we were fixing fences on the back forty."

At the same time, Sara pulled her head back and looked over at Garrison. "You didn't tell me about that. What happened?"

"Well, at least those assholes are consistent." Garrison made a fist and hit his thigh, then faced her. "Hank warned me to stay away from you from the other end of his gun. He also warned us to stay away from their property."

"Oh, God. So then this is because of…" She stared at the floor, her hand resting on Zach's shoulder.

"No. This isn't because of you." He snapped his fingers, and she blinked. "Look at me. They're nuts, and Hank's got a screw loose. Besides, we don't know for certain that the Brand boys set the fire."

"Seems more likely than not. Who else has a motive?" Kerr spit out.

Garrison shook his head. "Could have been an accident."

"Right." Kerr snorted. "Anyway. So what do we do?"

Eric's eyes went to the ceiling as his jaw locked tightly in place. He pushed off the wall. "I'm going to keep an eye on things outside." He stomped out and slammed the front door.

Zach startled and shifted, then fell back asleep as Sara trailed her fingertips over his forehead, soothing him.

Garrison's skin twitched. He wanted her soft hand on him, trailing over his starved flesh. The memory of unfulfilled desire at Sara's house tore at him.

Shit. What kind of fucked up parent was jealous of his child?

"I'll go with him." Kerr stood with a grimace, reached down toward his leg, but pulled his hand away. "We'll make sure every-thing is locked down tight. No one's getting close to the house tonight."

After Kerr shuffled out of the front door, ominous silence descended, punctuated by Zach's light breathing.

Sara stared everywhere but at Garrison. "You'll want to get him to bed."

"About earlier this evening—"

Her palm came up. "Stop. Take care of your family. Get cleaned up. Then maybe you can take me back home."

"You're not staying by yourself."

"I can make my own decisions. And you don't need more issues to worry about."

Oh no, he groaned inwardly as her chin came up. Son of a bitch, he didn't have the energy to argue with her tonight.

"What about your safety?" he asked.

"I'll be safe. Besides, you have way bigger fish to fry, by the looks of things. I'd be in the way and make more trouble for you." Her sad smile hit him in the solar plexus. "Already have caused trouble."

"No—" He crammed his hand through his hair. "Damn it. Okay, look, let me get Zach tucked in, and we'll talk. Just. Stay here."

"I'll meet you back here. Kerr said there's a guest bathroom down the hall?"

He nodded.

Her lips curled upward, tempting him to kiss that impish smile away. "Don't worry, I won't leave. No transportation."

A tiny spark of hope flared as he bent down. His front-row seat to her cute dimple made him forget how to speak. So, without a word, he picked up Zach and left the living room.

Garrison walked away. His attraction to this woman had the worst timing in the universe.

For the tenth time, Sara paced from the couch to the window and back. She'd memorized the location of the patterned rugs on the floor and how many steps it took to traverse them. The mellow brown log walls should have felt relaxing, cozy, but being so close to disaster made her shake in her shoes.

Between the ache of longing in her core from the interrupted sexy interlude and the fear of what would happen next with Hank, her insides were twisted into knots. Add to that her vow not to form any more attachments in Copper River, and she couldn't tell up from down. Yet the memory of Garrison's rough stubble and soft hair at the nape of his neck made her fingers tingle with the need to touch, connect. And his lips. Mother of all that was holy, what she would give to have those firm but strong lips on hers, his tongue dipping into her mouth and stroking her until…

Suddenly, she needed to rest her flushed face against the window. Closing her eyes, she flattened her palm against the cool glass and sighed.

Out there lay the destruction she had caused.

The remnant of the barn glowed as the twisted wood popped and settled in a heap on the far side of the ranch house. On the other side of the property, near the fenced area of livestock, the unlit bulk of a second, smaller barn absorbed all light, its dark hulk an echo of the larger structure that had been reduced to ashes.

Hank might have been behind this mess. How was that possible? Didn't matter how. The evidence pointed in his direction. This evening's display of anger revealed a dangerous edge she'd never fully seen before. If he was connected to the fire, then Sara and the Taggarts were in far more trouble than they realized. If.

She rubbed her bruised forearm. Damn Hank, he'd made his point. Now why couldn't he simply leave the Taggart family and her alone? This theory about him having a mental breakdown had gained real traction.

Because if he'd done all of these bad things and was sane? God help them all. They were all in deep, horrible trouble. Someone who could deliberately burn down a barn and put people in danger could sure as hell do even worse things. She rested her forehead on the window casing.

Holy Christ. Yeah, her goal of one day leaving this town and making a fresh start in Atlanta? Pretty good idea, after all.

"Penny for your thoughts?"

She spun around.

A freshly showered Garrison filled the entryway of the living room, his arms crossed and shoulders slumped. A few droplets clung to his wet hair combed back off his forehead. The sleeves of his plaid shirt were rolled up, revealing thick forearms dusted with ruddy hair. As he approached her, the smell of soap, the log home, and his warm spicy scent blended into a heady mixture.

In the dimmed light of the living room, his shadowed eyes drilled into her until her breath caught. Did he blame her for all the trouble she'd sent this family?

He stopped a foot away, consuming too much space. Behind her was the living room wall. She had no place to go. With the light source behind him, she couldn't read his expression.

But she sure as hell could feel the waves of pissed-off intensity crackling between them.

"I'm sorry." Damn, her voice quavered. She struggled to meet his shadowed gaze.

"What the hell are you talking about?"

She flinched. He might have a knack for telling the truth, but it didn't take a mind reader to figure out when a guy was barely holding his shit together.

"I believe that this," she pointed a shaking thumb back at the window, "is my fault, due to Hank."

He raked both hands through his hair, like he wanted to pull his head off. "Are you kidding me?"

"Well, who do you think burned the barn? And why?"

"First of all, I don't know for sure who's responsible. Second, even if it's the Brand folks, we aren't certain why or whether it even involves you. Hank threatened me earlier this week. There's something going on over on that property. And they've been trying to purchase our land. We saw mining equipment hidden on their ranch up in the hills."

"Hold on. Izzy said something a few days ago about mining."

"Izzy Brand?"

"Yes, I told you she's a friend of mine."

"You're still friends with a Brand?" He crossed his arms.

"She's not like them."

"How do you know?"

The third degree about her friendship with Izzy? So not happening. "Don't judge me because I don't have a knack for figuring out when people are telling the truth. How about trusting someone you've known for years? Ever heard of that?"

"Sure did. Bit me right in the ass." His glare glittered in the low light.

The ex-wife.

Sara mentally face-palmed herself. "Good point." Shoving her fists on her hips, she added, "But don't look so mean. Izzy is a nice, normal person. Nothing like her brothers, so don't lump her in with those guys."

Putting his hands up, he smiled. "Okay, message received. Do not mess with your friends. Got it." Then he edged toward her, close enough she felt the heat coming from his body. "But that is interesting information she told you. What else did she say?"

He stood so near, she spied a muscle jumping in his smoothly shaven jaw. How nice it would be to trace that hard line with her tongue.

"Sara?"

Caught. "Pardon?" Despite herself, she licked her lips, and then stopped as he stared right at her mouth. "I'm a little tired, that's all."

"So did Izzy mention anything else about her brothers?" His voice was mellower.

"Only that her brothers are keeping her in the dark about their plans. She's not allowed to go to certain places on their ranch. Her job is to take care of the house and their mom and leave the guys alone. It doesn't sound fabulous, but with her mother's health not being good, I think she feels obligated to stick around and help out."

"You think she's safe around a guy like Hank? Even if he is her brother?"

"Izzy looks out for herself pretty well. I believe she's okay."

He rubbed his chin. "Strange about what's going on at the Brand ranch. Even more unusual that folks in town either don't know about it or aren't talking about it. What in the world are our neighbors doing?" He blinked and stared past her out the window. "At least Kerr and Eric are keeping an eye on things." A muscle jumped in his jaw. "Damn it, I should be out there."

She fought the urge to straighten his tousled hair.

Or rough it up even more.

She swallowed.

"Garrison, you're exhausted. Let them help."

"Okay," he mumbled as he peered through the glass.

He stood way too close for comfort. Or rather, his proximity was *overly* comfortable. Which tilted her equilibrium even more.

"So, is Zach tucked in?" Maybe she should try to get him to focus on something good.

"He's out. Whatever you did to him, he's sleeping soundly. Have to say, I'm a little jealous."

"Jealous?"

"I'd like to fall asleep on your lap, Sara."

Her heart stopped dead in its tracks, flipped over, and then started scrambling for traction. "Oh."

A mere ghost of sound, his voice flowed over her. "*Oh* is right."

When he ran his thumb over her lower lip and leaned forward, she pressed her back into the wall. The rounded logs dug into her spine, the pain waking her the hell up. Got it. Suffering. More pain. Her future if she continued down this path.

She cleared her throat, breaking the spell. "I should get back home."

"No."

CHAPTER 15

*S*he nearly crawled out of her skin and into his.

"I can't stay here." Her voice sounded too breathy. Not a confident refusal at all. "You need to deal with the fire damage and everything, and I've got school in the morning. If I stay here, I will be in the way. A distraction."

"I want to be distracted by you, Sara." Even a deaf woman could hear the rumble of male interest in his low voice.

"I, um—"

"Please." Spoken like he ripped the word out of his chest. "I need you here tonight. Need to know you're safe."

Distraction? Safe? Disappointment crushed her heart. Yet despite his scowl, his eyes glinted and his chest rose and fell faster than normal.

Maybe she hadn't misread his interest. Maybe their close encounter earlier this evening wasn't a fluke.

Well, then. Nothing like throwing all caution to the wind.

When she leaned forward and laid a hand on his arm, the muscles bunched up. She looked up into his shadowed face. "You can think of no other reason for me to be here?" Her lips quivered despite her attempt to flash him a confident smile.

His jaw muscle jumped. Good.

She reached up to trace the lines of his strong mouth with her shaking fingertips.

His shudder cut the quiet atmosphere, but he didn't stop her.

Against her fingers, he said, "I want you. So badly."

Caressing his lower lip with her index finger, she said, "I don't have your knack of telling the truth. How do I know you're not lying to me?"

He caught her finger with his square, even teeth. Not hard enough to hurt, but he didn't let go.

In fact, the sweep of his tongue over the sensitive fingertip turned her bones to water.

Encircling her wrist in his hand, he held her hand still while he sucked one and then two fingers into his mouth. The swirl of his rough tongue sent a frisson of desire into her pelvis, where heat grew and expanded.

Her heart couldn't beat fast enough to compensate for her plummeting blood pressure.

Right as her knees gave out, he pressed her into the wall and stroked her neck with one hand. With his other hand, he teased the sensitive skin under the hem of her sweatshirt, drawing out goose bumps and shivers.

Well. She'd gotten his attention all right. She'd also deduced an answer to the question of why she should remain here. Message received, loud and clear.

His lips plied hers with a hot, building rhythm. Every inch of his tall, solid body leaned into her, including a hardness in his groin that hit at the perfect location on her lower belly. Delicious coils of happiness worked their way lower and lower until she pressed her hips into his. She was hungry, searching, wanting.

Rubbing her hands over the shifting bands of his arms, she sighed.

He groaned and plunged a hand in her hair, tugging her head back. His tongue slid between her lips, stroking inside faster and deeper.

She couldn't move. Didn't care. Wanted more. More touches. More kisses. More Garrison.

When his mouth moved to her earlobe, she whimpered. Holy Mary, they couldn't possibly...here in this house? With his family around? Heck, his kid was upstairs. That would make for an A-plus show-and-tell in class tomorrow if Zach saw her with his dad.

Tugging her hands free, she dropped her arms to his broad shoulder. "Garrison, what about...?"

"Sh. I need this. I need you."

"But your family—"

"Don't care. It's a big house. With a guest wing."

He stared at her like a low-carb dieter watching cookies rise. Images of chocolate chips melting on his body made her weak in the knees.

"You calm me." The words blew by her like a caress. "Being around you somehow makes the bad shit in my life seem bearable. Hell, being around you, I forget all my responsibilities and problems."

Hold on a minute. Didn't he want her because he desired her as a woman? Or did he want her as a stress reliever, like a pill or a soak in a bubble bath? Was he using her?

Decision time.

Enjoy the moment in a quick fling with the hottest man she'd ever met, or take the safe route and wait to see if a respectable relationship that no one would gossip about might develop later down the road? What about her plans for the future, beyond Copper River? Those plans were still there. A fling did not a relationship make. And no way was she creating entanglements here. Nope.

He brushed his mouth over hers, nipping at her lower lip until stars swam in her vision. Whatever he was doing with his hands, kneading and palming her breasts, it should be illegal. She couldn't breathe. How could she make an informed decision here?

Forget safe.

She'd done safe, and it bit her in the butt.

Rising on tiptoes, she met him, passionate kiss for kiss.

After a moment, he pulled back and held her head in his hands. "Damn. Listen to me before I lose my mind with you, Sara. It's not all about me. If you don't want...more, you have to let me know. I'll respect what you want, I swear."

If the pulsing sensations low in her groin were any indication, her body had made up its mind.

"I want you, Garrison."

Relief and intense need scrolled over his features like the news ticker on Times Square.

"Me too."

"But here? Kerr and Eric might come back inside."

"Good point. Guest room, let's go."

Still cradling her face in his hands, he kissed her again, drifting his mouth up her jaw and sucking gently on her earlobe. The puff of his breath in her ear shot a wave of excitement right to her clitoris. Sliding her hands up his corded forearms, she reveled in the hard muscles and the roughness of the hair under her fingers.

He stroked down her neck and under her sweatshirt.

Goose bumps rose on her skin, and she shivered.

"Damn it." He held her at arm's length. "We're never going to get to the guest room at this rate."

She grinned as he tugged her down the hall to an empty wing of the sprawling home. Old high school pictures on the walls and knick-knacks barely registered in her hungry mind as she followed him into a room with an antique dresser and a queen bed with a neat but worn quilt on top. He shut the door with a firm, final thud and flipped on the bedside lamp, bathing the room in a cozy glow.

"Last chance, Sara." He grinned and caressed her face with his rough fingers.

What would those fingers feel like elsewhere on her body?

Sara needed to know.

"Yes."

"Yes, what?"

Answering questions had become way too complicated. She gasped, "Yes. I want you, Garrison."

She grabbed the fabric of his shirt and tugged at him to bend down and meet her lips. Almost climbing up him, she worked her hands over his shoulders and then curled her fingers in the hair at the nape of his muscled neck. He didn't resist.

Quite the opposite. Clutching her to his frame, he pivoted and spun her toward the bed.

When he gently pushed her onto the quilt, she giggled and brought him down onto the bed with her.

On his side, Garrison slid a hand under her sweatshirt and stroked over the skin of her ribs.

"So soft," he murmured. He eased the sweatshirt over her head and away. "Shit."

Putting a hand on his shoulder, she pushed him away. "What?"

"Your arm."

He traced the purple bruise. His eyes darkened as his brows drew together. "Hank's going to pay for putting his hand on you." The line of his jaw went rigid.

She slid her hand to his shoulders and kneaded the muscles there. "I don't want to think about him," she whispered.

A full two seconds later, his eyes focused square on hers. "Your wish is my command."

His lips found hers again until he broke away to trail kisses down the center of her chest.

"You're gorgeous," he said, unclasping her bra and drawing it away.

Maybe she had been okay with the full frontal display earlier this evening, but this entire situation? Too immediate. Too intense. Too much to process.

"Lights." She gasped against his relentless mouth.

Like a man waking from a deep sleep, he blinked. "What?"

She blinked against the lamp's glow. "Turn off the lights, please."

A frown formed between his brows, but thank God he didn't ask questions. "Whatever you want." Moonlight filtered through the curtains, giving the room a soft, gray glow.

His hands roved over every inch of her skin, kneading, sliding, and cupping her.

He laved and gently nipped at each nipple, driving her pleasure to insane heights. And, clever man, while he occupied his mouth with one breast, his rough fingers worked their magic on the other.

Then, thank you Jesus, he switched sides.

Desperate to touch more of him, she unbuttoned his shirt, dodging his dipped head and ignoring the growls when he had to stop his magic. No question, he loved her breasts. She squirmed. Holy mother of God, they loved what he was doing to them.

By evading his hands, she created enough space to strip off his shirt. The expanse of muscled chest, sprinkled with rough hair, invited her to explore.

He groaned when she licked his hot skin. Bracing his arms on either side of her head, he hovered with his torso in easy range of her lips. So helpful. Her lips feasted on the taste of his heated skin. After a gentle bite over a hard muscle, she flicked her tongue over his flat nipple. His breath caught, and he lowered his hips, grinding his pelvis into hers until she couldn't distinguish her body from his.

She licked his other nipple; he reared up and drove his fingers beneath her jeans. In record time, he unbuttoned and pulled the garment down and away, leaving her in only her underwear.

Ugh. Had she known tonight would be filled with hot sex with a hard-bodied rancher, she would've chosen her foundation wear more carefully and changed from granny-panty cotton to a festive black thong. Her face warmed, and she slid her hands down to cover herself.

"No way. That's for me to enjoy." The possessive male growl curled her toes. "You're so damned sexy." He slowly eased her hands to the sides, then ran his hand up her thigh until he cupped her core.

His dark eyes glittered in the filtered moonlight. Every nerve in her body vibrated with longing to contact every inch of him, inside and out.

She couldn't move, held in place by that one big, warm hand. His skin was separated from her sensitive flesh by a mere scrap of fabric.

"Oh God, Garrison."

He bent down and blew warm air over the vee in her groin until she panted, on the edge, wanting more.

In the moonlight, she couldn't miss his masculine grin.

When she reached for him, he again guided her hands back to her sides.

And proceeded to remove her last article of clothing.

The heat in her sex pulsed in the cool air.

Until his scorching mouth covered her.

She shot upright.

He lifted his head. "Not good?"

"Oh my God. The opposite." She panted. "So good." She couldn't think or move.

In the dark, she could just make out his confident smile. "Well, why don't you just enjoy?" He palmed her butt and rotated her hips. Licking his mouth, he bent his head.

The swirl of his rough tongue on her sensitive skin left her unable to breathe.

When he darted his tongue up and down her folds, she sighed and let her knees drift to the sides. What he did with his mouth defied logic and gravity, but holy wow, he was great at it. With a flick on her clitoris, he pushed her right to the brink of orgasm, and he still had his jeans on, for heaven's sake.

She would have flown off the bed when he darted his tongue into her core, if his hands didn't anchor her in place. As he flicked and nipped, her back bowed and hips bucked against him.

"That's it. You taste so good." The rumble of his voice against her super-sensitive skin made the room spin.

He knelt over her, then ground his erection into her pelvis.

No way was she going to simply lie here and enjoy.

Dragging her nails down his back, she smiled when he gave a gut-wrenching shudder. She dipped her fingertips beneath the waistband of his jeans. Hard muscle rippled under her hands, and she swallowed.

"Your turn."

"Damn. Anything you want, I will oblige."

When he reclined on the bed, she undid the buckle and button. The ticks of the metal zipper, loud in the quiet room, set her nerve endings on fire. When she stroked his hard erection through the denim fabric, his back arched and a hiss of her name slid from his mouth. Good. Now for more fun. She pushed his jeans down, and he kicked them off, along with the briefs.

Circling his thick erection with her hand, she palmed him up and down its length until moisture coated the tip. He switched their positions, with her flat on the bed again. He lowered himself onto her and rubbed against her swollen lips, and she spread her legs wider, wanting so much more.

Then cool air and the squeak of mattress springs. She cracked open one eye.

"Shit. Please be there," he cursed as he ducked down on the floor. Clothing rustled. "Finally." A crinkle of foil and he was back, pressing every inch of his body against hers and kissing her until she couldn't tell where she ended and he began.

His voice, like rough fabric, tore over her. "Sara." At his nudge on her knee, she let her legs drop to the sides. Exposed and in need of him badly.

He stroked her wet core until she writhed.

The tip of his erection teased her entrance, and she whimpered and raised her hips.

He chuckled. "Patience."

"I don't want to be patient. I want you." She grabbed his head and pulled him down to her, sucking his lower lip, tasting her arousal on his mouth.

His breaths came out rough and wild as he entered her with one firm thrust.

He covered her gasp with his mouth and pushed into her harder and deeper, filling every inch of her body and stretching her farther than she had experienced before. After a moment of stillness, he slowly rotated his hips in a sensual rhythm.

A coil of pleasure spiraled up and up as she met his thrusts, until she couldn't handle any more. But, holy moly, she wanted more.

Then he grabbed one of her legs and sped up the rhythm.

She soared in his arms as the pace quickened along with his rasping growls.

The tension in her pelvis ratcheted up several more notches as she hooked both of her heels around his hard butt, seating him deeper inside. His half groan, half purr was all the approval she needed.

Higher and harder, he drove her, and she flexed against him, matching the rhythm and opening herself up to him more than she thought possible.

They crested within seconds of each other, her cries smothered as he entered her mouth with his tongue while driving into her sex below. Her vision dimmed, and in his arms, she shattered into a million tiny pieces.

CHAPTER 16

A whisper next to his ear woke him up.

"Garrison?"

Her voice, like sweet silk, slid over him, and he immediately hardened. Groaning, he pulled her deeper into the circle of his arms. As long as her soft body molded to his, maybe he wouldn't have to confront the stark reality waiting for him outside the guest room door. Maybe he wouldn't have to worry about everyone and everything. For the first time in far too long, he trusted his own feelings.

He would simply enjoy the beautiful woman in his arms.

"Garrison, wake up, please."

"With your sexy butt pressed next to me, who can sleep?" He dropped a kiss onto her neck, and she shivered. Good.

In the moonlight filtering through the window, her olive skin took on a luminous glow. Trailing his fingers over her smooth arm, he had a flash of what life would be like with her in his arms, every night, with her cries of pleasure filling his bedroom. Coming home to her each evening.

To do what? Have wild sex and create a future together? With his entire life in chaos? Hell, he didn't even know if they would have a home to live in next year, between buildings burning down, looming bankruptcy, and attempted takeovers of his land.

He had nothing to offer this woman. Or any woman. No financial security. No safety. Not even the promise of his undivided attention, if his duties on the ranch continued to expand.

Cold fear bit into him as he fought to hold on for dear life to his dream of a normal future. What the hell was he thinking?

He'd always be waiting for the other shoe to drop, waiting for Sara to betray him like Tiffani had done. Didn't matter if it was fair to Sara or not. At least he was honest with himself. His stupid ability, which he could use to verify that people told the truth? In the end, it only resulted in him not trusting anyone. He was damned if he used the gift, and damned if he didn't.

He would eventually get hurt. And that was a winning way to start a relationship. Complete lack of trust.

So. No dream for him. He needed to protect Zach and himself.

He rolled away from Sara and sat up.

"What do you need?" he said, trying to keep the snap of anger out of his voice.

She froze. Her wide eyes searched him.

Sweet Sara didn't deserve his self-loathing and doubt. But she did deserve a guy who had his shit together.

Basically, anyone but Garrison.

Clutching the quilt to her chest, she scooted up against the backboard.

"I need to leave."

He sat straight up. Was that a tremor in her voice?

"You need to leave?" He cringed. Wrong thing to say.

She lifted her hand to trace his jaw, making him shudder.

Her sad voice raked his nerves raw. "Why? Were you thinking of going, too?" Even in the shadows, her smile didn't make it to her eyes.

"No. Yes. Never mind." He rubbed his neck, wishing it were her hands there, not his. "Why do you want to leave?" Damn it, he couldn't stop himself from lashing out at her.

Sara Lopez was the last person who deserved to be the target of his anger. Hauling air into his lungs, he fought to calm down and wake the hell up before he said anything else stupid.

Time to tally up the score: He didn't want long-term commitment or to risk being hurt, but he had the gall to get mad if his sleepover buddy didn't want to stay until morning. Oh, and he wanted to use his sleepover buddy to check for strange behavior in his son, because Garrison couldn't be objective. So he would use her and then get mad at her for getting too close to him.

He had become the definition of a hypocritical asshole.

"It's four in the morning. I have to get ready for work." She swallowed. "And it might not be ideal if your family saw me here this morning. After...you know."

Shingle-peeling, brain-chemistry-altering terrific sex?

"You have regrets?" Too sharp of a tone, damn it. Like he was waiting for her to unman him, just like his ex had done.

Her head whipped around. "Last night was amazing, Garrison. But a mistake for our, uh, future. I know you were stressed out from all that's happened with Hank and the ranch." Without meeting his eyes, she said, "I am glad if...what we did...relieved your stress."

"What the—?" He bit back the curse. "A mistake? Relieved my stress?" Okay. He knew they shouldn't have slept together for his own personal messed-up reasons, but if she thought it was wrong, too, then they were doubly screwed up.

"Look, Garrison, it shouldn't have happened, okay?"

"Why? I thought we had something good going on here."

Wait. Now he argued in favor of the relationship? He really needed to make up his mind, for both their sakes, and quit see-sawing.

"You're a nice guy, Garrison."

"You're going to try the 'it's not you, it's me' bullshit again?"

She flinched. "Well yeah, actually, I am. That explanation makes the most sense, doesn't it?"

"No."

"Can we talk about something else, please? Like how you'll take me back home so I can get ready for work?"

"Fine."

He flipped on the overhead light. Screw her issues with the lights being off. Since this would be the last time he ever saw her naked, he wanted a good view.

Which also made him a different kind of asshole. So he clamped his jaw shut like it had wires running through it and turned his back to her while he shoved his legs into his jeans.

The light rustle of her clothes sliding against her skin nearly made him crawl out of his own. But he gave her what privacy he could.

Damn it. She regretted what they did last night. He didn't blame her one bit, but the rejection stung.

Hurt again by a woman. At least Zach hadn't become invested in Sara being part of their lives.

Garrison would not feel sorry for the woman whose shoulders slumped as she sat on the side of the bed. And he would not watch how she slipped her silky smooth arms into the bra and reached back to clasp it.

Damn. All he wanted to do was unhook that garment and run his fingers over her body until she screamed for him.

Clearly, he'd lost his mind.

Standing at the door, he crossed his arms. "Ready?"

"Almost." Her voice was strained.

He didn't care. Wouldn't care.

"Let's go."

"Okay."

He sensed her following close behind him down the hall; his shoulders twitched, but he wouldn't look back. She hadn't touched him, but he felt her disappointed presence, nevertheless, as they exited the house.

In the calm stillness of very early morning, the cold air clung to him with the undertones of damp smoke and impending snow. The scent of failure.

Out of the darkness, a shadow with an irregular gait signaled Kerr's approach.

If his brother thought anything odd about Garrison and Sara's early morning travels, he kept his opinion to himself. Thank God Kerr didn't have the ability to read emotion like Shelby did, or his brother's head would explode.

Garrison closed the truck door behind Sara and turned to his brother. "Where's Eric?"

"Resting on the futon in my room for a while. We'll switch off in an hour or so."

Right. Because the guest bedroom was occupied. Great. "Fair enough. You guys see anything?"

"No, it's been quiet. And I don't like it. Feels wrong, you know?"

His brother's psychic ability had nothing to do with sensing danger. His instincts had been earned and honed in the crucible of war, and Garrison took his younger brother's senses to heart. Nothing they could do right now, other than watch and wait.

Kerr tilted his head toward the truck, his expression lost in the last waning bit of moonlight behind him. "So?"

"So nothing. Sara's going home to get ready for school."

"That's all, Casanova?"

"All that's any of your business."

Kerr opened his mouth, but Garrison stopped him with a chop of his hand in the air.

"Not now. Keep an eye out. I'll be back in an hour or so."

"Roger, will do." Kerr's even white teeth shone in the darkness.

The bumpy ride down the dirt road and into town took place in complete silence. Garrison had to check to make sure Sara was still awake.

As they pulled up to her house, she opened the door before the truck stopped.

"Thanks."

She shut the door on any response and hurried into the house.

Damn. Well, at least he didn't have to endure messy discussion and hashing out their issues. No awkward good-byes. The relationship had ended before it started.

He wouldn't dwell on it. He had too many problems to work on right now.

Emptiness hollowed out his chest like a rat chewing a nice, cozy nest.

He threw the truck into gear and hauled ass back to his burnt property.

~

It might be Friday, but there was no Thank God included.

Sara dragged herself into the classroom, right on time but not bright-eyed. The thought of facing twenty energetic second-graders held no interest today and, in fact, filled her with dread.

How could she inspire her students if she couldn't pull her mind out of the mess from last night? After the roller-coaster ride between floating on a fluffy cloud of ecstasy and then being dropped off at her house like the UPS man couldn't make his delivery fast enough, she didn't have much left in the tank today.

The buzz of kids filtering into the classroom riled her irritated nerves.

"Hi, Ms. Lopez!" Zach trotted into the room and hung his coat on the hook before taking his seat.

Orange-haired Zach was a miniature of his father.

Garrison. Damn.

What did the man expect? She couldn't stay the entire night. And he only wanted her as a way to relax.

She shouldn't have been in bed with a good guy like Garrison in the first place. They had no future together. He had a loving family, a great son, the family business, and a solid reputation in town.

What did she bring to the table? A plan to leave this town and create a fresh, new life, untarnished by debt or her own past history.

Even if their evening ended with her pride in shambles piled on top of a heaping scoop of Garrison's regret, she didn't blame him.

As the bell rang, she shook the fog of unhappiness weighing her down, and pushed through the endless day.

After she got home that evening, Sara couldn't avoid her friend anymore. Time to fess up to Izzy. She thumbed the vibrating phone.

"Hi, Izzy."

"What the heck happened to you? It's like you dropped off the face of the earth."

"Long story."

"I'm listening."

"So when did we last talk?"

"Tuesday!" Yowch, her anger came through the phone crystal clear.

"I'm so sorry, Izzy. It's been a long week. You want to hang out?"

"Give me the highlights. I have to stay here with Mom tonight."

Sara left out the part where Hank came to her house and tried to break her arm. Izzy didn't need more stress with her already dysfunctional family life. Besides, knowing Izzy, she'd ream Hank out, and he'd make Sara's life even more hellish.

Still, the story flowed smoothly until Sara got to last night's wild ride.

"You did *what?*"

She held the phone away from her ear until it was safe to continue. "Yeah, well, yeah. We did it."

"Details. I'm almost a nun over here."

"It was very good. Too good. Okay, awesome." Stupid tears pricked at her eyelids. Not again. She'd been an emotional mess since meeting Garrison. "But it doesn't matter. We're done."

"What happened?"

How could she explain the ten-second implosion of everything good in her life?

She couldn't.

"It just didn't…work out."

"As in 'tab A doesn't fit into slot B' kind of didn't work out?"

Sara laughed despite herself. "No. It's not like a do-it-yourself project."

"Hey, don't knock it. Some of us have no problem doing it ourselves. No choice, either."

The tears rolled but not in sadness. "God, Izzy, you're so wrong."

"Sometimes a gal has to be her own boyfriend."

Air. She couldn't breathe for laughing. It was a small price to pay for this mood elevating conversation. She hadn't laughed this hard since one of her students shared that inappropriate joke for show-and-tell last week. "Well, now you've burned a totally new and equally as uncomfortable image into my brain to mull over tonight."

"Happy to help." Izzy sighed. "So what are you going to do?"

"Do? There's nothing to do."

"Wait. Stop. You met the hot rodeo star that happens to be a smidge emotionally unavailable and then had a passionate night of epic bronc-riding proportions with him? Who are you kidding with this 'there's nothing to do' bull?"

"But—"

"As a personal favor to you, I'm going to come over tomorrow evening. I'll be bringing a bucket of something greasy and covered in good stuff like lard or barbeque sauce. We're going to figure out a way to fix this mess. Because you and sexy rancher would be perfect together."

"I don't know…"

"About the light snack or the hunk of beefy man? Most women would like both."

Sara giggled. "How about put the two together?"

"You mean…barbeque sauce on a hot guy? Oh, yes, I've corrupted you but good now. That's fabulous! I'll see you at six."

"Okay."

The smile stayed on Sara's face after her friend hung up.

CHAPTER 17

*G*arrison's shitty Saturday tried to pulverize him into fine grit. To be fair, Friday hadn't treated him any better. The only good thing about Friday was that it was over.

Like his future with Sara.

Pausing in his work with Kerr and Eric to clear the remnants of the burnt barn, he leaned on his shovel. Her silky skin, her luscious curves, her taste like...

Ah, hell.

His jeans had become too tight again.

Gritting his teeth, he adjusted his stance and looked around. Hopefully, Kerr and Eric hadn't seen anything.

She'd made her rejection clear.

Hadn't she?

The details of their conversation had blurred. All he recalled was waiting for her to betray him. Like Tiffani.

Only Sara hadn't betrayed him, had she?

He cursed and flung a load of charred wood into the back of a trailer.

Damn it.

Shelby stormed out of the ranch house, carrying a tray of snacks and drinks. Shoving the supplies at Eric and Kerr, she came to a stop in front of Garrison. Uh-oh.

"You have got to stop." She wheezed then poked him in the chest with a finger. Hard.

"What?"

Kerr whipped his head around to stare at Shelby. Then he grinned and relaxed on his shovel handle as he took a leisurely bite of sandwich.

"This." She gestured wildly with her hands and shook her head, which only made her ruined curly hair fly out in all directions. "Whatever the heck is going on in your head over this woman, you have get a grip on yourself. I can't take—" She glanced over her shoulder at Eric. "Uh, the stress."

"Yeah, well quit invading my privacy."

"Quit intruding on my sanity." Waving her hand near her temple, she grimaced. "See? Right there. Stop that."

Eric frowned. As if he feared Shelby's jaw-jutted glare, he half-turned away from them and studied the gray pastures and hills as though he needed to memorize the terrain for a test later. Smart man.

Shit piled on shit. Garrison had had it up to here with the whole mess. "What the hell do you want me to do, Shelby? I can't control what I'm thinking."

Poke, poke. "Well, you can sure as hell grovel and apologize for being a total jerk."

If she poked him again, God help him, he'd break her finger, sister or not.

"Apologize to you?"

"No, idiot. To *her*."

"For what?"

"Freakin pick something. Just get it fixed because I can't handle any more of your depressed mooning."

He puffed out his chest. "Well, I'm not the person who was wrong."

"You are dumber than a sack of bricks." She glared at Eric when he sputtered on his drink. "First of all..."

Oh shit, she was warming up for a list.

"First of all, Sara's a lovely person and you'd be lucky to hang out with her. Second, she's a hell of an upgrade from Tiffani." Shelby raised her hand as his mouth came open. "And third, you're a guy."

"What's that have to do with it?"

"Your kind is always wrong. You should probably open every conversation with Sara by saying 'I'm sorry' if you know what's good for you."

Kerr piped up, "I already reviewed that information with him, sis." He pointed at his head and twirled a finger. "Didn't sink in."

"Obviously," she spat.

Eric, with his fist pressed hard to his mouth, looked ready to perform his own tonsillectomy. Unfortunately, it didn't keep his shoulders from shaking with suppressed laughter.

And Kerr, that traitor? His contribution included siding with Shelby and sipping on a pop. Give the man a scorecard and he'd probably rate this confrontation on a scale of one to ten, just for something to do.

"But it was her, not me—" He had no leg to stand on with this conversation, especially with Shelby kicking at his ankles.

"You freaking moron, don't you get it? It's always you."

Eric's mouth dropped open.

Kerr laughed his ass off.

"But—"

"Now I'm going back inside to take some ibuprofen because you're making my head hurt. If the two cells in your pea brain manage, by some miracle, to find each other in your empty, idiot skull, maybe you'll realize that you need to call Sara and beg her forgiveness."

She stormed off, righteous puffs of vapor in the cold air punctuating her stomping stride. When the front door slammed, Garrison jumped.

Holy cow, Shelby was a force of nature.

At least she was on his team. Mostly.

143

Sara didn't know which hurt more: stuffing herself with too much fried chicken from the Hungry Moose or laughing herself silly at Izzy's ridiculous jokes.

She didn't care, either. Izzy's generosity, combined with her warped sense of humor, worked wonders for Sara's bruised heart.

"So how did you two leave it, then?" Izzy leaned back and groaned as she nipped the last morsel of meat from a wing. She'd protested the last two pieces but kept eating like she had a hollow leg.

Sara shook her head. Amazing. Somehow Izzy managed to look country glam, with her tight jeans, form-fitting western button-down, and waves of long, blonde hair, all while she sucked sinew off a chicken bone.

Propping her arms on the table edge, Sara sighed. "Somewhere during that night, he mentioned how I calm him. And I ignored that statement until after the super-hot sex." She sighed. "Then I kind of ran with the phrase and might have embellished it and changed it to accuse him using me as a stress reliever."

"Lemme guess. Buyer's remorse forced you to use that stress-relieving line."

"Oh yes. But even if I was just a way for him to relax, I went along with it, eyes wide open."

"Can't claim bait and switch, huh?"

"If I'm being honest, no."

"So?"

"I kind of blew that statement way out of proportion about five seconds after he woke up from a dead sleep."

"Yikes. How'd that go over?"

"Like a lead balloon."

"So now you're having lukewarm chicken with a girlfriend on a Saturday night?"

"That's about right."

"Brutal." Izzy reached for one of the brownies she'd brought 'just in case.'

"Sounds like you have some fixing to do."

"No way. He was happy to get rid of me that morning."

"I doubt that."

Sighing, she muttered, "You weren't there."

She pinched off a dark brown morsel and popped it in her mouth. "No. I wasn't. But I know that you're a fabulous woman any man would be ecstatic to love. You should go over there and grab that man by his balls and make him realize that you're so much more than a stress reliever."

"Aw, Izzy, that's the sweetest thing you've said to me."

"It's not every day I can work your stellar character *and* a man's gonads into the same sentence."

"Speaking of pricks," Sara said.

"Speaking of pricks, nothing. We're not discussing my dumbass brother, and based on the way he's been acting this week, I have half a mind to dump a load of cow manure on the jerk."

"What's going on?"

"Getting the other guys riled up. Going on about his 'calling' or something weird like that. He got so mad yesterday, he shoved his hand through a wall in the house. Talking to himself and doing weird stuff."

"What?"

"Yeah. Fun times." Izzy scooped her hair out of her face. "Don't want to talk about it."

"Understandable. Want to watch *Bridesmaids?*"

Her friend pushed back from the table. "No, I need to get home and help Mom. Lord knows, the guys aren't going to do it."

Sara waved her off from tidying up.

As she opened the front door, a thick, tangy, sickening smell assaulted her senses. Sara flipped on the light and peered out into the shadowed porch.

A dead, rotted animal hung by a thin chain from the railing.

CHAPTER 18

A foul metallic and syrup smell knocked her back a step. She clung to the doorknob to remain upright.

"Stupid kids," Izzy muttered as she peered around Sara. After disappearing into the house, Izzy returned with pliers, paper towels, and several plastic bags. With a determined set to her mouth, she approached the corpse.

"Oh, God, Izzy, you don't have to do that."

"Not a problem. I've trapped and skinned animals before. I can handle a"—she used the tool to spin the body around—"prairie dog just fine. Here, come hold this bag for me."

In no time, Izzy broke the chain, and the whole mess fell into the bag. Sara double bagged it and tied twice. She ran around the house to throw the mess in the garbage can. Anything to make the disgusting smell stop.

Who would have done something like this? Oh no. Holy Christ.

As she returned to the front door, she darted glances up and down the street. The lack of traffic didn't reassure her. Even the shadows seemed to jump.

Bang!

She flew into the house and bolted the door, peeking out the side window.

Only a neighbor closing a car door.

A completely normal sound, unless you are losing your mind.

"Are you okay?" Izzy touched her arm, and Sara jumped again. "Okay, obviously not."

"Fine, I'm fine," she whispered, as they went to the kitchen to wash up.

"Doesn't look like it to me. You want me to drive you somewhere else to stay tonight?"

"No, not necessary. Say, Izzy, you don't think, uh…"

She grimaced. "Hank? I can't imagine him doing this. I swear. It has to be some prankster kids or something."

"Yeah, sorry to assume."

"Hey, you can think what you like. You've had a hellish week and capped it off with a dead animal on your porch." She dried her hands and hugged her. "Sure you're okay?"

Sara nodded. "Go on back home. I'm good. Promise."

"Call me if you need anything, okay?"

"Of course." She eased the door closed.

Long after Izzy drove away, Sara remained right there, hand on the locked deadbolt, her back pressed to the wall, frozen. Every creak of the house, every rustle of leaves, frayed her nerves.

She could always give Garrison a call. If he ever spoke to her again, he might let her stay at the ranch—

Absolutely not. No way could she burden him with another person to help and more work to do. Nope, it was time to pull up the big girl undies and manage things on her own. Exactly how she had done before and would do from here on out.

Five a.m. Sunday morning. Sleep wasn't going to happen.

Between periods of freaking out at little noises and shadows, Izzy's advice wormed its way into Sara's head. Maybe it was the loopy time of the morning where logic got all twisted and warped. Maybe she hadn't considered Garrison's insecurities and issues because she was too wrapped up with her own. Still, as fabulous as Izzy's recommendation to go over there and grab his balls was, a more circumspect approach might be better.

She flicked on her phone. Was she really going to do this? Yes. So what if the activity fell into the "mooning adolescent" category.

Sorry to leave it that way with you.

As soon as she hit send on her text, she scrambled to stop the message.

Nope. The message was now bouncing off of orbiting satellites. Damn.

On minute later, her phone rang. No text reply for Garrison Taggart, no siree. With a sinking sensation, she hit the button to accept.

"Hello?" she said, as though there was any doubt who called.

"Sara?" His voice turned her insides to melted goo, damn that man.

"I shouldn't have texted. Its early."

Silence.

Then he cleared his throat. "I'm glad you did. I was thinking about you."

She opened her mouth but no sound came out.

"Shelby said I was a jerk to you," he said.

"What do you think?"

"I think she's right." Rustling sheets transmitted through the phone.

He was in bed. Oh, God.

"Sara, I...Look, would you like to spend the day on the ranch? Nothing major, just two people hanging out together?"

Her heart expanded, about to burst. Then she reeled it in. "Depends. Am I there as a stress reliever for you?"

"Son of a bitch, I was an idiot, wasn't I?"

"I don't have much room to talk."

"Um, can we continue this conversation in person?"

After ten seconds of internal debate, she had her answer. "How's nine sound?"

"It sounds like I'll have to wait too long."

Three and a half hours later, Sara sat square in the eye of the hurricane.

What in the name of the Holy Spirit had happened? What happened to her decision to stay uninvolved?

Garrison had met her at the front door. Although their reunion had been cool but polite, the rest of the family had swept her away into their raucous Sunday morning breakfast. Zach peppered her with questions while Shelby studied her with an odd expression.

Meanwhile, Kerr dominated the stove, singing loudly as he pretended to take short orders. No one commented on how the elder Mr. Taggart was still in bed.

Kerr made only a few inappropriate remarks during breakfast—apparently, Shelby's and Garrison's dark expressions kept him in check. A few times, Sara laughed, despite herself.

After the meal, Garrison picked up her plate and dropped it in the sink. Then he walked over to where she sat.

Shelby coughed several times, then grinned, her odd, gold-glinting eyes so similar to her brothers'.

"Want the grand tour?" Garrison asked Sara.

"I thought you'd put me to work." She grabbed the hand he offered. Holy Mary, the connection of his big, warm hand with hers set her heart fluttering like she'd met her high school crush. Oh wait, she *had* met her high school crush. And they'd had dinner together, and more... In addition, she had enjoyed breakfast at his house.

"No promises I won't make you rustle cattle or run fence line."

"No promises I'll know what I'm doing."

Kerr snorted.

Garrison glared a hole into his brother's head.

And just like that, Sara smiled.

JILLIAN DAVID

Hours later, her mood wasn't so positive.

Mud and assorted animal by-products caked the bottom of her once-white tennis shoes. Her back and shoulders ached from tromping all over the ranch, holding a bridle so Garrison could clean a horse's hooves, handing him nails while he repaired loose boards on the house. She was pretty sure he didn't need any assistance, but he seemed to enjoy the company.

And she sure enjoyed his company. Damn. This was so bad for her future plans.

She had no problem appreciating how he concentrated on the task at hand, his gentleness with the animals, his raw strength as he threw around bales of hay. Garrison's energy appeared to have no limits. She really had no problem studying the press of his mouth as he puzzled out how to fix something, and as a matter of fact, she'd like those lips on her, pronto. He even seemed unaffected by the bite of cold air and the muddy, snowy ground as he moved from one job to another like a Stetson-wearing Energizer Bunny.

So, if she liked watching him work, and she liked him, then what was the problem?

Everything.

Even though she had grown up in Copper River, Sara was no rancher. She wasn't cut out for this life.

She had no future here. To follow her own plans, she shouldn't form entanglements.

Sure as heck didn't want to develop anything resembling roots.

Then why did she care what happened to Garrison and his family? She shouldn't.

Besides, the threat to the Taggarts would remain if she continued to see him. How far would the feud escalate?

Cold, harsh reality settled in: She needed to put an end to this… whatever had begun between them before more than a barn got destroyed. Before she lost her heart and her future. Before someone else in this family got hurt.

Garrison studied Sara's furrowed brow and stooped shoulders. Maybe she wasn't into the ranching. Maybe he'd worn her out. Not everyone was used to the work here.

He'd tried to get Tiffani to enjoy life at the ranch, catering to her comfort and needs as much as he could. It was never enough. She had finally gotten a house in town to stay "when the ranch got to her." In retrospect, that act was the beginning of the end with them. Their relationship had been broken long before she left him, years before she had mailed the divorce papers.

Yet here he was, going down the exact same road with Sara.

Today's "date" included repairs to the smaller barn on the property. What a real romantic location. Setting down his hammer after pounding the last board, he turned toward Sara.

"Are you doing okay?"

All right, that was a lame line.

Her full lips curled upward, enough to grab his complete attention. "Sure."

The smile didn't reach those beautiful brown eyes.

And damn him to hell, but he itched with the desire to use his power on her. Find out the truth.

At least he'd abandoned the idea of using her as his watchperson for Zach. Manipulating her to help Garrison be a decent parent? One look at her trusting face, and he knew he couldn't use her for his own selfish purposes.

"Let's sit inside the barn for a bit," he said.

She frowned and stepped back with a wary, shuttered expression. Probably waiting for him to say something equally as idiotic as he did the other night. Hopefully, he could keep from shoving his foot in his mouth, because damn it, he liked Sara.

But he wouldn't push her into a miserable life, either. They sat on a bench at the end of the barn, the warmer air punctuated by the sounds of horses in their stalls. A peaceful calm settled on him—something he hadn't felt for years on the ranch.

"I am glad if it relieved your stress." Her words from the ugly end to a beautiful night came back to haunt him.

Damn it. Maybe that was the problem: He needed to choose better things to say to this woman. He should probably try telling her how he felt, while he was at it. His skin crawled with the prospect of opening himself up to someone else. Yet another skill in which he was sorely deficient. But he'd give it a try for Sara.

"Um, listen. I don't want you to be on the ranch because of me."

She reared back like she'd been hit, her wide-eyed expression nearly destroying his resolve. "What?"

"Okay, that came out wrong. Damn it." He faced her on the bench. "I really like you. But life isn't great right now on the ranch."

"Oh, I see." The light in her eyes dulled.

"No, you don't. I had a wife who didn't like it here. You know how that worked out."

"I understand what you're saying."

He gritted his teeth. "No, you don't. I want you to like being here. On the ranch. With me."

"But I do. Garrison, I enjoy spending time with you."

"Yeah, but you're not cut out for this life." Son of a bitch. "That came out wrong, too. Damn it, I can't say the right things around you."

Thank God she giggled a little.

"What I'm saying is, I don't want to force you into a life you don't want. I can't handle a repeat of what happened before."

"We're talking about what you want?"

With that little smile, either she was teasing him or about to eviscerate him.

He swallowed. "Well, yes."

"Don't you think that's kind of selfish?"

His chest felt like it had caved in, and he opened his mouth, only to be stopped by her hand in front of him.

The wry twist to her mouth made his heart clench in response. "Want to know what I want?"

"Okay."

She opened her mouth but paused. Finally, she started. "I want for you and your family not to get hurt. And I have a future planned that doesn't involve Copper River. So, along those same lines, we are in agreement: I shouldn't even be here."

Whoa. Something had gone horribly wrong with this conversation. She couldn't even meet his eyes. "You want to leave? Again?"

"No." She twined her fingers in her lap. "And that's the problem."

"You're not making any sense."

"I know. Damn." She jumped to her feet.

His gut knotted. His heart lurched and twisted like a terrified, chained dog in his chest. She couldn't leave. Not yet. Whatever her future plans involved, he'd figure out a way to be involved, right? Standing up, he grabbed her hand, yanked her to him, ripped off his hat, and kissed her. He needed her in his life, without condition. He needed her. Like now. Groaning, he shifted his stance to relieve the sudden pressure in his jeans.

As he slid his arms around her back and neck, he ran his tongue over the seam of her lips until she opened on a gasp. The floral scent of her hair, her sweet taste, the silky slide of her tongue tangling with his—all shot sensations right to his hardening erection, which didn't give a shit about how much she did or didn't like ranch life. All he wanted right now was Sara.

As she shivered beneath his hands, regret stopped him. They had few options for impromptu sex on the suddenly much too crowded ranch, should the mood strike.

And damn, how the mood struck Garrison.

He worked a hand under her jacket and pulled her even closer, wanting more of her body pressed to his.

He slid a hand into her hair and tugged her head back, exposing her flawless neck. As he licked and nipped his way downward, her little gasps and sounds of happiness drove him to taste more skin. Until her shirt collar stopped him.

But he sure could improvise.

He dragged his mouth sideways over her lower neck and worked his way back up to her mouth. Keeping her head tilted, he plunged his tongue back through her parted lips. God, he could drink her in like this forever.

When he finally came up for air, they were both breathing hard. Her pupils had dilated, and her flushed cheeks put him about a second away from throwing her down on the barn floor and making love to her right there.

He couldn't do that. Sara deserved better.

Damn.

Sara. Who had as much as said that her life didn't have room for him in it.

Sara, who had told him she wanted to leave. Again.

After one more kiss, designed to get her attention, he stepped back, keeping his hands on her shoulders.

Her lips trembled. No force in this world would stop him if she gave him the green light to take things to a new level right now.

"So?" he asked.

"Well. Okay, then. Wow," she said.

"Um." Apparently all he could muster was a single syllable around her.

She blinked once. Twice. The passion on her face morphed into a sadness that looked suspiciously like regret. Damn it.

He had to salvage this conversation or he'd lose her. He needed to figure out how to give her time and space when he wanted her here and now.

"Damn it, Sara. I want you, and not just, well, because you're hot." They both cringed.

This time, he lifted his palm to cut off her response. No way could he deal with rejection. Not right this minute, with her smell and taste still tormenting his senses.

He dropped his hands. "So I agree with you. Yes, you should go home. Not that I don't want you here. I do. But you need to decide what you want. Decide if I fit into any type of future with you."

Damn her blank stare, her thinned lips. "Okay, then. You're right. I'll leave." Turning away from him, she took a few steps, then pivoted back around. "Stay here. I'm taking you away from your work. And I can't handle you walking me to my car."

"Sara—"

The side door closed with the dull thud of wood in the frame, leaving him alone with the disapproving eye rolls of several horses, a hard-on that threatened to squeeze off his blood supply, and sour regret in the pit of his stomach.

Nothing to do now. Garrison would give her space to think their relationship through, even if it killed him.

CHAPTER 19

$\mathcal{A}$s far as going over to the Taggarts' ranch yesterday and, as Izzy delicately put it, grabbing Garrison by his balls and making him understand that Sara was much more than a stress reliever, that performance stunk.

Not only had she not accomplished her goal, but the plan had also backfired. God bless him, Garrison had laid out his feelings, kissed her until she couldn't see straight, and then told her to go home and think about what she wanted. He didn't seem mad. More like he was tired of the indecision. Well, that made two of them.

Didn't matter. After that kiss, Sara knew damn well what she wanted, and it lived underneath a work shirt and a pair of tight jeans.

What about her own future that she'd worked so hard to create? She had another two and a half years, and then her loans would be repaid. Sara would be free of debt.

Free of Copper River.

And what about the problems with Hank and the threats to the Taggart family? God, what about her job? If she pursued a future with Garrison, she had an excellent chance of losing her job from Hank's sheer vindictiveness. If she pursued a future with Garrison, innocent people would be hurt.

By the time she made it to school, Sara had made her decision.

Now, if only she could get her sleep-deprived, aching body through a day filled with energetic second-graders.

At recess, she kept an eye on Zach.

When the Brand twins sidled up to him, her heart dropped to her feet.

Zach stumbled suddenly, and the twins stuffed hands in their pockets and looked everywhere but the kid sprawled on the snowy ground. Zach struggled to his feet and walked away a few steps, until he tripped over a booted foot and fell again.

Her heart ached when she spied his red face. He bit his quivering lower lip but got back to his feet again.

Get out of there, Zach.

A shove. She couldn't stop herself from marching over there.

Dropping her hands onto the Brand kids' shoulders, she kept her stance casual and friendly to the outside observer but squeezed the boys much harder than she should. She had to keep this discipline under the radar, or Butch would make good on his threat. These little Brand monsters were all but untouchable.

"Gentlemen?" she asked.

Zach fled to the far side of the yard.

One of the twins stuck his tongue out at her in a shocking display of disrespect. Figured, given the stellar character of their uncle Hank.

"Perhaps you should go play over on the monkey bars?"

"You can't tell me what to do—Ow!"

The second snot-nosed kid smirked. "What are you gonna do, send us to the principal's office?"

Touché, minijerk, touché.

"Uncle Hank says you're a slut."

She squeezed his shoulder until he yelped. Then she leaned down inches from the boy's face.

"Maybe I won't send you to the office, but you know what I can do?"

His eyes widened as she pulled the other boy close to listen.

"I will do evil things to evil boys."

"What?" one boy whispered.

"I will put you in detention until the end of time."

"So what?"

"Or if that doesn't work," she paused, making sure she had their attention, "you will hold hands with a girl for the next month."

"Ew, gross."

"Or...," she continued.

"Or what?"

She wanted nothing but to wipe the sneer off that boy's face.

"Or you will have cafeteria duty for the rest of the school year."

Two sets of raised eyebrows and pale faces. Good. The threat of cleaning lunch plates worked every time.

"Got it?"

They squirmed out from under her hands and ran over to their friends.

As she straightened up, she caught a face in a window. Damn. Butch.

Well, crap.

Ignoring the invisible daggers protruding from her back, she stiffened her spine and walked over to a brick wall to continue monitoring recess. Cold sweat pricked her forehead and chilled in the icy breeze. Her full body shiver had nothing to do with the wintry weather, though.

A few more hours and she'd be done for the day. Thank God.

As Sara stood at the front of her classroom an hour later, reviewing math with the kids, she couldn't keep from glancing out the window of her classroom. The snow fell in earnest now. Winter had arrived. A few inches of snow already coated the ground, and it was forecast for a good foot or so tonight, not unusual for early November in Wyoming. Normally, she loved when it snowed because she could get all cozy reading and enjoying the peace and quiet.

But everything irritated her. She was on edge. Too sensitive. Like someone watched her.

Probably because Butch had seen her with his nephews at recess.

Quiet time on her couch? Ha. Not tonight. The last thing she needed was time for introspection. Or time to recall Garrison's work-roughened fingers caressing every inch of her body and his lips working their magic. No. These thoughts led to short-term pleasure but long-term pain. She couldn't stay in Copper River after her teaching assignment ended.

She sighed. For a minute, though, she considered it. What would life be like in a normal relationship, where she saw her boyfriend several nights per week and on weekends? Dinner, movies, sleepovers. Normal couple behavior.

The fantasy floated, within her reach.

It was up to her to grab hold of it.

She shook her head and returned to the lesson.

A movement outside caught her attention as a truck growled around the back of the school. Probably a parent, arriving early, eager to get home in the weather. She couldn't make out the figure in the truck with the thick snow falling.

Typically, she didn't pay much attention to vehicles around the school.

Until Garrison.

Damn it. Finish the day already.

"Ms. Lopez?" Zach had his hand up. "Can I go to the bathroom?"

If his jiggling legs were any indication, he'd been holding it for as long as possible. She glanced at the clock on the wall: 2:45.

With no energy to argue today, she gave in. She couldn't argue with anyone right about now.

"Quickly."

He dashed out of the room, the sound of his rapid footsteps fading as he ran down the hall.

Focused on teaching the kids multiplication by fours, she startled when the dismissal bell rang. Students chattered, put away their school supplies, and donned coats as they headed to their parents' vehicles or the buses.

One desk still had pencil and paper on it. Sara gripped the edge of her desk. One coat still hung on the wall.

Garrison's Monday started out foul and quickly progressed to downright crappy. Never mind that he hadn't heard back from Sara; he hadn't slept at all last night to boot. So his attitude had pretty much circled the drain all day long.

In the early morning, while riding out to check the property boundary, Kerr had found footprints leading away from the ranch house, through the edge of a pasture, and into the national forest. There, deep ruts, likely from an ATV, took off up into the foothills.

Unfortunately, they had to stop the search due to the snowstorm that started up around midday. Now a few hours later, the tracks were long covered. Any proof had been buried under the snow.

Garrison would bet his best horse that Hank was somehow responsible, but he had no concrete evidence, same as before.

Son of a bitch.

Even as the issues with the ranch tried to drag him down, his thoughts kept going back to Sara.

The more he tried not to think about her, the more her sweet smile and tempting body intruded front and center in his mind.

The situation was out of his hands now. He'd cope with disappointment in the best way he knew how: hard work. He'd start by feeding the horses and making sure they were safe and warm in the smaller second barn.

If he got a spell of clear weather in a few weeks, he might be able to get the big barn rebuilt, or at least get a shell up that was functional enough to store supplies.

Supplies he'd have to buy all over again.

Damn it. Time and money. Two things he didn't possess right now.

He needed to check on his dad, too. His old man looked almost gray during the last few days. Even though he'd been slowing down for the past year, fighting that fire must have knocked him down. Might have even hurt him.

It was nine in the morning. His father never slept in, ever.

Garrison should try again to get him to go to the doctor. If Vaughn were here, Dad would listen to him.

It killed Garrison to watch his dad fade away in front of his eyes.

He peeked in on his father, who snored, his work-worn face relaxed for the first time in forever. Decision made. Dad was going to get a checkup. If that didn't work, he'd sic Shelby on the old man. One way or another, a medical professional would evaluate his father before the week was out.

Shelby, too. When he had passed through the kitchen earlier, she looked like manure warmed over. Her wet cough echoed in the kitchen.

"You going to get that cough looked at?" he asked.

"Stuff it," she said, wheezing on her way out the door.

His sister and father were cut from the same stubborn mold. Fine. Those two could stay in the house and be sick together.

After trudging back through the house, he shoved his hat on and went back out in the cold morning air.

Hours of mindless work made the rest of the day pass in a snowy, muddy haze. He put hay out for the cattle, the herd's grumpy lowing reminding him that he was late. Thankfully, he'd stored some of the hay in the second barn, but it wouldn't be enough to get them through this winter.

More money, down the pipe.

While checking on the horses, he looked over Shelby's horse again. The gelding was singed in a few places, but other than a shorter mane and tail—like Shelby—the horse had escaped what could have been a deadly disaster.

Hours later, with shoulders aching from the endless pile of work, Garrison scowled up into the blank, gray sky. Snow continued to fall. Damn it. Snow wasn't bad. The fact that snow would slow him down and make more work? That was bad.

It was already 4:00 p.m. now. He needed to head down to the highway and pick up Zach.

After driving to the end of the ranch road and parking the truck,

Garrison took off his hat and rubbed his face and head. Shit, what a day.

The flat-nosed yellow school bus rumbled up to the ranch road and stopped. With a hiss, the doors opened.

No one exited.

A fist of cold fear strangled Garrison.

Dashing out of the truck and up the three stairs into the bus, he scanned the interior. A few kids were left to complete the route.

"Where's Zach?" he asked the matronly woman at the wheel.

Her eyes widened as she twisted around. "I don't know. I thought he was here."

"You don't know if he got on the bus in the first place?"

"No. I don't take attendance each day. By now, the kids know which bus to get on. None of the other kids said anything." Tears pooled in her eyes. "Oh no."

The foam on the padded rail shredded beneath his fingers.

His heart raced. Where was Zach?

Maybe still at school? Did Sara keep him late and was bringing him home? Surely she would have called.

"Mr. Taggart?" The driver sniffed as she finished dialing her cell phone. "I'm going to call this in to the superintendent's office right now, but then I have to take these other kids home. I'm so—"

Garrett stormed off the bus before she could finish her sputtered sentence.

Zach.

As the bus hissed and rolled down the road, Garrett's cell phone rang. Blocked caller.

He ignored the snow landing on his head and answered the phone.

"Yes?" he shouted.

"Hey, asshole."

CHAPTER 20

"*H*ank." He'd recognize that grinding voice anywhere. "How are things on the ranch? Extra crispy?"

"You taking credit, dickhead? Want to make an official statement?"

"Concerned for my neighbor, that's all." He breathed heavily.

"My ass, you're concerned. What the hell do you want?"

His laugh oozed like slime through the phone. "Besides your ranch? Oh, I don't know. How about you figure it out?"

"I don't have time for games, Hank."

"How about you think about our offer on the ranch?"

"Or what?"

"Or I won't be extra nice to a person you love."

Holy shit. Zach.

"What have you done?"

"I have a little friend over for a visit. And how nicely I treat him depends on how well you keep your big mouth shut."

The phone went dead.

Being kicked in the balls wouldn't hurt this much.

Before Garrison could get into the truck, his cell phone rang again. Sara's number. Shit, this was not the time. Hank had his kid. Garrison had to deal with that issue first.

Should he backtrack to the school and see if anyone could give him a lead, or should he go back to the ranch house?

His father couldn't take more stress right now. Shelby would try to help, but she couldn't form a sentence without wheezing. And Kerr and Eric were exhausted.

He vaulted into the truck and threw it into drive, wheels spinning as he exited the ranch road, and floored it down the highway to town. Maybe Sara knew something.

Stupid. He should have answered when she called. He grabbed his phone, which now blinked a message. Ignoring the message, he called Sara's number, and it went straight to voice mail. *Please let this be Hank's stupid joke. Let Zach be okay.*

Zach had been gone fifteen, twenty minutes, max. Sara glanced at her watch. How far could he go? Maybe he was in the bathroom, ill. If so, someone would have found him and alerted her, right? Maybe he was hurt. Or in the principal's office. Or ran away. Who knew?

She couldn't breathe. Couldn't think. Where was he?

Grabbing her phone, she dashed down the hall, checking all of the bathrooms and even ducking into the gym and cafeteria. Nothing. Only a few remaining kids waiting out front to be picked up.

God, she'd have to tell her boss that one of her students had gone missing.

Well, there went the last nail in the coffin of her teaching career. Butch had it in for her, and losing a kid was beyond unacceptable. To be fair, she didn't deserve to be a teacher if she couldn't keep her students safe.

Might as well pack her things now.

First, though, she had to find Zach and make sure he was okay.

Panting as she ran through several inches of snow, she circled around to the back of the school. And stopped dead.

A different truck was parked on the far edge of school property near a stand of trees.

Sara stared at the vehicle and shivered. She should have put a coat on before leaving the building.

The buzzing in her hand startled her.

She recognized the number, even after a year.

With shaking hands, she answered the phone. "Hello?"

"Hi, baby. Miss me?" A figure in the truck waved at her.

"What do you want, Hank?"

"Come on over to the truck, and I'll tell you."

"What?" She began to back away toward the building.

"Get over here, bitch," he growled. "If you want Zach to live."

A wave of nausea smacked into her.

She crossed the snow-covered asphalt in no time, and Hank motioned her into the truck. After a good twenty seconds of debate, she approached the vehicle. Zach's life was worth the risk. She got in, closing the door. The air was thick with her fear and Hank's seething breaths.

"Okay. Where's Zach?"

"I'm in charge here, Ms. Skank. I know you're running around with that Taggart. What do you see in him, anyway? He's a stupid fuck."

"This is a bad time for the jealous ex-boyfriend crap, Hank. If you can't help me find Zach, then I have to go."

"No, I don't think you should go. You'll want to hear what I have to say."

"Why?"

"Missing anything?" he snickered. "I mean, missing *anyone?*"

Her heart dropped out from under her, like coming off the top of a roller coaster, only there was no more track left. "What did you do?"

"Nothing. Yet." His harsh laugh grated on her nerves—nails on a chalkboard.

"What do you want?"

Cold calm settled over her like a heavy, wet blanket.

He grinned. "Your ass right here in front of me, right now. Begging."

"What?" She'd lost her voice.

He'd lost his mind.

"You think your life is worth the life of a kid?"

Tears burned behind her eyelids. "Don't hurt him!"

"We haven't. Yet." He belched. The stomach acid odor made her swallow back her own bile. "What happens next to young Mr. Taggart depends on you."

"Please don't hurt Zach. He's just a child. You want me to beg? Fine. I'm begging you."

"You'll do a lot more of that before I'm done. I will please the Great One tonight."

A wave of light-headedness grabbed her, and she put one hand on the dashboard and the other on the door handle.

"Ah, ah," he said, waggling a finger. "If you leave, Zach dies."

"How do I know you're telling the truth?"

He dialed a number on his cell phone, never dropping his smile, and held it up to her ear. The sound of a boy's frightened whimper stopped her heart.

"Zach?" she whispered. "It's Ms. Lopez."

A sniff. "I'm cold."

"Oh, honey, I know. I'll be there soon to help, okay?"

"Ms. Lopez?" His thin voice brought tears to her eyes. "I'm scared."

"Me, too, Zach. Be brave and I'll find you soon."

"Yes, ma'am."

Before she could answer, Hank grabbed the phone back.

She faced all of the crazy, head on. What else could she do? "Fine. I believe you. You want me to beg? I'm begging you. Now can you let him go?" Maybe she could distract Hank. Keep him talking while she thought of something.

"Not quite."

"Why not?" She eased her cell phone out of her pocket and tried to thumb it on.

"Because I have work to do."

There. The text box came up. She tried to type. "What kind of work?"

"The special kind." Fast as lightning, he grabbed her wrist in a painful grip and yanked the phone away. "Ah, what's going on here?" He peered at the screen. "A text to your lover? Sorry. Not going to happen, little traitor."

He rolled down the window and made as if to throw the phone out. Then, with an eerie calm, checked himself. "On the other hand, this could come in handy."

"Handy?"

"For a special surprise later." He blinked and scrabbled under the seat until he pulled out duct tape. "This will work perfectly. Your hands, please." So terribly calm.

Wincing as he taped her hands together, she darted glances around. Most of the teachers had left right after the kids. No cars remained here behind the school. Oh God, this situation had gone from bad to a disaster.

"I don't get it, Hank. Look, whatever beef you have with me, you need to let Zach go."

"All depends on how nice you are to me."

Acid rose in her throat. "All right." She swallowed. "Where are we going?"

"To a special place."

"Where—"

His hand reached her shoulder in record time, and as he gripped painfully, he said, "No more questions. It's time to go."

As he glanced at his watch, she read the time: 3:15. Cold fear wrapped a bony hand around her spine and squeezed. It would be tomorrow morning until someone realized she'd gone missing. Too much time. Hank could do anything.

As he pulled out of the nearly empty parking lot and casually drove toward the mountains and the national forest, it took all of her strength not to cry. She wouldn't give him the satisfaction.

Forty-five minutes later, he pulled the truck onto the shoulder of a county road and turned on her cell phone and his.

"Two bars. Just enough for what we need to do." He put a finger to his lips and winked as he dialed a number. "Hey, asshole." She recognized Garrison's voice through Hank's phone. "How are things on the ranch? Extra crispy?"

Panic hit her full force and her vision grayed for a moment. She barely registered Hank's nasty voice as he threatened Zach. He turned his phone off with a satisfied flourish.

Hank wanted to mortally wound Garrison, and she was a pawn in his scheme.

Sweat beaded her forehead. She needed to get out of here, but even assuming she escaped Hank, they were miles from town. It was snowing. She'd die before she reached help. Besides, she had to hang in here long enough to help Zach.

Hank chuckled and handed her the phone. "Here's what you do. Call lover boy and tell him that you two are over. You've decided your life is better off without him in it."

She dropped her jaw. "I can't do that. And not after what you just told him about Zach."

"You can. I will hurt that boy if you don't do as I say."

Damn Hank to hell. Awkward with her taped hands, she dialed Garrison's number. After five rings, it went to voice mail, thank God. Also odd, considering Hank had just talked with Garrison. After his terse greeting, she left a message. "Garrison, it's Sara. I…I thought about it, and I can't be with you. My life plan doesn't involve Copper River." At Hank's circling "go on" motion, she added, "Or your family. Or the ranch."

She froze as he repeated the gesture. Hank wanted her to say more? Damn it, she had to sell this or Zach might suffer.

She swallowed. "And frankly, my life is better off without you in it."

As she gave a choked sob, he turned off her phone, got out of the truck, and threw the phone into the woods. He turned off his own phone and chucked it out the window as well.

He slammed the truck door closed, put the vehicle in drive, and traveled another few minutes before turning on an unmarked dirt road that led into the forest. The terrain continued to worsen as they bumped along the road up into the mountains. With the snow falling heavily now, their tracks would be covered within an hour.

Night began to fall, and the truck's lights against the narrow road became a tunnel leading to her doom. Everything about him scared the hell out of her. His intense calm, his nonsense chatter as he maneuvered the truck deeper into the forest, his random giggles – all freaked her out.

Goose bumps rose on her arms as they pulled into a clearing and parked next to another old truck. She spied a light deep in the woods to the right.

When he opened her door, he stepped from one foot to the other. "I'm waiting," he rasped.

She wanted to scrub her ears with alcohol. Reluctantly, she slid toward his beckoning arms.

All the air left her lungs as she stepped down into a deep patch of snow.

Forcing her heavy legs to move, she struggled to follow Hank. The last place she wanted to go was anywhere with him. At least he cut through the duct tape so she wouldn't do a face-plant every time she stumbled. The snow melted in her shoes, and the bottom of her slacks was soaked. Soon her hair became damp. She shivered but pressed forward.

When she knew she couldn't take another step, they reached a structure. The glow of light filtered from the cracked and dirt-smeared windows of a trapper shack.

She stopped dead in her tracks. What would she find inside? Her heart pounded.

Hank stopped and crossed his arms.

"Ladies first."

The last thing she wanted to do was enter what could realistically become her coffin.

But she had to go inside for Zach.

God knew what Hank would do to them.

God knew what he'd already done.

Her slacks froze against her ankles. With trembling fingers, she touched the rough wood door. Could she hear anything inside?

No.

The door gave a harsh creak as she pushed it inward. Blinking against the relative brightness inside, she saw exactly what she dreaded.

Zach.

CHAPTER 21

Zach sat on a thick wooden chair in the middle of the room, his back to her. His head came up as the door opened. Was he okay?

Hank's brother, Wyatt, hovered nearby, his bulging eyes darting all around. Despite the chill, sweat beaded his forehead.

Terror locked her legs into place.

"Damn it—move!" Hank shoved her through the doorway, and she fell, banging her knees on the uneven dirt floor. As she struggled back to her feet, she spied a Coleman lantern hanging from a nail near the door and a low pallet on a metal bed frame.

Zach's whimper spurred her to action.

She spun around, no longer caring about her own safety. "Hank, how could you do this? To a child?"

"All Wyatt did was make sure the kid didn't try to run off."

Not caring about Hank, she knelt in front of Zach and hugged him. Poor kid. His nose ran; his hands were frigid. He reared back, and his eyes went wide with terror when Hank approached. Zach tried to move, but couldn't.

His feet were tied to the chair legs.

Hank flicked his wrist, and a deadly looking blade popped out from a knife handle.

"Bro, stop." Wyatt held up a hand. "You said you wouldn't hurt the kid."

Refusing to move, Sara stood in front of Zach.

"Step aside," Hank growled.

"Absolutely not."

"Sara, you always were a dummy. Relax, I'm cutting him loose." Hank shouldered her to the side and sawed at the ropes tying Zach's feet to the chair.

"Hold still, buddy. You'll be fine." Keeping her hands on Zach's shoulders, she tried to pour reassurance into the boy.

His lower lip quivered, and he flinched as Hank sawed through the tight ropes.

Once free, Zach flew into Sara's arms. Holding tightly to the boy, she glared at Hank over Zach's head.

Hank snorted. "See? All better, son."

"Let me take him home," she said.

Zach had a death grip on her shirt, and every inch of his thin frame quaked.

"Oh, no. You're not leaving, Sarita," Hank said.

"Are you taking him home, then?"

"Nope. He's going to do that himself," he snickered.

"Come on, Hank. He's a child." She tightened her arms around Zach.

"He's a Taggart. He can walk home."

Even Wyatt's jaw dropped. "Hank, you can't be serious."

She glared at Hank. "No. He can't be out by himself. It's dark. It's snowing."

Hank snorted. "He'll be perfectly fine. It's not that far. I'll even point him in the right direction."

She whispered, "No, Hank. He'll die."

"Not by my hand, he won't."

Oh God, he had lost his mind. "What?"

"I'm not okay with this," Wyatt said.

"Get out." Hank's voice boomed across the room, unnaturally loud. His eyes bulged, and for a second, they glowed red.

Sara and Zach flinched at the sound.

His brother sputtered. "No, I'll stay and help, but don't make that kid walk home."

"You're done here, Wyatt. One day you'll understand the commands from the Great One. For now, get in your truck and go home." Holy moly, Hanks eyes had turned a weird reddish black. *"Now!"* The walls shook.

As if controlled by a puppeteer, Wyatt snapped his feet together, spun around, and marched stiffly out of the shack. Moments later, the distant sound of a truck engine roared and then faded into the night.

Hank reached for Zach.

When Sara tucked him deeper into her arms and didn't let go, Hank held the knife over Zach's head and grinned.

"Step away now, or I'll gut him."

Mother of God, he meant it.

"Ms. Lopez?" Zach sniffed, not releasing his desperate hold around her waist.

"You know what to do, Sarita," Hank crooned, his singsong voice making her blood curdle. "Young Zach has one chance to survive, and you holding onto him isn't it."

She knelt in front of the boy and put a shaking finger under his chin. Somehow, she held herself together, projecting a calm she did not feel. "Listen to me, Zach. You keep going until you get home, understand? Do not give up. Don't stop. You hear me?"

His voice quavered. "Okay, I'll be brave and strong like Dad always says."

That one statement broke her heart. Zach wanted to make Garrison proud, even in this untenable situation. Garrison. Hank was using Zach and Sara to get back at Garrison. The worst part? There was nothing she could do.

"Let's go, boy." Hank grabbed Zach's upper arm and dragged him out the door and into the night.

Sara followed, trying to dislodge Hank's cruel hand on Zach, but

Hank backhanded her. She came up spitting snow and blood. Her cheek throbbed. Scrambling to her feet, she stopped short as he held his hand up.

"If you want this boy to live, don't come any closer."

She didn't move.

Hank pulled out a compass, dialed it in, and turned Zach to face downhill, into the thick forest. "You want to go home?"

"Yes, sir." Zach sniffed and closed his mouth on a sob.

"Walk that way. For about fifteen miles."

"You'll rot in hell if you do this, Hank!" Sara called out.

His grin flashed like a deranged jack-o'-lantern. "Why yes. Exactly. That's the point."

"What?"

He ignored her and growled in Zach's ear. "If you don't get out of here now, I'm going to hurt your nice teacher. Got it?"

"Yes, sir." Zach took off into the forest. The snow came halfway up his legs. His thin frame faded into the night.

"Oh my God, you just sent that kid to his death. He's not going to last, wearing sneakers. He doesn't even have a coat."

But when she stumbled toward Zach's retreating figure, Hank yanked her into his chest and dragged her back to the shack.

"That's no longer your problem, Sarita. I am."

Ripping the classroom door open, Garrison rushed inside and scanned inside his son's locker.

A backpack and coat still hung inside the metal box.

At Zach's desk, supplies littered the surface, like his son had stepped away for a moment and planned to return to finish the worksheet of multiplication tables.

Garrison's mouth turned into a desert.

He searched the rest of the room. At the teacher's desk, a coat still rested on the back of her chair. Her planner open on the flat surface. Opening the drawers, he blinked. Why was her purse still here? Her car keys? It made no sense. Unless she had some involvement in Zach's disappearance. No, that didn't make sense either.

And what about her message? Maybe she had taken off with Hank.

Why hadn't he jettisoned his ethics and used his power on her in the first place? Or second place? Or third? Hell, he had ample opportunity to catch her lying, and he'd held back on his power out of misguided morals. Stupid decision.

Butch Brand jogged down the hall toward him, out of breath. "What the hell are you doing, Taggart?"

Son of a bitch, wanted to punch every Brand guy, including this oldest brother, with his thinning hair and paunch and all. By some miracle, Garrison kept his hands at his sides.

"Look, man. Zach's gone."

"I know. The superintendent called a few minutes ago."

"Your psycho brother is behind my son's disappearance."

Butch rocked back on his heels. "Whoa, there. Let's not go throwing stones."

"Who's throwing stones? Hank called me and threatened Zach's life."

"He did not."

"Are you kidding me? Don't you think he's been acting weird lately? He's nuts."

Butch stared at the ceiling for a moment. "He's a little vindictive and driven, but not crazy."

"I wouldn't be so sure." Garrison repeated the interactions with Hank over the past few days, which culminated in the phone call a half hour ago.

Butch smoothed strands of hair away from his sweaty forehead. He might be only ten years older than Garrison, but he looked much older than that. "My God. If you're correct, we need to find them, fast." He shook his head. "I never thought he'd do anything like this."

"So you knew he wasn't acting right?"

"I chalked it up to him being super focused on a project recently."

"Project?"

"Hank's been cooking up a new scheme to get rich or something like that. He hasn't let me in on the details, though. Ever since I took the job here as principal five years ago, I haven't been on the ranch as much, so I don't see my mom and brothers and sister as often as I used to."

"He wants to get rich?"

"Well. Not in as many words. Mining for ores. I presume for gold or silver. So I figured that meant he was trying to make money. Kind of obsessed by it over the past year. Why? What else would they be digging for?"

"You tell me."

"No idea. But right now, we need to find Zach." He tapped on his cell phone and put it to his ear. "Nope. No answer from Hank. Went straight to voice mail."

"Did he mention anything to you recently? Anything that seemed...different? A clue?"

"I haven't seen him for a few weeks. A while back, he'd gotten wrapped up in a long-distance relationship that went south six months ago, so he was off in Salt Lake City a bunch with his lady friend. He'd been seeing her since around this time last year. After that, he mumbled some about a mission or a calling. Like he found religion. But not exactly." He rubbed his jowls. "I'm sorry, Garrison, I had no idea he'd do something stupid like this."

"Pardon me if I don't believe you, Butch."

Garrison grabbed the man's wrist and unleashed the power of his surreal lie detector. The power burst out of him, harder and more determined than it ever had manifested. Butch stiffened as Garrison's mind invaded, expanding like a bubble to surround the other mind. Then the sphere shrank and confined the essence of the man. As Garrison hijacked the man's thoughts, an animal groan slid out of the man's gritted teeth. Butch in pain? Couldn't care less.

He pushed past the polite veneer that formed Butch's public persona and looked at the inner self. Only a bright red aura, truth tinged with anger. No blackness, no deception.

Butch Brand had nothing to do with Hank's actions. That was a good start.

"What the hell was that?" Butch rubbed his temples.

Garrison mirrored his movement. "Nothing, man. Forget it. How are we going to find Zach?"

"Well, we need to contact the police. It's getting dark. God knows where he is. We need to start a search."

"Agreed. But where should we start looking?"

Butch rubbed his forehead. "Heck if I know. Listen, I'll call the police and get things moving. Then I'll run home and see if my family knows anything else that would help us find Hank."

Find. They had zero direction to begin a search, and by now, Hank could be many miles away from Copper River.

Garrison snapped his spine straight.

Find. That was the key.

The Taggart family might just have a miracle for this situation.

"Fine. Do that, Brand. I don't have time to stick around."

Garrison stormed out of the school, flung himself into his truck and flew back to the ranch, where he parked the vehicle and pounded up the stairs and into the house.

"Shelby! I need you now! Help! Shelby!"

The sound of multiple running footsteps on the floor and down the stairs preceded everyone's arrival. Shelby paused at the bottom to catch her breath, her shoulders folding over with jagged coughs. When Eric raised his eyebrows, she glared at him until he scooted over to a wall and crossed his arms, a hand clenched over his opposite bicep.

Their father shuffled from the living room and leaned on the banister. A stiff breeze could blow him over.

Kerr entered the foyer last but hurried in his own way. Christ, his brother looked like he'd just woken up to an Afghanistan ambush. A twinge of guilt sliced through Garrison, but damn it, he needed to focus on the task at hand.

Shelby coughed into her elbow, then lifted her head. "What is it?"

He filled them in on what he knew.

"Zach's out there?" she said, her lips whitening.

He nodded.

"What about Sara?" she asked.

"We're done." The words tasted sour. "She left a message saying it's over. Which was weird, because when I went to the school to look for Zach, her purse and coat were still there, but I never saw her. Maybe she was just avoiding me until I left."

Kerr absently rubbed his right thigh. "What time did she call you?"

"I don't know. Maybe a minute after Hank called."

"Don't you think that's kind of a coincidence?" Kerr asked. The gold glinting in his eyes hardened.

"Oh, shit." Ice poured through Garrison's veins. "You don't think he's got her, too?"

"Hank's crazy enough to do anything to cause us grief," Dad mumbled.

"You actually thought that Sara left you for good? Or that she was callous enough to break up with you on voice mail?" Shelby said, her mouth twisting into a grim half-smile. "Which is it? Are you blind or deaf? Because it's gotta be one of those problems with you."

He wanted to sink into the floor. Shit. How had he completely missed the point of her call? The stress in her voice. How could he have placed so little faith in Sara?

"Stop it, Garrison. Please." Shelby winced and pressed her thumb and third finger into her temples.

"Yeah, cut it out," Kerr said. "Even I'm getting feedback from Shel."

Eric frowned. "What are you two talking about?"

Shelby glared at Kerr and Garrison. "Nothing. Just sibling talk."

Garrison clamped down on his emotions. "We have to find them. There's no telling what Hank's going to do, but it won't be anything positive."

"Good God," his father whispered. The circles beneath his eyes gave him a haggard appearance. He rubbed an arm and leaned on the banister.

Grabbing her arm, Garrison begged, "Can you find them, Shel?"

"I don't know, but I can try. But not here. You know." She lifted her chin sideways at Eric and then back to Garrison.

"Fuck it, Shel," Garrison gritted out. "I don't care if Eric knows your secret. We need to get to Zach and Sara before they die."

"What secret?" Eric said, pushing away from the wall he held up. "The one where you can find people?"

"How do you know?" she gasped.

"Guessed it a while back." He tapped his temple. "Geezus, I knew there was a reason why your search-and-rescue success rates were so high."

Her mouth dropped open. Fury painted her cheeks red and made her scowl deadly.

Eric shook his head. "So will that trick help us find Zach and Sara?"

"Damn you." Shelby glared at Garrison while Kerr winced. That crazy twin link again. "Thanks for outing me. That was a secret."

"Don't care. We've got people out there to rescue." Garrison turned to Eric and shrugged. "Yeah. It's true. Shelby can find anyone, anywhere."

"So you're good at hide-and-seek?" Eric's brows furrowed.

"I'm actually the one who can hide. She seeks." Kerr raised a hand. "Long story. But I also never get lost, as you may have noticed from my fabulous trip leading without using a map. Shelby can find anything. Mom used to call us Lost and Found."

Shelby shoved her hands into her hair, like she was trying to hold her head in place. "Damn you all, okay? That's personal stuff." She spun toward Eric. "Yeah, so I'm a mental freak. Keep it to yourself. No one's supposed to know."

Eyes wide, Eric shut his hard jaw closed with a snap.

She glared twin holes into Garrison and Kerr. "And you two, shut the hell up, please. No more secrets. You've done enough damage for one night."

Garrison cleared his throat.

She rounded on Garrison. "All right then. Fine. Which one?"

"What?"

"The radar only works on one person at a time. Which one do you want me to find?"

Son of a bitch. He had to choose.

She waved her hand. "Close your guppy mouth. I'll work on Zach."

"Hurry."

"It takes as long as it takes. Stop talking and let me concentrate."

Garrison ground his teeth. She needed to hurry. But she was right —her power worked at its own pace.

His father swayed on his feet, and Garrison motioned to Kerr, who pressed his mouth into a hard line and guided their father into a seat in the living room. It was a testament to how bad his dad felt when he didn't protest the help.

Shelby hung on to the bottom of the stair railing, her eyes closed as her body rotated from side to side, like a human dowsing rod. Garrison would catch hell later. She had never told anyone outside the family about her powers. Until he spilled one of her most guarded secrets.

Didn't care. He'd use any tool at his disposal to find Zach and Sara and get them out of harm's way.

The people he cared for.

Of course he loved Zach. He'd move heaven and earth to get his son back.

The image of Sara's sweet, smiling face with that cute dimple on one cheek, rose up. The sounds of her enthusiastic passion, the depth of the trust she'd placed in him.

Yep, he cared for her, and possibly more, but this wasn't the time to examine his defective emotions.

And Hank was going to use Garrison's feelings for Zach and Sara to inflict the greatest pain. Shit.

With her back ramrod straight, Shelby's right arm lifted, as if of its own accord. Although her eyes were open, they had gone unfocused as her index finger pointed a path that led directly into the national forest and up into the mountains.

"That way." She whispered, putting her hand on the top of her head again, as if holding it together through the pain.

He'd find a way to make it up to her later.

If they found Zach and Sara.

"How far?" he asked.

"Never can tell. All I can give you is direction, dude. That's the best I can do."

"Good enough." He'd ride in that straight line for as long as it took to get to his son.

"Let's go," she said. Then she stumbled, legs buckling.

Eric snagged her under her arm, his frown deepening.

She moved away from him and took a few breaths.

His hand dropped. "Okay, come on. This is stupid. Shelby, you have to stop." He stared over her bent head at Garrison. "She's not going anywhere. She's obviously not healthy."

With a weary smile laced with pain, she spun back to Eric. "Look, I'm going to track them. End of discussion. *Capisce?*"

"It could be dangerous," he said. "Hank has it in for this family. Anyone in this family."

"You don't get it. I'm the only one here who is a freakin' bloodhound. I have to go." She laughed, then went into a wheezing spasm until she bent over, clutching her chest.

Garrison said, "Shel, I agree. You shouldn't be out there."

"You asked for a tracker, you got one. Don't try to dictate how I use my ability, okay? We have to let it run." She rubbed her temple and grimaced. "I'll be ready in five minutes."

The sound of her footsteps receding up the stairs and down the hall was followed by another coughing fit.

Eric's dark blue eyes turned grim as he stared up the stairs and shrugged. "I got nothing for that, man. I tried to keep her from doing something stupid."

"Not your fault. She's pissed that I outed her, but she'll wait to rip me a new one until after we find Zach and Sara. I have a reprieve for a while. So, you up to coming with us? I might need some help."

"You bet. Let me get some things." He ran out the front door. The sound of a truck gate opening and closing filtered back into the house.

It was agreed. Kerr would stay with their dad in case anyone came to the ranch or called. The youngest Taggart had protested remaining in the house, but Garrison insisted. Whatever was going on with their father, he shouldn't be left alone.

Several minutes later, Shelby, Eric, and Garrison saddled and mounted the horses.

"All right. Which way, Shel?" Garrison asked.

She tugged the zipper of her synthetic search-and-rescue jacket up to her chin and exhaled vapor. Bowing her head with another wince, she pointed into the snowy night.

"That way."

CHAPTER 22

*H*ank had left her to die.

After he had tied her arms up and left her to stand on tiptoes, dangling by the hook in the middle of the shack, Sara had expected horrible things to occur. She had a good idea what he was capable of as she watched Zach stumble away.

So when he secured her to the roof beam, she anticipated his next move. Would he beat her up? Gut her with a knife? Rape her?

Then he'd left.

Every so often, she caught his muffled voice and crunching foot-steps as he paced near the cabin. Each time his voice rose, her heart thudded faster and harder.

Okay, so Hank had lost his mind. Sure, a year ago he'd had an edge to him, but he had acted like a generally decent guy right up until they broke up. Today's Hank barely resembled that man.

She caught a few muttered words. "Great One" and "make the blade," but she had no idea what that meant.

Might never know.

Poor Zach. Anything could happen to an eight-year-old. Animals could attack him, leaving him bleeding in the wilderness. What if he fell and broke a leg? To say nothing of hypothermia. Did he lie in the snow now, lost and frozen?

She had to figure out how to get out of here or at least get a message to Garrison.

Or die trying.

Anyone searching wouldn't know where to look and wouldn't easily find the trapper shack, especially with the small forest roads quickly becoming impassable in the early winter storm. No one would get to her location until spring.

No need to worry about spring. No way would she last that long.

Garrison would be sick with worry. He'd tear up the countryside looking for his son, but by the time anyone found Zach, it would be too late.

What about her? No one knew that she had gone missing. No one would check up on her tonight.

Her eyes burned. No. She would not break down.

Why not? What would it matter if she lost it and started crying?

It wouldn't.

God, her arms burned. Her hands had lost circulation a while ago, and her legs quivered with the effort to remain upright. Her cold, numb feet barely touched the ground, and to take pressure off her arms, she had to stand on tiptoes. When her calves cramped and she lowered her heels, her shoulders and arms ached, bearing most of her weight.

Hank might be outside talking and taking a stroll now, but at some point, that would change. She twisted her wrists, trying anything to free herself from the ropes. The cords didn't budge. Damn.

The muttering outside stopped. Silence.

Footsteps crunched close by then stopped at the door.

Her heart leapt. Maybe someone had come to get her out of here. Maybe it wasn't Hank.

The door creaked open.

"Time for some fun."

His leer lit up his entire face in a sick glow.

"Come on, Shel. We've got to move faster." When Garrison tensed, his horse shied sideways.

"Lay off, man," Eric said from the horse behind him. "Whatever she's doing is hurting her. I can't believe you're making your own sister do this."

"I have no choice," he said, his jaw tight, neck muscles tensed to the breaking point. "What else can I do?"

Eric gestured toward Shelby, her groans audible as she fought to maintain control of her power. Garrison knew how much the prolonged use of her ability hurt. She'd returned from search-and-rescue missions completely wrecked by headaches. But she always found her lost hiker or climber. Always.

Sometimes even found the missing person alive.

Which was why he was betting everything he had on her skill. His sister was Zach's only hope.

Full dark had fallen, replaced by a rising moon in cloudy skies. At least the heavy snow had faded to flurries. Every second that ticked away was a second closer to death for Zach and Sara. As for Shelby? A few Tylenols and a nap and she would be fine. He hoped.

Zach and Sara might not okay, though, if he didn't hurry.

He'd push his sister's psychic ability to the limit, if it meant finding his son and…

What was Sara to him?

Girlfriend? They really hadn't dated.

Lover? Too harsh.

He would give her no label. Couldn't. Not now.

"Shel. Anything?" He tried to temper his voice to be less demanding. But he gritted his teeth and glanced at his watch again. Damn it. Almost 7 p.m. It had taken way too long to get out there.

Neither Zach nor Sara had coats. How long could someone last out in the elements without warm clothing?

The three of them guided their horses deep into the forest, where the terrain became steeper. Picking a line up the slopes that the horses could manage had become challenging.

Was Shelby even pointing them in the correct direction?

"Yeah. We're going the right way." She coughed, a harsh, raking sound, pressed her hand to her chest, and then cried out and grabbed her forehead beneath her hat.

Eric nudged his horse near Shelby's and scowled at Garrison.

Couldn't help it. Garrison needed to find his kid. Needed to find Sara.

Needed to kill a certain rancher.

"Can you sense both of them?" Garrison asked.

"No. I'm locked into Zach." Kneeing the horse to a slightly different angle, she led them toward a thick, dark stand of trees. "Oh my Lord, he's really cold, Garrison. His legs hurt, feet are numb. Good God." Her shoulders slumped, and she grabbed the pommel to stay in the saddle.

"Geezus." Eric put a hand out to keep her on the horse. "Stop making her do this."

"No. We have to get to him soon. Keep going. I can tell what he's feeling," she said.

By the time her voice reached Garrison, it was a mere thread of sound, and it took him a second to process what she'd revealed.

"Wait a minute, Shelby. What did you just say?"

"I said...Zach is cold. And...he's scared." Her wheezes were getting worse.

"How do you know?" Garrisons blood froze in his veins.

"Damn it, I don't know. I just know he's cold."

"Before, could you ever tell what your target felt?"

"Yeah, no. Oh, wow. This might be something new." She rubbed her gloved fingers, like they had suddenly become cold. "Whatever is happening is definitely weird, but we'll deal with it later. Let's find your kid."

"I'm right behind you," Garrison said.

Stiffening as she looked around, she said, "Hey, guys. Something's not right out here. I don't know what, but it feels off."

"Like, with Vaughn?" Garrison asked. Everyone in the family knew the oldest Taggart sibling could detect danger.

She coughed. "Not exactly danger. Well, yes...I don't know. No. The feeling is just...wrong."

Eric muttered something about this being bullshit and drew his gun as his horse followed hers. His head swiveled from side to side, scanning the woods.

Garrison wanted to do the same and watch for danger, but he could only stare ahead, into the darkness, imagining that every shadow was his son.

Was Sara with Zach? God, he hoped so.

Shelby's wheezes punctuated the crunch of hooves in snow and wind in the upper branches of the trees. Maybe she'd go faster if Garrison moved closer to her?

Eric's rigid posture warned him off. For now, Garrison would trail his sister and trust her instincts.

With a gurgled cry, she slid off the horse.

Eric vaulted down and grabbed her upper arm, ignoring her attempts to wave him off.

"What?" Garrison said.

As she crumpled to her knees in the deep snow, slowed by Eric's grip, she pointed to a dark shape next to a tree.

"There."

CHAPTER 23

*G*arrison's pulse pounded in his head as he ran twenty feet and crouched down next to a huddled, motionless form.

His heart stopped.

"Zach? Buddy?"

He pulled his son into his lap and cradled his head. Zach murmured and raised his arm. Alive.

Holy shit, his son was alive. But was he injured? Sick? Would he survive?

"Dad?" That incredulous whisper was imprinted on his soul forever.

Helped by Eric, Shelby staggered over and knelt down as well.

At her instruction, Eric yanked Shelby's saddle off, and she brought the horse-warmed saddle pad to tuck around Zach.

"Hi, Zach Attack." Her smile, bright in the icy moonlight, contrasted with the circles under her eyes.

"Auntie Shelby?"

"Anything hurt?" Shelby ran her hands over him, using her EMT skills.

"Tired. Can't feel my feet."

"We'll get you home, buddy." Garrison had to force the words out around the lump in his throat.

He clutched his son to his chest, holding on like Zach was a life preserver and Garrison about to go under for the last time.

Shelby's hand on his shoulder kept Garrison's anger in check. "He needs to be warmed up, pronto. Maybe frostbite on his feet. We'll take him straight to the hospital," she said.

"Okay." He searched the area around them. Nothing moved. No sounds. No one else around. Sweat popped out on his forehead. "Zach, where's Ms. Lopez?"

"Back there." He pointed with a shaky finger.

Garrison peered into the dense forest that pushed into mountains. Out there? "How far? Was she with you?" Was she lying in the snow as well?

"No, she stayed at the little house," Zach said.

Maybe his son was confused from the hypothermia. No one lived out here. "What house?"

"Mr. Hank's house." He whispered, "He's not nice, Dad."

"Did he hurt you?" With effort, Garrison kept his voice low and even.

Shelby flinched and bit her lip as she drew the pad farther around Zach, took off his shoes and socks, and tucked his feet beneath the thick, warm material. She pulled a jacket out of her bag and wrapped it around his shoulders.

Eric froze in his vigilant stance, head cocked toward them, his hand still on his gun.

"Mr. Hank tied me to a chair until Ms. Lopez came to get me."

"What?" Garrison gritted out.

"When she got to the house, Mr. Hank let me go. He told me to keep walking until I got home."

Above them, Eric stared. "Geezus."

Shelby gasped.

Son of a bitch. "Did Hank hurt Ms. Lopez?"

"He yelled at her and hit her and made her cry."

Garrison's hearing faded as his vision blurred. He needed to get to her. Now. He would make sure Hank couldn't threaten anyone else ever again. As a bonus, he'd love to make certain Hank couldn't walk or talk again, either.

But Zach needed him, too. His son wasn't out of the proverbial woods yet. He might still need medical help.

Damn it all to hell. Too many plates spinning. He stood up, clutching his son in his arms.

"Garrison." Shelby startled him out of his black thoughts. "We'll take Zach back to the ranch and then on to the hospital."

"What about your saddle?"

"Not the first time I've ridden bareback. It'll be fine."

Eric holstered the gun. "We'll take good care of him. But we have to go now." He darted another glance into the woods. "I don't like any of this weird situation."

"Shel, can you get a direction for Sara?"

"Geezus, man, she's done enough." Eric glared at him, gesturing toward Shelby's slumped shoulders. "This…radar shit…isn't good for her."

When Eric held out his hand, she took it this time, a testament to how bad she felt. Squaring her shoulders, she reached for Zach, who rested in Garrison's arms.

"All right, Zach Attack, one more question, then we're going home and getting you warmed up. Did you walk in a straight line?"

"Tried to."

Dropping her forehead into the palm of her hand, his sister sighed. When she looked up at him, tight lines around her mouth and eyes spoke to the extraordinary stress Garrison had placed on her. And he wasn't done being a shitty brother.

"Okay. That makes it easier." Shelby fished a compass and flashlight out of her pocket. She mumbled, "Sara," and held out an arm as she turned in a quarter arc in the general direction Zach indicated. With a whimper, she stopped when her body snapped to a fixed position, and she held still while she spun the compass direction arrow into position. "Got it. That way." She handed it to Garrison. "Oh man." A whimper escaped her lips.

"What?" he yelled.

"Oh, God. Pain. So much pain and fear. Cold, numb…please, no. Ahh." She dropped to the snow, limp.

"Shelby?" Eric pulled her boneless body up to his chest. "Dude, she's out. When is enough, enough?"

Another minute of Eric chafing her arms, and Shelby woke up, grabbing her head. "Ow. Damn it all to hell."

"Sorry, Shel," Garrison said.

"You couldn't…help it," she gasped, staggering to her feet with Eric's help.

"You two okay to get back home?" Garrison asked, shifting Zach's weight in his arms.

"Possibly. No thanks to you." Eric glared as he held onto Shelby's upper arm.

Her face turned eerie in shadow, like a ghost. "Go find Sara. She needs you."

"Will do."

Eric's grim smile stretched his face too tight. "Try not to do anything stupid."

"No promises." Second order of business after finding Sara involved committing a felony, and Garrison cared exactly zilch about any repercussions.

"Call when you've got a location. We'll send the police." Eric said.

Thumbing his phone on and off, Garrison shrugged. "No signal out here."

"I can go with you," Shelby offered.

"No!" both Eric and Garrison said.

She frowned. "Fine. Help me up, jerks. Let's get out of here." Eric boosted her onto her horse.

"Hand me the saddle, Eric. I'm taking it back with me."

"Why can't you just ride on the saddle without the blanket?"

"It'll rub Bob raw."

"You're worried about the damn horse?" he sputtered.

"Don't listen to him, Bob." She petted the neck of her horse as the animal jiggled the bit. "This is my baby, and I will not rub sores on him."

Eric looked about ready to throw his hat into the woods. "Geezus. Then we'll come back for the saddle. It'll take over an hour to return to the ranch."

Shelby's glare could be classified as a lethal weapon. "Like hell we're coming back for it. It's was a gift from Dad. I'm taking it back with me."

Eric looked to the night sky and shook his head as he handed her the saddle. She clutched the leather in a big, awkward bundle in front of her.

Garrison wanted to hang on to his son forever and never let him go. But no way would he expose his son to more violence. Plus, Zach needed medical attention.

Tilting his head toward a pissed-off Shelby, he passed Zach up to Eric. "Take care of my boy, please."

"Will do."

"Love you, son." Garrison swallowed another lump in his throat.

Zach sagged as Eric held him securely in his arms. His son, covered by the saddle pad, had nodded off.

Shelby called to Garrison, "Be careful, please."

"Thank you, sis."

Hopefully, his son's ordeal was over.

But Sara was still in hell.

Swinging up into the saddle, Garrison faced in the direction of the compass arrow and followed the general direction of Zach's footprints in the snow.

"I'll be fine," he murmured. "Can't say the same about Hank, though."

Hank paced in circles around Sara, his breathing harsh. The shape of his face danced and changed as he passed in front of the lantern, but his wide eyes never left her. With deft wrist movements, he flicked a knife in front of him.

Open.

Closed.

Open.

Closed.

Like the tick of a bomb timer, counting down the seconds.

Cold had long since permeated her bones until every inch of her body felt like solid ice. Shivering hurt her shoulders too much, so she tried to suppress the urge. When she tried to wiggle her toes, she no longer could tell if they moved or not.

Hank came to a halt directly in front of her and grabbed her chin.

"It's been two hours since he left. You think that little boy is still alive?" he sneered.

Her jaw ached beneath his pincer grip. "Damn you, Hank." Her tears created tracks of heat on her cold cheeks.

"Big question is: will lover boy find us before you die, too?" The pressure on her face increased. "My opinion? No one knows where we are. No one knows you're missing. No one cares. And you told Romeo to take a hike." Hank snickered. "Maybe when you don't make it to work tomorrow, someone will realize you're gone. Even then, they might just think you're a slacker."

"Why are you doing this, Hank?" Maybe she could keep him talking. Stall for time.

But it only delayed the inevitable.

He shoved her face back, and she lost her footing, which yanked at her upraised shoulders. She bit her lip, refusing to scream. Refusing to give him the satisfaction.

"Why am I doing this, lover? For so many reasons. Garrison had what should have been mine. Something wonderful. I finally took it from him, but it was already spoiled."

"I don't understand."

"You wouldn't." He patted her hip, and she flinched. Hank chuckled. "I've hated him for as long as I can remember. He's always had the best of everything: land, luck, women. I'm sick and tired of being second place to Garrison Taggart."

"Second place?"

"Yeah, but now we have the upper hand. Not only have I ruined his life, but now I have the power to destroy his family and all of the rats in that nest. I've been given a mission, you see." He glanced around, eyes bulging. "Sh, don't tell." He grinned like he'd half-cracked. "Don't tell. Now that's funny. Like you'll survive to tell anyone. I'm mining for something special. Something that will make me powerful for the Great One."

"What are you talking about?"

He snapped his hand up, and she braced for the slap that didn't come. Opening one eye, she saw that he'd frozen right before contact.

He blinked and frowned; a flash of the old, normal Hank flitted over his features, then disappeared again. "Can't tell you. Only we need the Taggart ranch property. Any way we can get it. And if it hurts Garrison Taggart, even better. That's part of the mission."

"Hurt Garrison?"

"Oh, yes. Hurt all of them. Hurt the legacy."

What in the world? "But how does this involve Zach and me?"

"Well, see, I've asked very nicely for old Austin Taggart and his kids to sell the ranch. Many times. And they keep saying no."

"Okay..."

"No. Not okay. If they're not going to help me get what I want, I'll have to destroy what the Taggarts have and take what I need." Spittle formed at the corner of his mouth.

"That's crazy," she whispered.

The crack on her cheek made her see stars. Her face throbbed like a hot iron pressed into it.

His face hovered inches from hers as he screamed, "Not crazy. Not crazy. No one is crazy. You don't even know half of what I've done and what I'm capable of doing. The Great One has given me a calling. No one messes with us."

Holy mother of Christ. Apparently he had obtained an all-consuming, deity-based, destroy-the-Taggarts ideology. Not good.

Trying to hold her ground, such as it was, she said, "So. The barn?"

He pointed a thumb at himself. "Yep, that was me."

"The dead animal?"

"Guilty." He chuckled.

"My kitchen window?"

"Didn't you like my ball and chain coming through the glass? It was a little excessive to make a joke but so completely worth it."

She rolled her eyes. "You and I are broken up, you know."

He squeezed her breast and snorted when she cried out. "Thank goodness and good riddance. You're trash, and everyone knows it. Fat, too." Patting her on the hip, he continued, "No, I didn't want you. I only wanted Garrison to think that you and I might get back together. I just wanted to screw with the guy."

Asshole. May he rot in hell. She bit her cheek to keep her face expressionless.

She wasn't trash, Hank was. He had no right to judge her. Screw him. An intelligent, cute woman like her could attract a sexy guy like Garrison. Hank needed glasses and his head adjusted.

However, now was not the time to tell him to where to stick his stupid ideas.

Now was the time to pray.

"So if I'm not worth anything, let me go."

He pressed a thumb into her still-throbbing cheek and grinned. "That hurt? Good. You're here because lover boy wants you. Why, I don't know. But here's the deal: Anything the Taggarts wants, I will make sure they cannot have. And I will make sure they suffer the loss. Every. Single. Time."

"Fine, I'll stop seeing him. Problem solved. Now let me go."

"Not that simple. I'm going to use you to send a clear message."

"Message?"

"No one fucks with us. Time for respect. Even more important, it's time for the Great One to emerge."

"God."

"No, God isn't here, my chunky ex-girlfriend."

He flicked open the blade again and drew it down the neck of her blouse until the rip of fabric echoed too loud in the shack.

His insane eyes danced in the lamplight.

She couldn't feel her hands, but she sure could feel the cool air on her chest.

He grinned. "You're all mine now."

CHAPTER 24

*T*he flurries had stopped, and frigid, dry air now gusted through the forest. Garrison's lungs burned with each icy inhalation.

It had been more than an hour since he left Zach with his sister and Eric. Would Zach be okay?

Too much time wasted, and Garrison still hadn't found Sara.

Time was running out.

Hope threatened to knock him off the horse—a faint glow of light on the snow!

He followed the light to a rough trapper-type shack. Zach's footprints had long since faded before Garrison had arrived at his destination. Thank God for Shelby.

Leaving his horse tied to a tree several hundred yards away, Garrison grabbed his shotgun and crept up to the structure. He sidled around to the single window and peered through the hazy, cracked glass. A familiar figure paced in the center of the room. Son of a bitch, he would break Hank's hands in a million places so he couldn't touch her again.

Sara hung from her arms but stood on tiptoes. He could see only her profile, but from the way her head tipped back and forth like she was writhing, and the fact that she bit her lip, she had to be suffering.

On her cheek, not a shadow but a dark bruise colored the skin.

Pressed against the building wall, he took deep breaths. Shit, he was already in a crouch, muscles tight, ready to burst in there and drive his fist through the back of Hank's skull. But he couldn't. If went in there, proverbial or literal guns blazing, Sara could get hurt. He had to plan carefully.

He might not be able to bring Hank to justice in the next ten minutes, but Garrison would gladly settle for getting Sara the hell out of here right now. Hank's turn would come.

Without taking his eyes away from the view through the window, he set down the gun and removed his coat.

Between gusts of wind, the voices inside the shack filtered through to his ears.

"No one fucks with us. Time for respect. Even more important, it's time for the Great One to emerge." Hank could take his Great One talk and shove it up his ass. Even better, Garrison would be happy to do it for the guy.

"God."

Sara's strained voice shredded Garrisons heart. He couldn't risk firing in there with a weapon. Not with Sara inside.

Hank leaned in close to her face. "No, God isn't here, my chunky ex-girlfriend."

Goddamn Hank. Sara was beautiful, smart, and sweet. And her curves were amazing.

Then Hank flipped open a knife, and Garrison went on instinct, edging toward the door. He heard him say, "You're all mine now."

The sound of fabric tearing…Garrison exploded into the structure, knocking the door off a hinge on his way to Sara.

At a dead run, he tackled the guy. Hard to say which satisfied him more: the shock on Hank's face or the bone-crunching *thud* as he drilled the asshole into the floor. They rolled together until slamming into a wall with a shower of dirt and splinters.

Garrison drove a knee into Hank's chest.

Hank shifted and kicked Garrison's knee, collapsing it.

Shit, where was the knife?

Hank loomed over him, punching and swearing. Garrison's head snapped back hard enough to see stars. Only Sara's panting gasp kept him conscious.

Which was good, considering Hank was now trying to slice a horizon line into Garrison's face.

He kicked the knife out of Hank's hand and head-butted him, dropping the guy to the floor where he lay, unmoving. Long may it last.

Garrison staggered to his feet, head throbbing, his knee trying to buckle again. Although he couldn't walk a straight line, he was determined to reach Sara. His forehead stung, and he wiped away blood that blinded his left eye.

"Oh my God, your head," she gasped. White lines of pain surrounded her mouth.

"Forget my head. You're getting out of here."

He picked up Hank's knife on the floor and sawed at the ropes around her wrists.

As the ropes fell free, she crumpled to the ground with a gurgled moan. He patted her on the shoulder, and she flinched and cried out.

Kneeling next to her, he chafed her purple, cold hands until some color returned.

"Better?" he asked.

She shook her hands, but then her expression contorted from relief to pain. She hissed, "So sting-y. Oh my God, they hurt." Studying her hands in her lap, she said, "I can't lift them."

Rubbing more gently, he kept up the friction on her hands. He wouldn't be responsible for his actions if Hank had permanently damaged her nerves. "You'll be able to soon, I promise."

Careful of her bruise, he dabbed her tears with his sleeve. Unable to clutch at him, she flopped her hands near the front of his shirt. Her effort to hold him? Heartbreaking.

"What about Zach?" she whispered. Her eyes were wide and searching.

"We got to him in time. He'll be okay."

"Oh, thank God." She sagged against him.

Her sobs cracked open his heart. Tonight, he had nearly lost two people who meant the world to him.

A groan got his attention.

"Don't move," he ordered Sara. Bad news if the blow to Hank's head hadn't kept that man down. Garrison didn't know how much more fight he had left in the tank. "What the hell, Hank?" he yelled as the man sat up and then got to his knees.

He spat to the side. "This is all your fault, Taggart."

"You're out of your mind."

"If you'd fucking sold me the ranch, none of this shit would have ever happened."

"Excuse me?" Such twisted logic defied reason.

"You had your chance to end this peacefully. Sell the ranch and everyone would have been happy. But no, you people are stubborn. Attracted too much attention." Hank whispered between bloody lips, "That's why we're going to destroy all the Taggarts."

"One, we're not interested in selling anything. It's our land. Two, why do you want it so much? And three, why do you want to destroy my family?"

"That's for us to know and you never to know."

"Anything to do with the mining?"

"The fuck you know!"

Like coming off a springboard, Hank launched himself from a crouched position and drove his head into Garrisons midsection, knocking him to the ground. Unable to breathe, Garrison blinked back dimming vision. The fists pummeling against his head helped to wake him the hell up as stars burst behind his eyes with each blow.

Hank's well-placed blow shot pain straight through to the back of Garrison's skull. His nose made a sickening, wet crunch.

The guy was getting the better of him. This bastard was stronger than any person should be. But Garrison couldn't fail.

Because if he went out of commission, who would protect Sara?

Hank had departed the realm of insanely pissed off and irrational four punches ago. Homicidal would be the next stop. If he neutralized Garrison, then he'd kill her for sure.

Garrison was the only thing that stood between Hank and Sara.

A snap of wood registered in the periphery of his hearing. When Hank turned toward the sound, Garrison landed a solid uppercut on the man's jaw. Damn, that stung the knuckles. Where was Vaughn when he needed him? His brother loved brawling and MMA shit. He'd be perfect in this fight.

Garrison blinked against blurry vision that created four Sara's and four awful Hanks.

Speaking of which, the man sprawled back against the wall, then like the damn Terminator, sat back up again and crawled to his feet. Blood dripped from his mouth, and he wheezed. But he kept coming.

Sara swayed on her feet. She held a wooden leg from a chair, pressed between her two palms. The tip of the wood drifted toward the floor. She had no grip strength. If Hank got his hands on the weapon, the nut job would bludgeon them both.

"Sarita, put that down," Hank crooned. He spat a glob of blood onto the floor.

Sweat beaded her forehead as the wood piece shook.

Move, damn it. Move. Get over there and help her. How long until Garrison's head would be clear enough to function?

Hank had turned his back on him. Bad mistake. Garrison blinked away blood and slowly worked himself to his knees, inching closer to Hank.

Sara flicked a glance at Garrison and stood straighter. "So, Hank, why'd you kidnap me, anyway?"

Good job, Sara, buying more time. He fought to get the cobwebs out of his head. Son of a bitch, it felt like he was moving through sludge.

Hank barked what passed for a laugh. "Like I said. If the Taggarts want it, I will have it. Or take it away from them. That includes you."

"Why?"

"Part of my calling."

"You said that before. What do you mean?" She frowned.

"The calling is from the Great One." He wheezed. "Since neither of you will leave this shack alive, I'll let you in on a secret. I'm about to become the most powerful being in the world."

"What?" she said.

"You'll see. My lord whispered the plan to me one night. If I follow instructions, I'll be the new Great One."

"Okay, that sounds interesting," mumbled Sara.

"Ah, you don't believe me. That's okay. Let me tell you what else I've done." Hank rubbed saliva and blood from his mouth onto the back of his sleeve. "Pretty boy here used to have a wife, right?"

Garrison froze.

"That was a year ago, right?" Sara asked.

"Yeah, his bimbo wife left him." He laughed and spat. "For me."

Surely, that knife had just been plunged into his chest and then twisted. Tiffani? With Hank? Ridiculous.

"What?" Garrison roared.

Hank spun around. "Hey, look who's awake. Who do you think told her to clean out your bank account before she left you?" He crooked a thumb at his chest.

Garrisons head started to throb, and it had nothing to do with the concussion. "You're lying."

Sara dropped the end of the chair leg to the floor and leaned over on it. How was she even remaining upright?

The insane asshole had the gall to sneer. "She never loved you, Taggart."

"What do you know about it, Hank?"

"Oh what a tangled web we weave." His singsong voice grated on Garrison's nerves. "She should have been mine all along, Taggart. I wanted her from the get-go. But our love had to wait."

"In what alternate universe?"

"When you brought her home that Christmas break from college to show her around town—that's when I knew I had to have her for myself."

"Why?"

"You always got the best of everything. You were the most popular guy in school. You always got the girls. You have the best property for

—" He clapped a hand over his mouth. "Anyway. Enough was enough. It was time for me to get something *I* wanted."

Blood drained out of Garrison's head until he shook it to clear his muddled mind. "So, you and Tiffani…?"

Hank snickered. "First of all, let's be honest here. In the beginning, she really wanted your brother, Vaughn. Not you or me. Anyone could see it. Maybe that's part of why your brother left town last year."

"What?"

"Oh. Oh? You didn't know, did you? Oh my, oh my. That's why big brother left. Affair. Couldn't keep his hands off your wifey. Too bad his noble gesture to exit stage right didn't matter in the long run."

"You're lying." A strange pressure began behind the temples. Insistent. A force begging to be let out. Begging to discover the truth. Begging Garrison to rip the truth out of the asshole's head.

"No, no. As time went on, after Vaughn left, you paid far more attention to the ranch than to Tiffani, and she grew to love me, as it should have been in the beginning. And how she loved me! Over and over. Said I was way better in the sack than her dull husband." He licked a cracked lip.

Garrison had to breathe hard to control the sensation pushing out from the inside of his mind. Almost like hands reaching out to Hank. "Where is she?"

"No longer with us, sad to say."

If Hank could be believed, this explained why Tiffani hadn't contacted him in over a year. "Tell me."

"Nope. Sorry. End of story. She died in Salt Lake City. Fell in with the wrong sort of people, sadly." Hank advanced, grinning. "Look, you want bad things to stop happening? You want to keep your family safe? Sell the ranch. Leave. It's real simple."

"Why are you so fixated on the ranch?"

"I gave you a chance, Taggart. You lose."

When Hank lunged at him, the blow ricocheted Garrison into the wall.

Hank wrapped a hand around the front of his neck until a train-engine roar of sound filled Garrison's ears. He could not pass out. Not now. Not with Sara vulnerable.

Blackness tunneled in on him; the howl of pressure in his head turned into a desperate force.

Then he heard a loud sound that refocused him for a split second before losing consciousness.

With a scream and an ungraceful lurch, Sara clocked Hank on the back of his head with the broken chair leg.

Hank crumpled, once again still.

Hopefully, it had hurt. He deserved to suffer after what he'd put her and Zach through. Not to mention hurting Garrison.

She dropped the piece of wood, fell to her hands and knees, and then rolled onto her side, shaking, as the reality of the situation sank in.

Blinking, she stared at the man who slid down the wall and sagged into a sitting position. The enormity of the near-death experience made her gut churn.

"Garrison? You're here?"

Blood trickled down his forehead. "No place I'd rather be." She winced in sympathy at his lopsided, bruised grin.

"But how did you find me?"

"Very good directions."

A hot flutter in her chest choked her. "What about Zach? He's out there! You have to find him."

He lifted a bruised hand. "We got him, Sara. He's okay." He grabbed the wall and shoved himself back to his feet. "Now it's your turn. I'm getting you out of here."

"No!" She rubbed her face; the bruise hurt like hell. "I mean, yes, I want out of here. But we can't leave Hank here."

The sudden darkness in Garrison's eyes raised goose bumps on her arms. "You're protecting him?" His voice came out dangerous, low, deadly.

"No, not exactly. I want him to pay for what he did. But we can't leave him to hurt more people."

Garrison staggered toward her. "What do you suggest? Killing him?"

She bit her lip as she studied Hank's unmoving form. Maybe he was dead from her blow? "No, but shouldn't we, you know, call the cops or something?"

He exhaled and shook his head. "Sara, his family *is* the police in these parts. And the cell phone doesn't work out here." He rubbed his neck. "Please, let's just get out of here. I need to know that you're okay."

Her heart skipped a beat. "I'm good. You found Zach. And you're here now."

"Sara, I—"

She held her breath.

Glancing over his shoulder, he said, "I'm glad I found you before Hank could do worse damage."

Her breath whooshed out. "You're glad. Yeah. I got it."

He dropped to his knees in front of her, his deep groan filling the hut. "Damn, I'm getting too old for this crap." Taking her chin in his hand, he stared at her, like she was an algebra problem to solve. "I need you away from this place. Away from Hank. For me. Please. I—" His jaw went hard. "If I stay here, there no telling what I will do to Hank for hurting my son. For hurting you." When he looked at her like that, she wanted to drown in his gaze.

Every muscle in her body went slack as she leaned into him. He pulled her into his arms. She didn't even care that he was crushing her to his chest.

Because it was Garrison's chest.

He had found her.

"You're a tough woman, you know, whacking Hank over the head."

"Pure skill," she mumbled into his shirt.

His chuckle turned her bones to liquid. "God, I'm glad you're all right." He whispered those words like a prayer. Like he tried to convince himself.

"I'm okay, thanks to you."

Holding on to her upper arms, he leaned back. "Please. Let's get out of here."

She wanted to soothe the hurts and kiss away the bruises on his face. But she and Garrison were in the middle of the woods. In winter. Two feet from a guy who had tried to kill them both. "Okay. We can go. We'll send the police back here and hope they will do their job."

"Good deal." He stood, pulling her up and into his side. Where their frames met, familiar, comforting warmth flooded her skin.

As she took a step, a hand closed around her ankle.

CHAPTER 25

*H*ank moaned and rolled over, bloody fingers digging into Sara's lower leg. What the hell? He wasn't out? The guy had superhuman strength and endurance. Garrison had never seen anything like it before.

The power flared to life, blanked out all other rational thought, and took over Garrison's will.

He wanted to kill Hank, but first he had unfinished business with the guy. And that unfinished business required the asshole to remain conscious.

Using the edge of his boot heel to encourage Hank to let go of Sara's leg, Garrison retrieved the pieces of rope and trussed Hank's wrists and feet.

Sara stared at him with wide-eyed horror. Hank writhed within the bonds and spat curses. Garrison paused, torn.

Son of a bitch. He should get her out of here and to warmth and safety, but damn it, his fingers of truth itched to connect with the man's head.

In fact, the roar of his power built up to a cyclone inside his skull. The spinning pressure pushed against his mind. Cracks started to form. He'd never experienced anything like this with his ability before. Stress pushed him to a new level. So much did the power consume him, he set her to the side and scooted a few feet away, worried he'd hurt her.

He kicked Hank's foot.

The hog-tied man yowled. "Fuck off."

"Good. You're conscious enough for me." He knelt and locked Hank's sweaty, bloody face between his two hands, then released every ounce of power in an arrow of psychic energy, anchoring himself to the other man's mind. Hank screamed but kept his eyes fixed on Garrison.

"Hank, I'm going to ask you a question."

"I'm not answering anything, dickhead."

The building pressure felt different tonight. Maybe he didn't need Hank to say anything. What if he didn't need to ask a question to get the answers?

He'd try it the normal way first. "Where is Tiffani?"

Hank's jaw clamped down. The anger boiling in Garrison's body ratcheted up his newly hungry power several notches. The ability wanted to be released, needed to be released. The roaring in Garrison's head would give him a stroke unless he let it out.

So Garrison did something he'd never done in his life. Not only did he simply read Hank's lying aura. This time, Garrison shoved his power into another person and reached inside. Under the invasion, Hank writhed and howled while Garrison's ability freakin' *looked for* the answer to the question. His power had never acted like this before.

Then, like it stumbled onto an idea, the ability shifted, as if it found what it came for and throttled back. He simply read Hank's memories of Tiffani like a sick, disjointed story. The truth.

While working at the county office, Tiffani had found out about the Brands' mining and property acquisition plans a year ago. At first, Hank had tried to sweet-talk her into keeping her mouth shut, but later resorted to blackmail.

So Tiffani had posed for nude pictures in a men's magazine back in college? For this she bent to Hank's will?

Not only that reason. There. The truth in Hank's mind glowed bright orange.

Garrison's brain pulsed like a bass drum, making it difficult to concentrate, but he pressed forward. He needed to know the complete truth about his wife.

Hank whined like an animal stuck in a metal trap, writhing in pain with nowhere to run. Good. Garrison dug deeper.

Not only had Hank held the specter of public humiliation over Tiffani, but he'd found out about her fixation with Vaughn. Then Hank had threatened Zach's life. Blackmail and threats kept piling up, deeper and scarier. So, little by little, Tiffani had covered up important information about the Brand's mining operation, helped Hank, and siphoned county funds to him.

When that hadn't been enough, Hank cashed in all of the blackmail. He wanted to ruin her family, her career, and her reputation.

Similar M.O. to how he treated Sara. At least the asshole remained consistent.

Then, Hank forced Tiffani to become his lover eleven months ago. His sexual tastes were…uniquely twisted…but when that relationship didn't work out, he forced her to empty the joint bank account she had with Garrison.

Then she gave the money to Hank.

That was the awful day, right after the divorce papers arrived, when Garrison went to withdraw cash and had zero dollars in the account.

He had thought that moment represented his rock bottom. Until today.

Hank started to scream, his eyes rolling back, fighting against the invasion. A shadowed zone remained in Hank's mind, still closed off the Garrison. Maybe there was even more. Garrison plunged in farther until the man howled.

Big deal. Let the guy scream. He deserved the pain, and Garrison ignored his own pounding headache as he pressed the man further. He couldn't care less if he exploded the foul pulp of that guy's brain in the process. More pressure. More answers.

The dark area remained closed. No truth existed in that black wasteland, a voice whispered. *Withdraw. Or else.*

Refocusing on the information he wanted from Hank, Garrison gritted out, "You didn't answer my question. Where is Tiffani?"

"She's dead, you loser."

Garrison strained with every muscle in his body to maintain control of his power and not twist the man's head off his shoulders. "Did you kill her?"

"No."

Truth and fury glowed a desperate, lava red in Hank's mind.

"Who killed her then?"

"Not sure. I kicked her to the curb early this year, after I had your money and had sampled all the rest of her goodies. I think she ran away to Salt Lake City and hooked up with some bad people there."

Truth, as much as Hank possessed, continued to glow.

"What about this talk of your calling and your mission?"

Darkness within his mind pulsed. Seethed. Forced Garrison back. "Fuck. You."

The black area formed into a thick wall inside of Hank's mind. The truth lay behind that wall. The second Garrison's power brushed against the darkness, an explosion of sound, light, and evil flung him out of Hank's mind.

How long he lay in the fetal position on the dirt floor, Garrison had no idea. Only that the roar had gone away, replaced by a muffled feeling in his ears, like he'd stood way too close to a speaker at a concert. His head throbbed so badly even his hair hurt. Were his ears bleeding? Felt like it. Son of a bitch, every piece of his body ached like hell.

Right, because he'd used his power, times a million. He'd have a migraine until he could apply for AARP membership. Shit.

A questioning sound from Sara and he dropped his hands and pushed to a seated position. Every cell in his body ached.

Hank groaned...*Join the crowd.* Garrison couldn't give a shit.

Instead, Garrison crawled over to Sara and took her in his arms. Even though his head pounded, being near this woman soothed his pain, balanced him, and reconnected him to something good after being coated in the slime of that bastard's mind.

"God," she cried. "What happened? It was like you were in a trance for a half hour."

"I'm fine now."

"I don't understand what going on. What did you do?"

"Something I vowed never to do and hope not to ever do again."

"Garrison?" Her quavering voice made him haul her in for a long, hard embrace. The soft, trembling body in his arms felt like bright light and possibilities and life. He'd been given a second chance here, and damned if he would squander the gift this time around.

He kissed her until neither of them could breathe, burying his hands in her tangled hair. Careful of the bruised areas, he dropped kisses on her neck, chin, lips, and forehead. Even now, in a freezing, dirty cabin in the middle of God-knew-where, he couldn't get enough of her.

"You two should get a room." Hank spat.

Garrison helped her to stand, picked up the wooden chair leg, and whacked Hank on the head once more. Those bulging eyes rolled back in his head.

"I'm sick of listening to him talk."

Sara sighed and wrapped her arms around Garrison's midsection. "I couldn't agree more."

Once he confirmed that she could walk on her own, they exited the shack.

He retrieved his coat and put it on her, and then he pulled out his cell phone. No reception. No help coming. So it was up to him to get them out of here safely. He could feel the temperature dropping, they had minimal supplies, and were both injured. He picked up the gun. Not that he could aim for shit, with his vision blurry.

None of that mattered. He would stay strong for Sara. He'd get her out of this mess.

How was Zach doing? Did Shelby and Eric get him back to the house? He couldn't do anything until he got back to the ranch. With Sara.

Before they'd made it more than a few feet, an ear-splitting scream erupted from the shack.

"You will not win!" a voice screamed.

Garrison turned and shoved Sara behind him.

"Oh, Great One, yes. I will still give you a sacrifice tonight." The howls split the darkness until a blast of light and a percussion of sound sent them flying back on their butts in the snow.

What in God's name had happened? Garrison helped Sara to her feet and, against her protests, ran back to the shack.

The inside of the building had been scorched like a flash fire had touched every inch of the structure, all at once.

Hank was nowhere to be seen. No burned remains, no bones, nothing. All that remained was a circle of charred ropes on the floor.

Garrison backpedaled out of the building. Whatever happened to Hank couldn't have been good. The creepy crawly sensations on his neck made him pull Sara toward his horse as fast as she could go. Whatever happened in there wasn't normal, and hell if Garrison would expose Sara to more danger tonight.

Dragging her to the horse, he gave her a quick hug before helping her up into the saddle. Her arms wrapping around him personified heaven and hell.

What he wanted.

What he had almost lost.

CHAPTER 26

*T*he sturdy horse stomped one hoof and whuffed a breath of vapor as Sara grabbed the saddle horn.

"Sorry, fella, you've got more work to do tonight before you rest." Garrison patted the horse's neck. He turned to Sara. "Rode much?"

"No. But I'll become an expert if this is our ticket out of here." She glanced over her shoulder, imagining a shadow form running through the forest, stalking them.

Garrison grasped the reins and led the horse through the snow-covered terrain. His gait remained unsteady.

"What about you?" she asked.

"I'll walk until we get to safer terrain."

"But—"

The warmth of his hand on her leg dispelled the shivers of fear shaking her body. Yes, they could do this. They were going to get out of here, in one piece. Alive.

"But nothing. Let's go home." He tilted his face up with a mangled smile. "And don't get cocky. We've got several hours of travel ahead of us." He checked his watch. "It's 10:30. Going to be a long night."

"Can't be much longer than it already has been."

He nodded. "We'll be home soon, don't worry."

Home.

Her gut clenched.

Sure, Garrison had risked his life to save her from Hank. But the facts remained. Her relationship with Hank had laid the groundwork for the deadly actions this night. Zach had nearly died.

Didn't matter how much the Taggart family had welcomed her, she had no place in this family. To be fair, she had no place at all. Not in Copper River. Not anywhere.

It also didn't matter how much she adored Zach. Didn't matter how much she...cared for Garrison. She couldn't stay in his life. Her own life lay before her. Her plans.

And after tonight, she had even more reason to want to leave Copper River the minute her contract ended. Time to stop hurting the people around her.

Her legs ached, and her face throbbed. Thankfully, the sensation had returned to her hands, though the rope burns on her wrists stung when fabric brushed over them. But after what Garrison had done for her tonight, no way would she complain. Mother Mary, if he hadn't come for her, she'd be dead. No question.

Limping in front of the horse, he led the way through the rough, snowy terrain. He bent into the frigid wind. A lump formed in her throat. Here she sat, wrapped in his toasty sheepskin coat. There he walked, coatless, dealing with the dropping temperatures like it was no big deal.

Damned if his essence didn't permeate the coat. The simple act of ducking her face into the collar and taking a deep breath brought memories of his rugged face and their night of passion. His masculine scent made her nerves tingle.

His scent made her heart ache.

"Garrison, do you want to ride for a while? You've been walking forever."

He paused and looked up, his face hidden in the darkness. "You know what? Yes, I'd love to ride. My knee's killing me."

"Absolutely." She removed her right leg from the stirrup to swing over the saddle.

His hand on her leg froze her in place and then sent a zing of excitement straight into her belly. She had to remember to breathe. Holy cow, all that from touching her leg?

His quiet voice split the still air. "I'd like to join you, if you don't mind."

"Of course." Her voice came out way too thready. Riding double with Garrison was dangerously like other things they would never do together again.

"Um, if you hop down for a second?" One corner of his swollen mouth lifted. "Oh."

He helped her down, swung up into the saddle, and kicked his left foot out of the stirrup. In an ungraceful move of impressive proportions, she hiked her aching leg so that her foot could rest in the stirrup, grabbed his hand, and stepped up as he helped her settle behind him.

"You may want to hold on," he said.

What woman wouldn't?

Maybe she wouldn't see him again, but the memory of her time spent with Garrison would keep her warm for many lonely winter nights. She wrapped her arms around him, bringing her chest up flush against his back. His body heat radiated through her skin, even through the coat she wore, and her head swam as she pressed her cheek to his neck.

"You can't do that," he murmured.

She started. "What?"

"It makes me crazy."

Life plans be damned. She wanted to taste his skin, at least once more. "Like this?" She licked an exposed area of his neck, and he shuddered.

"Keep it up, and I'll get pulled over for drunk riding."

His chuckle rolled through her in a soothing wave of comfort, settling over her like a warm blanket. Nice feelings while they lasted, but her time with Garrison was drawing to an end. She wouldn't think about it. Instead, she would rest for a few minutes. She laid her uninjured cheek on his upper back, tightened her grip around his muscled waist, and closed her eyes.

Sometime later, his voice drifted back to her.

"Wake up, Sara."

Disoriented for a moment, she clutched at the man in front of her as panic shot through her like a bullet.

"Whoa."

Did he say that for the horse or for her?

"Sara, we're almost home."

Damn that word again. *Home,* Yes, but not for her.

As they approached the main ranch yard, a figure, shadowed in the porch light, limped over to them. Kerr.

Sheriffs' vehicles were parked in front of the house, and officers wandered out of the front door at Garrison and Sara's arrival.

Kerr opened the gate from the fields.

The horse walked a few steps, then stopped.

Kerr whistled. "Holy fisticuffs, Batman, what the hell happened? Sara, goddamn it, your face. Shit. Are you all right?"

"Glad to see you, too, man. Can you help her down?"

Sara managed to move her wrecked body enough to hook a toe in the stirrup and swing her other leg over the horse's rump. Thank God for Garrison's support and Kerr's steady hand when she landed on the ground.

Garrison dismounted, also landing heavily. Both men clutched each other around the neck and pounded upper arms.

As Kerr led the horse away, Garrison pulled Sara into a tight embrace.

"Thank you," she mumbled into his chest.

He kept moving his arms to new holds around her head, neck, and back, like he couldn't hang on to her enough. Little tremors rippled through his muscles. "Son of a bitch." His voice cracked. "I thought I'd lost both of you."

After a moment, they leaned back.

"Zach," they both said together.

Moving as quickly as their aching and abused bodies permitted, they sidestepped a deputy to enter the house.

"Zach?" Garrison called. He turned into the living room. "Zach? Dad?"

No one sat in the living room. Where was his father? Kerr entered the house. "They're at the hospital."

Garrison spun and ran out the door to the truck, ignoring the officer again.

Sara followed. "Garrison!"

"Get in." He paused. "Please."

The sudden need in his voice stopped her cold. Was her future worth this man? Later. She'd deal with those thoughts later.

"If you're sure..."

"Yes. I'd like you to get checked out at the hospital, too."

"No, I—"

"Please." Again. He held a hand out across to the passenger side. "I almost lost you and Zach today. I need to know that you're both okay."

A lump made her throat ache. He wanted to see Zach. Understandable. He wanted to make sure her injuries weren't serious.

Practical and reasonable.

Her chest ached, and her eyes burned.

She got in and buckled up as Garrison revved the truck and sped away.

No. She wouldn't feel sorry for herself. She'd made her decision; time to cut ties with Garrett and the Taggart family. She would finish out the semester, but this week had made it obvious she needed to be someplace else.

Where? How?

Anywhere. No way would she stay here with all of the bad blood from dealing with Hank. From the damage done to the Taggart family.

What about her school loans? She would deal with them. She'd talk with the board members. Figure something out. If necessary, she'd simply pay off the loan, however long it took. She could get a second job if she had to. Hard as paying off $100,000 would be, at least she could give the Taggarts some space. She could move on with the plan she'd mapped for her life.

The best decision, right?

So why did it hurt like a bomb had just exploded inside her chest?

For right now, though, she would make sure Zach was all right.

In no time, they pulled up to the ER at Bondurant Valley Hospital, just outside of Copper River.

Her heart pounded harder as each step carried them closer to the doors.

The receptionist startled at Garrison's and Sara's rough appearances.

"Oh my word, are you two all right?" the older woman said.

"Fine," Sara said.

"Not fine. She needs to be checked out," Garrison interrupted. "But I'm looking for my son, Zach Taggart. Is he here?"

The receptionist picked up the phone, mumbled into it, and then pointed through the double doors. Sara held back.

"Stay with me. Please." The words seemed ripped from him. His haunted amber eyes bore into her face, like he memorized her appearance. A shudder drilled through her.

She'd miss his eyes, his intensity.

Her heart broke into little pieces. Maybe she could stay at his side for a bit longer. Maybe it wouldn't hurt him.

Sure as hell would hurt her.

Garrison pushed down nausea as he shoved open the ER doors, Sara right behind him. He'd watched his mother die of cancer in this hospital five years ago. Now Zach was somewhere inside. Alive? Dead? Sweat broke out on Garrison's brow.

At the direction of a nurse, he rounded the corner of a patient room and tore the curtain aside. Eric and Shelby looked up from their seats in hard plastic chairs next to a hospital bed. They both looked like day-old leftovers, barely reheated.

Zach sat up and smiled. "Dad!" His bright orange hair stood straight up from his head. Smudges of dirt speckled his forehead and cheeks.

Garrison's chest tightened as he hugged his son hard to his chest. He'd almost lost the most important person in the world to him. Never again would he take his kid for granted.

He shifted his grip, careful of the electrodes and IV lines coming out of his child.

"Kerr said Dad's here," Garrison said over his son's shoulder.

Shelby rubbed Zach's head and, with a tilt to her head, led Garrison and Sara out of the room and down the hall a few feet. Eric stayed with Zach.

A sinking feeling settled in his gut.

Shelby pinched the bridge of her nose and sighed. "Dad's in the CT scanner right now. Doctor thinks maybe it's a stroke."

"From tonight?"

"He might have been going through a series of ministrokes over the past few days. Apparently his blood pressure is sky-high. Damn it. I should have known."

Sara's tired eyes widened, but she pressed her lips together.

Garrison rubbed his head. "Not your fault. He's stubborn. I'm amazed you got him here tonight."

"He had a seizure; police and EMS were already at the house. So we didn't give him a choice."

"Will he be okay?"

"Not sure. But they're taking good care of him. Might admit him, if he'll allow it."

"Oh, he'll allow it," Garrison growled.

"Kerr'll be here soon, and he's planning on staying with Dad. All night if necessary."

"Good." He faced Sara. "Please get checked out. I need to know you're okay."

She opened then closed her mouth. "Sure. Okay."

Waving a nurse over, Garrison handed her into the medical professional's care. He wanted to go with Sara, but he needed to be with his son. With twin unhappy expressions, Shelby and Eric withdrew from the exam room.

"Doing better?" Garrison rested his hand on Zach's head and shoulder.

"Lots. Know what?"

"What?"

"They gave me hot chocolate. In a big cup." He demonstrated with hands.

"Awesome." He kept his hands on his kid. Couldn't stop smoothing his son's orange hair. Couldn't stop rubbing his kid's warm skin.

Zach was alive.

Son of a bitch, at some point he'd have to explain to Zach about his mother's death. Not right now, though. He needed his son to recover from his ordeal first. Garrison needed time to process what he'd learned, too. Grieve for the marriage he had never really had in the first place.

Zach leaned forward and whispered. "Know what else?"

"What?" He played along.

His eyes widened. "They put bags of hot water, you know, down *there*. I think some girls saw...stuff."

Garrison stifled a laugh and hugged him. "Probably worth it, if you're alive."

"Yeah."

He didn't know how long he held his son, but it wasn't nearly long enough.

A petite doctor popped into the room with a quirk to her eyebrow. "Hi, I'm Dr. West. So, sounds like you two have had an interesting evening. Mr. Taggart, is Ms. Lopez part of these festivities as well?"

Garrison nodded. "Yes, Ms. Lopez was mixed up in a kidnapping. She managed to get Zach free. Can you take care of her?"

"Next on my list. Your family is keeping me on my toes tonight." Her shoulder-length brown hair swung forward.

"Are you new to the area?" he asked. "Sorry, it's a small town."

"No worries. Yes, I've been here since August, first job out of family medicine residency."

"Not ER?"

"It's a small hospital, Mr. Taggart." She grinned. "Welcome to rural medicine. We have to cover a lot of bases."

"I can see that. What do you think about Dad?"

She frowned. "Won't know for certain until the CT is completed. If we can get his blood pressure under control and help him relax, we can limit any damage that is occurring."

"You think stress brought on his symptoms?"

"Didn't cause the problem but sure didn't help."

A stab of pain flashed behind his left temple. Reducing Dad's stress. More to manage.

"And Zach?"

Her green eyes danced as she wrinkled her nose at Zach. "He's going to be just fine."

Bless him, but his son smiled and blushed.

"Thank you so much." Garrison shook her hand.

A nod. "If you don't mind, let me go work on your dad and Ms. Lopez now. Um, can I get the officer in for a statement? He asked to talk with you."

"Sure."

A few minutes later, an older officer, with a notebook ready, entered the cubicle. The officer gave him a professional smile and took the statement. Thank God the law enforcement guy wasn't Tommy Brand. Garrison couldn't take any more of the Brand clan this evening.

He provided the officer as much detail as possible regarding the events leading up to Zach's kidnapping and what Hank had done to Sara. He gave directions based on what Sara had told him and where Shelby had indicated.

"Hank might have escaped or burned up." He shrugged. They could throw Hank in jail for kidnapping and attempted murder. Or they could throw a funeral for him. Garrison would bring confetti and noisemakers to make a real party of it. He couldn't care less as long as Zach and Sara were safe. "We left him tied up, but then there was some weird flash fire or something in the shack. I didn't see him after that, but frankly, I wasn't searching very hard."

"Understandable."

Garrison rubbed Zach's head as his son nodded off.

After the officer left, Garrison rested his head on the pillow next to his son. He might have even drifted off for a few minutes there.

The doctor ducked back in and answered Garrison's unspoken question. "Don't worry. I took a look at Ms. Lopez. We're running a few tests, but I think she's just banged up. She'll be fine."

Garrison released a breath he hadn't realized he held.

"What about my dad?"

"Needs to be admitted tonight for neuro checks and to get his blood pressure under control. We'll have physical therapy evaluate him tomorrow."

He nodded. "And Zach?"

His son peeled open his eyes at his name and yawned.

Dr. West smiled. "He can go home tomorrow. Let's get another him another bag of warmed fluid goes in. When he got here, his temperature was much too cold and he was semiconscious." She tugged on the stethoscope around her neck. "His feet will end up with frostnip, but your sister got him warmed up nicely on the way over here. Probably saved him from long-term tissue damage."

"Before we got in the ambulance, Auntie Shelby put my feet in her armpits! Ewww!" Zach obviously wasn't too grossed out to tell the tale.

"Smart thinking," the doctor said. "So, let me make sure all our tests are wrapped up, and then we'll get you and Zach on the road as soon as is safe."

"Sounds great," Garrison said.

Shelby poked her head in as the doctor left. With her wild, singed hair sticking out in all directions, the lines of exhaustion etched on her face, and her audible wheezing, Garrison wanted her evaluated as well. But his sister was too hardheaded to accept help.

"You should get rest, Shel."

Her voice came out rough. "I will, soon. You too."

"What about Dad?"

"Not your fault."

"I know, but I'm sorry." He cleared his throat. "And I'm sorry for what I made you do, sis."

She waved a hand like she was brushing away lint. "Don't even think twice about it. You had to do whatever it took to get to Zach and Sara. I don't blame you."

"But your head?"

"I'll be fine." The smile didn't light up her face like it normally did. "It'll be good to have you two back home."

He shifted in his position on the side of the bed. "Sounds like we're getting out of here tomorrow."

Zach lifted a paper cup. "I want more hot chocolate."

Shelby rubbed his head. "I'll see what I can do, bud." She paused. "Um, Garrison, someone wants to talk with you. It's Butch Brand."

Heat fired up his skull until it throbbed. "God da—" He glanced at Zach's raised eyebrows and swallowed the curse. "What does he want?"

"He seemed pretty torn up. He really needs to speak with you, I think."

After debating for a full minute, Garrison hauled air in and out of his lungs to try to calm down. "Fine. Stay here with Zach?"

"You bet."

Garrison stormed down the hall and banged through the double doors to the tiny waiting area.

Butch looked up and immediately backed away, hands raised. "Hold on, man."

"No, you hold on. If you don't recall, your psycho brother tried to kill my son and my...Ms. Lopez."

"I'm here to apologize, I swear."

Like hell. All he wanted to was drill into the man's head to figure out the truth. But damn it, but after Garrison's brain had nearly exploded this evening, no way could he use his power right now. He'd have to take Butch at his word, such as it was. "Fine."

The older man rubbed his balding scalp. "I had no idea what Hank and Wyatt were up to. Hank hasn't involved me in the offers on your ranch, or I would have told him to shut up and leave you all alone. And Wyatt's along for the ride, doing whatever Hank says."

"So you claim."

"I swear. If I get to my brothers first, I'll personally take them to the county jail."

"Again, your word is weak." He softened his tone. "I never saw Wyatt out in the woods, so God knows where he is now. And frankly, I'm not sure if Hank's even alive."

Sweat beaded Butch's forehead, and he swallowed. "I see. Wow. Well. Okay, we'll check the place out and see if there's any sign of him." He played with the bottom of his jacket zipper. "I need to let you know I've fallen down on my job as principal. I'm going to tighten up security with visitors in the school."

"And?"

"And I will make sure the bullying is under control. For all kids. Period."

"Noted."

"I'll do what I can do keep my family in check. Again, I haven't had a lot of involvement with them lately, but what happened tonight is not acceptable." He stuck out his hand. "On behalf of my asshole brothers and my lack of leadership, I am taking personal responsibility. I apologize."

Garrison waited a beat until grasping his hand.

"Go back to your son, Taggart." Butch walked away, shoulders slumped.

Reentering the ER, Garrison flagged a nurse outside of Zach's space. "Excuse me. Where is Ms. Lopez?"

"I believe she checked herself out of the hospital."

"What?"

"Eric took her home," Shelby called from behind the curtain.

"What? Why?" He reentered Zach's room.

"She claimed she didn't want any more medical attention and that she needed to leave our family alone. Something about us being 'better off if she didn't hang around.'"

"Exact words?"

"Yup."

"Damn."

"So, what are you going to do about it, big brother?"

Black, heavy, sucking emptiness settled over Garrison, but it couldn't be helped. Family first. His Dad, Zach, Shelby. He had too much to take care of.

Besides, he'd given Sara an ultimatum and told her to think about her decision, hadn't he?

Her choice was obvious, and apparently she'd made it clear tonight.

Frankly, he couldn't blame her. Insanity and danger if she stuck with the Taggart clan or peace and quiet with her own life, free of land feuds and drama? Pretty simple choice for a nice person like Sara.

"I'm going to take my son home to rest in the morning, we will find out what's going on with Dad, and then we're going to have a family meeting."

Shelby punched him in the arm, hard, right over a bruise. "You're a real idiot, you know?"

CHAPTER 27

*I*t was well past midnight when Sara finally arrived back at her rental. Eric kindly checked her house before she entered. Nothing would be wrong, of course. No one would be there. She shivered. Thank goodness she'd had the kitchen window repaired over the weekend.

Eric offered to stay until morning, but she thanked him and politely sent him away.

After a long shower, she changed into pajama pants and a t-shirt. A quick look in the mirror and she sucked in her breath. Her left eye hadn't shut completely, but the bruises and swelling were impressive. She shivered. Hank had hard fists, and if he had used them any more, she wouldn't have survived the night.

Garrison took way more impacts than she had. How bad were his injuries?

What about Zach? Eric said Garrison's son would be okay. *Please, Lord, let that be so.* With good care and some good luck, hopefully he wouldn't have lasting damage, physical or emotional.

The pain in her own chest had nothing to do with the bruises and torn muscles.

Chasing four ibuprofens with a glass of water, she collapsed into bed and tried to sleep. But even though her aching body had gone beyond exhaustion, her mind wouldn't shut down.

Could it be only a few days ago she and Garrison were wrapped each other's arms in steamy passion? She trailed her hand over a breast, recalling his touch, his mouth, his...

She rolled on her right side, hugging a pillow to her chest. Contrast that hot and heavy night of pleasure with last night's horrors. Holy mother of God.

What in the world had happened when Garrison went into that weird trance with Hank? She'd never seen anything like it before. Almost like the two men's minds were linked together for a long time. Whatever had happened, Garrison's haunted expression spoke of horror and pain.

Oh God, he had almost died last night. She had almost died. Hank might be dead, and sorry to say it, but good riddance. Zach had almost died because Sara had failed at her job.

Her career had imploded.

She literally had nothing but the roof over her head, which soon she wouldn't be able to afford.

Nausea churned in her stomach, and her cheekbone ached like hell. Every inch of her body hurt. Like, run over by a Mack truck hurt.

Too bad she didn't have any tears left.

The late morning light did not raise her spirits.

Confusion clouded her thoughts. What day was it? Tuesday. Yesterday—Monday—she had been teaching. Before...last night...in the shack...

Oh God, she had missed work!

With a lurch that jarred her aching body, she managed to reach her cell phone. A message blinked. The number from school.

Holy Mary, it was too soon to be fired. She couldn't handle more heartbreak today.

But her class was her responsibility. With a sob, she hit the message button.

"Sara, this is Butch Brand. I'm, ah, so sorry about what happened with my...with Hank. I took the liberty of calling a substitute for you today..."

Blackness tinged her vision. Such an awful way to get fired.

"You take your time and get better. When you've recovered, your job will be waiting for you. And again, I'm sorry for my...for not being a better principal in this...with what happened. Yeah."

What?

Incredulous, she stared at her phone and hit replay, in case she'd hallucinated the entire message. Nope. Her job was safe.

Long enough for her to finish the semester and move away from Copper River and Garrison Taggart.

Relief flooded her limbs until she couldn't move, so she did the next best thing and sank back into the mattress.

A few hours later, Sara finally got out of bed. Every joint in her body creaked. Hard to tell which her muscles hated more: movement or gravity.

Checking her messages, she read a text from Izzy.

I'm sorry. If you ever want to talk to me again, please call. If you don't, I understand.

As much as Sara wanted to call her friend back, she didn't have the emotional energy to spare right now. Of course she didn't blame Izzy, bless her friend's sweet heart. Izzy had nothing to do with Hank's insanity or Wyatt's part in the kidnapping.

I'm okay. Call you later.

Trudging into the kitchen, she made herself tea and a sandwich. Damn, even chewing made her jaw hurt.

At one point in the early evening, Sara jumped out of her skin at a knock at the front door. After the footsteps faded away, she cracked the front door and pulled a still-warm casserole dish into the house, along with a note from a coworker with wishes for Sara to get well.

Get well? Nothing would cure this entire situation. Not even tasty, cheesy casserole.

Empty sadness hollowed out Sara's chest until she struggled to breathe.

Only one thing to do.

So she went back to sleep until her watch informed her that another night had elapsed. Wednesday. Fabulous. She was losing huge chunks of time to her misery, pain, and exhaustion.

Feeling slightly more human, she took a ridiculously long bath and changed into actual clothes, jeans and a sweatshirt, at least somewhat ready to slog through the day.

With sore arms, she assembled and taped cardboard boxes and laid them around the house. Might as well pack now.

She'd be leaving at the end of the semester, just over a month away.

Couldn't face her students. Couldn't deal with her own role in the Taggarts' troubles.

Couldn't bear seeing Garrison again.

Couldn't remain here in Copper River.

She'd implement her exit strategy early. Somehow, she would pay off the debt owed to the school district. She'd call her friend in Atlanta and try to get a foot in the door with the district there. Heck, Sara could substitute teach until a permanent position opened up.

Anything to survive.

Anything to get out of this town.

Thirty minutes into box creation, she gave up and curled up on the couch, head aching, muscles weak. Time to feel sorry for herself for a minute. She rubbed her hip, recalling Garrison's tender touch. She imagined his warm gaze consuming her as he made love to her.

Damn it. Now the tears came, welling up from deep inside of her soul.

And they didn't stop.

Waves of sadness swamped her, blocked out all of her senses.

A tapping sound began. It had to be coming from her throbbing head.

The sound persisted.

The front door. Damn it, she didn't want any more well-wishers.

She didn't want any prying eyes evaluating how badly she'd been beaten up. It was none of their business.

She tried putting the throw pillow over her head, but the tapping continued.

Dear Lord, could these people not take a hint?

As she winced her way to the front door, she clenched her teeth, ready to be polite but firm. She yanked open the door.

Garrison filled up too much space on the front porch.

He had a bouquet of lilies in one hand, a steaming bag full of what smelled like Hungry Moose chicken, and keys and her purse dangling from his other hand.

He'd healed up about as well as she had. Butterfly bandages bridged a cut on his temple and purple bruises covered most of his face. A patch of swelling distorted one corner of his grimly set mouth.

Too exhausted to react, she stood there and stared at him.

His burnished eyebrows shot up, and a wary smile grew on the half of his face that wasn't swollen.

Time slowed. How long had she stood there, mute?

He shifted from foot to foot. "So…"

"How is Zach?"

"He's fine. Complete recovery, amazing kid."

"Good. Um, your dad?"

He nodded and pressed his mouth into a line. "He ended up having a stroke prior to arriving at the ER. Too late to give him the clot-busting medicines, so they observed him in the hospital here. He'll be coming back home tomorrow. Refused going to the rehab facility and all, stubborn man."

"Will he be okay?"

"Not sure how much he'll recover. We'll take care of him at home, where he belongs."

"Shouldn't you be at home, then? Where you belong?"

A light glinted in his gold-flecked eyes. Well, the one eye that wasn't swollen, anyway. "That's an interesting comment. I've done some thinking. It's time for me to readjust priorities."

"Well, um, that's good, then." Quiet and cold air filled the lonely space in the conversation. "So why are you here?"

When he stepped to the side, she did a double take.

Her car was parked in front of her house. She'd left it at the school. He'd brought it back here for her.

"Garrison?"

His brow furrowed, and then he stood up straight, like he'd made a decision.

"So, Sara. Here I am, standing on your porch with my hands full of stuff I don't normally carry. I'm sore and really tired, and it's cold outside." He cleared his throat, and a hint of a smile crossed his bruised face. "Here you are, standing in a warm and toasty house. Your hands are empty. And your mouth is open, by the way."

She closed it, head spinning. An odd shadow flickered near her car, then was gone. Probably a trick of the light.

A cold chill came and went through her spine.

"Um, come in?" *Smooth, so smooth.* She shut the door behind his tall, solid frame.

"Don't mind if I do." When he limped on the leg that Hank had brutally kicked, her heart twisted. After depositing the food in the kitchen, he set the bouquet, purse, and keys down on the coffee table.

"Thank you. Wow."

"So I was feeling guilty about what you went through. Figured I should return your stuff." He grimaced. Damn him, how the glint in his eye made him even more handsome, despite the swollen lip and bruises on his face.

But she didn't live in a fantasy world. She needed to address reality. "Pardon me for asking the question, but why the heck are you even here?"

When she sat on the far end of the couch, he gave her a lopsided smile and sat right next to her.

Her heart tripped several beats.

Dealing with saying good-bye to Garrison with all that heat from his muscled thigh brushing against hers added a degree of difficulty she couldn't handle today.

However, she'd own up to her part in the disaster. "Look, Garrison, I'm sorry."

"You're sorry?" His smile froze on his bruised face.

Her neck warmed. "The mess with Hank. Losing Zach at school. Oh, God."

"How hard did you get hit on the head?"

"What?"

"You're obviously delusional." He touched her uninjured cheek, and damned if she didn't lean into his hand. "The way I see it, I owe you an apology."

"How you see it?" She tried crossing her arms, then gave up when it hurt too much.

"Hank's had my number for a while. He hated me because of his own insecurities. He had a real screw loose with all that talk about a Great One. Then he resented me because of Tiffani. Frankly, the feeling is mutual."

"I'm so—I don't know what to say about Tiffani."

He pressed his lips together and bowed his head. Then he pinned Sara with an intense gaze. The corners of his mouth dropped. "There's nothing for you to say. It's history." He swallowed. "I feel bad that Zach has to grow up without his mother. But she and I had no real marriage and no future. I should have known. It was within my skill to know."

"I don't understand."

"My ability to detect the truth? My psychic power." He tapped his head. "I'm not like other people."

She scooted over, like being a few more inches away from him somehow would protect her. "Wait. What are you talking about? What do you mean you're 'not like other people'? You were serious about the lie detector thing last week?"

"Okay, that came out wrong. Please. I'm like other people, but I can tell when folks are telling the truth. Get into people's heads."

"Like invade their minds?"

"Yeah. Kind of."

"So you just...do this thing...whenever you feel like it?" Her hand fluttered up over her forehead, like she needed to protect herself.

From him.

"No, not like that. Yes, I went into Hank's mind to find out the truth. And more. But that was different. I don't normally go around doing that to folks."

"What about me?" Her ears buzzed as if hornets swarmed nearby.

A pause. "Yeah, I did it on you before." He stared at the floor, up at her, and then quickly back down again.

She rolled her hands into fists to keep them from shaking. "You didn't believe me? And somehow you can justify the invasion of my mind with your ability?" Pushing to her feet, she had to get some distance between herself and Garrison.

He remained on the couch. "Please, let me explain. I'll tell you everything, and then I'll leave if you want me to. I swear."

Waving her hand, she backed away another step. "Fine. Go on. But stay over there."

His grim expression almost made her pause. Almost.

He cleared his throat. "So I never told anyone, and didn't want to admit it myself, but before she left, I used my power on her. One of the times I truly regretted using the ability."

"So you knew she was cheating?"

"No, I couldn't go that far. I was too chicken. But I asked her several questions. She lied to every one of them. Way too easily." He stared at the floor. "I couldn't ask her the hard question."

Anger bled away. What price did he pay to use his power? What price had he paid avoiding its use? An image formed of Garrison in the cafeteria in grade school, eating a PB&J sandwich and drinking his chocolate milk, all by himself. Then an image of a lean, tall, jeans-clad Garrison in college, resting on the arena fence rails, far away from the other rodeo teammates.

"What do you mean?"

"I couldn't ask her if she loved me. Didn't need to. I knew the answer."

He stared into the space in front of him.

The silence hurt as much as her bruises. He had been through so much with a woman who had betrayed him. The ability he hated but had been forced to use took something away from the proud man before her.

Could she trust him?

Could Sara be with a guy who would know if she ever lied?

No problem, since she had no intention of lying to him, ever.

Maybe they had a future after all.

Sara couldn't ask him the hard question, either, so she settled for something easier to handle. "Were there other times you wished you hadn't used your gift?"

"Yeah. The parent-teacher conference with you. And I apologize. It was an invasion of your privacy. It was wrong."

She touched her temple. "Is that why my head hurt?"

"I'm so sorry. You have no idea." He stood up and faced her. "After I used it on my ex, I vowed never to use it again. But obviously I broke that promise. Several times."

"So you didn't trust me?" Damn it if tears didn't prick at her eyes. Here she thought she was all cried out.

His eyes raked her face, then looked away. "No, I didn't."

"What about now?" she whispered, crossing her arms.

"Sara…" He reached toward her, then dropped his hand.

"Well, it makes sense in a twisted way. You did what you had to for your family. For Zach."

"The ends didn't justify the means, and we both know it. I can't promise I won't use my power again."

"Wow." She let disappointment drip off the word.

He turned his palm up. "But I can promise I won't use it on you ever again."

"Well, um, that's honest, I guess." Her heart thumped. "So what now?"

"Sara, why are you still here?"

She dropped her hands to her sides. "In Copper River? Or in my house?"

"Standing here in front of me. Not running away. Not kicking me out."

Blood pooled at her feet until she swayed in place. "I don't have a good answer."

"I do." He swallowed. "Maybe you're still here to give me a tiny bit of hope."

"Hope?"

"That maybe we have a future." He pointed to the boxes littering the living room. "But then I see all of this and wonder."

Holy mother, he was going to make her actually say it? "It's for when, you know, I'm gone at the end of the semester. Because. Zach. You. What Hank did. And everything here." Since when had stringing words together become so difficult?

She clenched her teeth together.

When he took her hands, the dam burst and she pulled away from him, burying her face in her hands, working to get hold of her emotions. God, she didn't want him to see her cry. She was stronger than these tears. She could yank off the Band-Aid. Walk away from Garrison, once and for all. She could do this.

Warmth seeped through her sweatshirt into her skin. When she turned her head, she spied his hand resting on her shoulder.

After a few minutes, she wiped her eyes. "So why all the questions? What's the deal?"

"You're the deal." He took her hands again.

"Okay, now you're talking in riddles."

"Sara, I don't need my ability to know that you've never lied to me." He rubbed his thumbs over the backs of her wrists until her skin tingled. "You're so great for Zach and for me. You're a light in my darkness. You're smart and sweet. And you're the sexiest woman I've ever known. I will never get enough of you." He took a deep breath. "But here's the deal. I wouldn't blame you if you told me to go to hell for everything I've put you through, for the lack of faith I had in you."

"I would never—"

He slid his finger over her lips, stilling them. "I have some serious baggage, no question. There are major trust issues, and I haven't had a healthy relationship because of that lack of trust. But I realize that the problem is with me, not with my partner."

When he tilted her chin up, the focus of his eyes locked onto hers, knocking her equilibrium half a degree off plumb.

Could she do it? Could she believe him? Try again? If she tried, how badly could he hurt her?

Badly.

She stared at him.

Clearing his throat, he said, "You don't have to agree to forever with me. But I want another chance with you, Sara, if you'll give it to me. I want the chance to convince you to stay in Copper River."

"But what about my own baggage?"

"We all have pasts. I couldn't care less about yours."

"Really?"

"Really. I care about who you are now. And the woman in front of me is beautiful, intelligent, and hotter than molten lava. If you think that we could have a future together, I want to try. I love you, Sara Lopez."

Hope swelled inside of her, pushing out the emptiness and doubt. "I don't want anyone else, Garrison." She took a big breath. "I love you, too."

Gesturing around the room, he smiled. "Maybe one day we can fill up those boxes together?"

"Oh." Her heart flipped. "Yeah, I'd love packing boxes with you."

She fell into his strong embrace and kissed him, careful to avoid the bruised areas of his mouth and hers.

Based on the intensity of the kiss he returned, cuts and bruises were the last thing on his mind.

When he guided her to the bedroom, she shivered. Apparently, there wasn't much that bothered him today.

Come to think of it, her bruises didn't hurt nearly as much, either.

The glint in Garrison's eyes promised to take away any pain.

And that suited her just fine.

The End

LEGACY LOST

COWBOYS OF COPPER RIVER, BOOK 2

Wait until Eric found out she could read anyone's emotions.

Not that she'd ever tell him.

It was bad enough he knew about her homing beacon skills.

A wave of something else wafted over her filters. Warm, smoky caramel. The scent of Eric's concern and worry about her.

Great.

His light brown brows drew together. "So, how's your breathing? Really?" By the way he asked, he damn well knew the answer.

"Fine."

"Want to try that answer again?" The curve of his sensual mouth pressed into a hard line as he studied her. Did he seriously move into a wide alpha-dude stance? Not that she was affected by him. No way. Her disgust stemmed from the fact that hard muscled, denim-clad legs like those should be illegal to display without a license.

"Sure." She suppressed a betraying wheeze. "How about it's none of your business and let's get back to work?"

He barked what passed for a laugh and moved not one inch. "You bet it's my business." He extended a work-roughened hand toward her then dropped it. "I can't believe you're on call for Search and Rescue in this condition."

"In this condition?" Virtual heat steamed from the top of her head. "Now you're checking on my condition?"

"I'm an EMT, same as you. Someone should assess how you're doing since you refused medical treatment after the fire."

"Don't need to assess anything. I'm fine."

He rolled a gloved hand into a fist and propped it on a central beam, leaning like he wanted to shove down the entire structure. "Damn it, Shel, you're going to get yourself killed if you don't take care of yourself. I'm one of the team leaders on Search and Rescue. And I will pull you from a mission if you're not healthy."

Irritation crackled along her nerves. No way could she give in to the undertone of concern in his voice. "That would be the last thing on earth that you did, getting in my way of doing my job."

His mouth barely moved. "If it's a medical call, I'll do it."

This conversation was getting too serious too quickly. And she couldn't detect a rock bottom for this uncomfortable chat. "So now you're a medical expert?"

"As close as we're going to get right now."

Spin the topic, damn it. Change the subject. Now. "No way, dude. You're not evaluating my medical condition. Because then I'd have to make you wear the stupid nurse costume and call you 'ma'am.'"

He paused then shook his head. With a glint in his dark blue eyes, he shot her a broad grin that made her heart flop. "How about I wear the hat?"

"Well…"

"And nothing else."

Today's verbal judo wasn't working like it normally did. Her cheeks warmed up at the thought of an exam by Eric. With him wearing only a nurse's cap. That image cast her childhood friend in a whole new and uncomfortable light. She broke eye contact. Nope. Nothing would ever happen beyond friendship, and life was better for both of them that way.

Because, with her crappy gift to detect emotion, Shelby's problem wasn't intimacy, it was the aftermath, the judgment, the inevitable disapproval, the garbage and static that came along with even the nicest thoughts. Way too much closeness.

She and Eric were friends. That's the way it had been for years, and that's how it would be for years to come. Period.

"Fine, Nurse Patterson." She sniffed. "But I get to decide how to use the stethoscope and blood pressure cuff."

∾

LEGACY LOST
Available at Bookstores and Online Retailers Everywhere

ACKNOWLEDGMENTS

As this new series begins, I want to thank the indomitable Gwen Hayes for her wit, insight, and fabulous brainstorming. Thank you also to Julie Sturgeon for her amazing guidance and patience as she helped mold (shove) this book into the current form.

Thanks to my hubby for the support, even though he believes a paranormal cowboy story is "the most ridiculous thing ever."

P.S: He's just jealous that he doesn't get to be on the cover.

ALSO BY JILLIAN DAVID

The Cowboys of Copper River Series

Legacy of Lies

Legacy Lost

Legacy of Danger

Legacy Found

ABOUT THE AUTHOR

Jillian David lives near the end of the Earth with her nut of a husband and bossy cats. To escape the sometimes-stressful world of the rural physician, she writes while on call and in her free time. She enjoys taking realistic settings and adding a twist of "what if." Running or hiking on local trails often promotes plot development.

www.JillianDavid.net

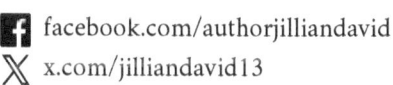

facebook.com/authorjilliandavid
x.com/jilliandavid13

www.ingramcontent.com/pod-product-compliance
Lightning Source LLC
Chambersburg PA
CBHW050509260626
47157CB00004B/1248